JACKSON

A Reed Security Romance

GIULIA LAGOMARSINO

Cover Design courtesy of T.E. Black Designs

www.teblackdesigns.com

❃ Created with Vellum

This book is dedicated to me. I wrote this while potty training my twins and it was exhausting! I'm giving myself a round of high fives. I hope you all enjoy!

Jackson is book 2 of a 3 book arc and needs to be read in order.

Sniper
Jackson
Chance

CAST OF CHARACTERS

Sebastian "Cap" Reed- owner
　　Maggie "Freckles" Reed
　　Caitlin Reed
　　Clara Reed
　　Gunner Reed

Team 1:

Derek "Irish" Cortell- team leader and part owner
　　Claire Cortell

Hunter "Pappy" Papacosta
　　Lucy Papacosta

Rocco Turner

Team 2:

Sam "Cazzo" Galmacci- team leader and part owner
　　Vanessa Galmacci

Sofia Galmacci

Mark "Sinner" Sinn
    Cara Sinn
    Violet Sinn

Blake "Burg" Reasenburg
    Emma Reasenburg
    Ryker Reasenburg
    Beatrix (Bea)

Team 3:

John "Ice" Peters- team leader and part owner
    Lindsey Peters
    Zoe Peters
    Cade Peters

Julian "Jules" Siegrist
    Ivy Siegrist
    John Christopher Hudson Siegrist

Chris "Jack" McKay
    Alison (Ali) McKay
    Axel McKay
    Elizabeth (Lizzie) McKay

Team 4:

Chance "Sniper" Hendrix
    Morgan James (Shyla)
    Payton James

Jackson Lewis
    Raegan Cartwright
    Parents: Susan and Robert Cartwright

Gabe Moore
  Isabella (Isa) Moore
  Vittoria
  Lorenzo (Enzo)

Team 5:

Alec Wesley

Florrie Younge

Craig Devereux

Training:

Hudson Knight- formerly known as Garrick Knight
  Kate Knight
  Raven Knight

Lola "Brave" Pruitt
  Ryan Jackson
  James Jackson (Cassandra Jackson- mother)
  Piper Jackson
  Ryder Jackson

IT Department:

Becky Harding

Robert "Rob" Markum

Chapter One

RAEGAN

One year ago...

"I want that shipment by the end of the day. I don't care what you have to do to get it."

I listened from the bedroom as Xavier talked with his supplier. He was into dealing weapons and over the years I had known that, but I had looked the other way because I thought I loved him when we first got together. Of course, he had been different then. When he started getting into dealing, he had changed into a different man, one that liked to keep me in line with his fists. If I hadn't been so weak, I would have walked away, but I waited too long and now he knew exactly how to keep me in line. Unfortunately, I let my mouth get away from me a time or two and had paid the price. I just couldn't help myself sometimes. I tried to keep my mouth shut, but sometimes my thoughts just slipped out. One of these days it was going to cost me my life.

Like I actually had a life the past few years.

But I couldn't stay now. He was making a deal with his supplier to try and overthrow his largest competitor, a man that I had only heard of, but knew that he wasn't someone that you messed with. Anyone who did, died a very slow, very painful death. And that was only the beginning. He sent messages to his buyers that he wasn't to be fucked with by using families as examples. I had seen it with my own eyes. Women and children had been literally burned at the stake when someone double crossed him. That was what Xavier was planning on doing, and if he was caught, he would be the least of my worries.

"I'm not willing to put my ass on the line unless I get a bigger cut. You know that if you get caught, I'm going down too. Taking weapons from this guy is as good as signing our death warrants," his supplier said.

"Not if you do it right. Get rid of those asswipes you use and get some real men to do the job."

The supplier sounded irritated, but even he knew that he could only push Xavier so far. They were both playing a dangerous game.

"I'll have it for you by the end of the day, but you need to find a different location for the drop. We have to assume that any place we've used in the past could be known."

God, these guys were fucking idiots. They were going to get everyone killed.

"Fuck," Xavier laughed. "The payday off this is going to be incredible."

"Are you sure you want to do this? This guy has eyes everywhere."

"I'll have people all around watching. If they see anything unusual, I'll know immediately and take care of it."

Famous last words. God, he's such an arrogant prick and it's gonna get him killed. Not that I cared. I'd be happy to be rid of him at this point, but that was easier said than done. I couldn't just walk away from him and too many people knew that I was his girlfriend. If I ran away, anyone would snitch on me just to get a better deal on their weapons.

His supplier didn't seem like he really believed him, but he agreed and continued to make plans with Xavier. I crept over to the other side of the room and pulled the burner phone from the back of the closet. It had been slipped to me by someone that stopped by once after Xavier had beaten me. He was concerned for me and knew that I wouldn't be able to make it out on my own. I hadn't used the phone yet, but I was going to now. The only people that I knew would help me were my parents. I didn't want to put them in danger, but they were my last hope. I dialed the numbers that I still knew by heart and waited for someone to answer. My heart thumped wildly in my chest and when my dad's voice came over the line, I started to tear up, I was so choked up over hearing his voice after all these years.

"Daddy," I whispered. I gasped as my breathing seized in my chest. I had to hold it together.

"Raegan?" The shock and hope in his voice came through loud and clear. I hadn't talked to my parents in years and the last time I had, they begged me to leave Xavier. But I knew that would likely never happen. "Baby girl, are you okay?"

"Daddy, I need you," I plead. "Xavier is doing something stupid." My voice trembled with anger as I thought about what I had overheard and the danger he was putting me in. "He's doing something dangerous and..." I swallowed down the fear that was causing me to choke up. "I don't think I'll make it out of here if he goes through with it. I don't want to die here."

My voice broke as I spoke the words, knowing the truth of the situation was staring me in the face.

"Baby, tell me where you are. I'll make sure you get out."

"Uniontown. It's on 7th Street and Harris Street. It's the brown house on the corner."

"Hold tight, baby. I'm coming for you."

I nodded, trying to convince myself that he could make it in time to get to me, but deep down, I was pretty sure this was the last time I would speak to my father. "Daddy, if this is it, if I don't make it, tell Momma I'm so sorry. Tell her that I love her and I'm sorry that I didn't listen to you."

"Baby, I will make it or I'll find someone that can get to you. I swear, I'll get you out."

"I know, Daddy. I love you," I whispered. The phone was yanked from my hand and I yelped in surprise. I hadn't heard anyone come in because I wasn't paying attention, and that was my biggest mistake yet. Xavier backhanded me and I flew against the closet wall, trying to hold in my scream so I didn't scare Dad.

"Who the fuck is this?" His eyes shifted as he listened and then he glared down at me, his fists clenching in anger as he stared at me. "She won't be contacting you again."

He threw the phone against the wall and it broke apart, crashing to the ground. My last lifeline was gone. All I had now was hope that my Dad could come save me. Xavier cracked his knuckles and bent down on his haunches, his jaw hard as steel as he looked at me.

"So, you thought you'd try and leave. That's never gonna happen, bitch."

"Better to die escaping than stay here and die because of your stupidity," I snapped.

He grabbed my hair, yanking me to him. My eyes watered and my scalp burned as he pulled me from the closet. I tried to crawl out so that I wasn't dragged, but I couldn't get my hands under me as he hauled me up higher. I felt my hair being ripped from my head as he threw me against another wall. My skull cracked against it with a sickening thud. Everything in front of me went blurry and I tried to blink my vision back, but before I could, his fist caught me in the jaw, sending me back against the wall again.

God, I was stupid. I just couldn't keep my mouth shut. I cowered away from him, knowing this could be the worst it had ever been. His foot connected with my ribs and I gagged and then threw up on the floor. He kicked me again and again until at least a few of my ribs were broken. I was wheezing and sucking in air as best I could, but black spots were forming from lack of oxygen. When his foot struck out and hit me in the face, my nose broke and blood gushed into my mouth. I started choking on my own blood. I pulled my knees up, ignoring the pain in my chest, doing anything I could to protect myself.

When he didn't hit me immediately, I thought maybe he had left me and my beating was over. I slowly opened my eyes just as he walked into the room, shoving his brass knuckles onto his hand. I whimpered in agony as his fist came toward me again. Two hits was all it took and I was out.

I thought I heard voices, but that couldn't be right. I was dead. I couldn't possibly still be alive after what Xavier had done to me. Something touched my face and I moaned, jerking away from whatever it was. I knew I hadn't moved far, but my instincts were to get as far away as I could. The problem was, I could barely move. I felt myself being lifted and prayed that someone was here to help me. Either that or just shoot me and take away the pain.

As I moved through the air, my arm hung limply next to me. I tried to pull it into my body, but I didn't have the strength. My head was resting against something, but as we moved, it flopped backward, straining my breathing. My strangled breaths became too painful and just when I thought I would pass out, I was moved again in a more comfortable position. I heard what sounded like gunshots and then there was bright light behind my eyelids. The voices were back, but they were so muffled that I couldn't make out what they were saying. I couldn't focus on anything and I kept floating in and out of consciousness, not sure what was real and what was a dream.

I wanted to call for my dad when I thought I heard his soothing tone, but I couldn't make my voice work. Something touched my face again, but this time I didn't flinch away. I could feel rough fingers brushing my hair from my face, but I wasn't scared. Either I felt safe with these hands or I was too far gone to care at this point.

"Hang on, Raegan."

The male voice was fierce, but comforting, and I wanted to beg him to stay, but I was too late. He was gone. I could feel it.

Something wet dripped down my cheek and something soft was swiped across my face. It felt so good, so refreshing that I moaned in appreciation. My body felt light, almost like I was floating. For all I knew, I was lying on a cloud in heaven right now. I vaguely remembered my last encounter with Xavier, but I couldn't be bothered with the outcome right now. I wasn't in pain like I thought I would be. Yeah, there were some aches and pains, but overall, I felt pretty good. I tried to open my eyes, but it was like they were stuck together. I raised my eyebrows and lowered my jaw, hoping that it would help peel apart my eyelids.

"It's okay, Raegan. Just give me a minute."

Wetness coated my eyes and slowly, I felt my eyelids starting to loosen from the attachment they had to each other. I sighed my contentment as the gluey substance was cleared from my eyelids. After blinking a few times, clouds appeared in front of me. But the more I blinked, the more I realized that I wasn't actually surrounded by clouds. My vision cleared enough to see people. There was a woman sitting on the bed beside me.

"You're so pretty," I sighed. "You have really nice hair and your teeth are really white."

She was holding a cloth in her hands and smiling down at me. I felt really good, kind of loopy, but it felt so nice.

Another figure appeared behind her and I gasped. This man was terrifying, with black hair and the darkest eyes I had ever seen.

"Psst." I struggled to lift my finger and motioned her toward me. "Don't look now, but there's a really scary man behind you. I think he might be a killer, but he's also kind of hot," I croaked. God, had I become a frog? Was that possible?

The woman chuckled slightly and the man just raised an eyebrow at me.

"Do you think he's any good in bed?" I blinked a few times and narrowed my eyes to see him better. "Nah, I bet it's all for show. Look at the size of his muscles. He's compensating for something."

I winked at her, which was actually more like blinking at her. "That's my husband," she laughed. "Raegan, meet Hudson."

"Hudson? That doesn't fit him. Shouldn't he have some badass name like O'Roark or The Butcher?"

"Well, everyone calls him Knight," she chuckled. "And I'm Kate."

"Ah, Knight definitely fits him better. He's like the Black Prince," I said dreamily. "His name was Edward, which definitely doesn't fit you, but he was a knight. Get it? A knight named Knight." I attempted to laugh at my own joke and Knight shook his head at me. "But he died of dysentery, which I would think would really suck because diarrhea in the 1300s couldn't have been fun."

"Diarrhea would suck, but death was okay?" Knight questioned.

"Hey, Doc, tell the Black Prince about infectious diseases in the 1300s," I whispered conspiratorially.

"How about instead we get you over to my clinic and get you some x-rays?"

"Do you know how they went to the bathroom back then?" I said to the Black Prince. "They built garderobes on the outside of castles and their excrements fell down into a hole. Imagine walking under that and diarrhea falling on your head," I laughed.

"How about we talk about this on the way to the clinic?" Kate said. She held out her hand to me and pulled me up into a sitting position. The room tilted around me, making me feel drunk.

"And people hung their clothes in the garderobes because the smell kept the moths away." I grimaced and feigned gagging. "I think I'd rather have moths than smell like shit." I stood and leaned heavily on Kate. "That's where wardrobes came from. Such a lovely picture."

Kate started walking with me toward the door where another man was standing, leaning against the doorframe with his hands in his jeans pockets. I stopped where I was, smacking Kate in the arm. "Do you see him?" I hissed. "He's so gorgeous."

A smirk spread across the man's face and he shook his head, walking out of the room.

"What's with all the really good looking men? Are we at a hot man convention?"

"No, that was Jackson and we're at his house."

"Why?"

"Because he pulled you out of your boyfriend's house today. Is it hurting you to walk?"

"Doc, I gotta be honest. I'm not feeling much of anything right now."

"Well, then the drugs are doing their job."

"How much further? I kinda want to take a nap."

I started to plop down on the floor and Kate quickly helped lower me to the ground. I sighed as I laid down on the rug that covered the hardwood floor and closed my eyes.

"Jackson!"

I heard Kate call for the handsome man and I yawned sleepily. The floor shook like an elephant was running toward me and then I felt a hand on my arm shaking me. I batted it away and brushed at something that was tickling my nose.

"Go away," I grumbled.

Arms lifted me and I opened my eyes to see who it was. The handsome man that was in the doorway was carrying me. I blushed and snuggled against his chest, feeling his heart beat wildly against my cheek. I could get used to being around this man.

"You okay, Raegan?"

The deep rumble of his voice reverberated through his chest, sending tickles down my spine. "As long as I'm in your arms," I replied. I heard him sigh and smiled. He obviously loved me in his arms as much as I loved being there.

I groaned as I tried to roll to my side. That obviously wasn't happening, so I flopped onto my back, a move I instantly regretted when pain shot through my body.

"Are you in pain?"

I blinked drowsily, trying to figure out where I had heard that voice before. It was a low rumble that sent tingles down my spine. A man came into my vision, a look of concern on his face. It almost seemed like I was seeing double and that's when I realized that one of my eyelids would only open halfway. What the hell had happened?

"Are you in pain?" he repeated.

"Yeah. Where am I?"

"At my house. I'm Jackson. Do you remember me from yesterday?"

Yesterday? What the hell happened yesterday? Did I get drunk and pass out at some guy's house? That would definitely explain the headache and the pain in my stomach.

"No, sorry, did I sleep with you?"

"No," he said, looking at me funny.

"That's good. Xavier would be pretty pissed." I closed my eyes and let my head sink into the pillow again. At the thought of Xavier, I popped up in bed, yelping in pain when my whole body screamed. The man quickly grabbed me from behind, supporting my back as he lowered me back to the mattress.

"Take it easy. No one's going to hurt you."

"Where's Xavier?" I asked in confusion.

"He's dead," Jackson said. His eyes were almost cold as he gazed over my body. Had I done something? I glanced down, making sure that I was dressed, which I was. Well, that was a relief. Although, I had no idea where I got a man's dress shirt from.

"What happened to Xavier?" It was practically an afterthought. I didn't really care about Xavier anymore. Years of him treating me like a punching bag really marred my opinion of him.

"He beat you within an inch of your life. We were there to get you out and one of my team shot him."

"Huh." That was interesting. He was dead and I didn't have to worry about him anymore. It was like a weight was lifted off my shoulders and the world had opened up to me. I was free. I could do whatever I wanted.

"That's it?"

Jackson broke through my thoughts, drawing my gaze to his. "What more is there?"

"I don't know. I guess I expected you to cry or...hell, I don't know. Fall apart."

"Is that what I'm supposed to do? Because he was kind of a bad person and I can't say that I'm actually sorry that he's dead."

And I wasn't. Xavier was nothing like he used to be and the furthest thing from my mind was whether or not Xavier was okay.

"No, you're not supposed to do anything. That's just what I thought would happen. I guess I thought that a woman that gets assaulted regularly would be on edge."

"You would think," I snorted. "But after you get beat up for the hundredth time because you opened your mouth, you just learn to roll with the punches. No pun intended."

He smirked at me, his lips twitching in such a way that his eyes seemed to sparkle at the same time. The light blue of his eyes pierced me like steel and I couldn't look away from their hypnotizing color. A flush crept up my neck the longer I stared at him. I was watching him like a schoolgirl watches her crush. Only I was an adult and that just made me look creepy.

I quickly averted my gaze, clearing my throat uncomfortably. I tried not to think about his dark hair that looked silky soft or the muscles that were obviously trying to escape the sleeves of his shirt. And I really tried not to think about the tattoos that made me want to rip off his shirt just so I could get a better look. "You said that I was beat up?"

"Yeah, when I got to you, you pretty much looked dead."

"That would explain why my body hurts so much."

"I'm gonna grab some pain pills for you. I'll be right back."

He stood and walked out of the room, giving me an opportunity to breathe and take stock of my body. I lifted my arm and grimaced when I saw all the bruises and cuts that marred my skin. Pressing against my face, I felt more cuts and the swell of my skin around my eye. It must have made me look like I had a tiny orange sticking out of my eye.

"Lovely," I muttered. And I of course looked like this in front of the most gorgeous man I had ever met. Wasn't that just my luck.

"Here," he said as he walked into the room with a bottle of water and some pills. I went to sit up, but quickly came to the conclusion that it wasn't a good idea to sit up yet. "Yeah, I wouldn't try that on your own. You have four broken ribs."

"One more and I'll have a basketball team," I quipped.

He grinned at my wry humor and slipped his hand under my back to help me sit up. He shoved another pillow behind my back so I was propped up and then handed me the pills and water. I drank down the water because I was so thirsty, but then wondered if that was a good idea since eventually I'd have to get up to pee. That was gonna suck.

"So, can I ask you something?"

"Shoot."

"Why'd you stay with him so long if he was hitting you all the time?"

I shrugged and smiled at him. "I was going for the world record for the number of beatings I could take."

He shook his head, scrubbing a hand across his face. "Do you take anything seriously?"

"Sure, hygiene is very important. Not washing hands after using the bathroom is my biggest pet peeve. Also, I'm very serious about my pictures all hanging straight on the wall. If they're off even a skosh, I seriously lose my shit. And then there's general courtesy to others. People can be so rude nowadays and that really bugs me."

He studied me, leaving me fidgeting under his scrutinization. I didn't like anyone watching me so closely, afraid they would see who I really was underneath, an idiot that hadn't left when I should have. Who was I kidding? A man like Jackson probably thought I was some crazy woman that thought I could change my man. Which I wasn't. I knew as soon as Xavier started to change that nothing I did would make him who he once was. But I didn't leave. I loved him too much. So, yeah. When a good looking man like Jackson started asking me personal questions, I was going to use my best defense mechanisms to ensure that he didn't see the pathetic woman that hid beneath all the armor.

Chapter Two

JACKSON

After Kate had done all her x-rays and exams, I brought Raegan back to my house. Her father was insisting on being with her every step of the way and it pissed me off. What kind of parents watched as their child got sucked into a life that was so obviously killing her and did nothing? I didn't want him anywhere near Raegan. He hadn't earned the right to be back in her life. I realized that I may have been a little harsh on both her parents, but when I pulled her out of that house, bloody and broken, barely alive, I was filled with a rage so strong that I really wondered if I would be able to keep from killing someone.

She had been high on drugs when Kate took her for x-rays, but she had backed off the good stuff and gave her a different drug when she saw how much it affected Raegan. I had decided to stay home with Raegan for a few days and made sure that her parents got settled. I basically had two wings of the house, not like a mansion, but the layout of the house had the master bedroom on one side and two other bedrooms on the other side. And since I wasn't home that often, it wouldn't really affect how I lived. Or, so I told myself.

After a week of staying with me, Raegan finally ventured out of her room. She must have been expecting me to be gone, because she startled when she saw me. I could see the uncertainty in her eyes, but then she walked over and took a seat at the counter. I watched her for a moment, trying to figure out what she looked like when she wasn't all banged up. Her eye wasn't swollen anymore and her blue eyes were bright and cheery. She had dark brown hair that had to go to the middle of her back. I hadn't noticed when we brought her here because there was so much blood everywhere. She was a small woman, skinny with pale skin, but I wasn't sure how much of that had to do with the situation she was in. When she walked out of her room, I could picture her hips swaying as she moved. I'd bet my life that when she put on some weight she would have great curves.

I pulled my gaze from her before she started to think I was psychotic and turned back to the stove. I had already started on bacon and eggs, so she was right in time. I gave her my best smile and said gently, "Hi, Raegan. It's great to see you up."

"Well, after years of not being allowed to have a job, I figured I deserve a vacation, so I stayed in bed."

"Uh..." Right. I wasn't sure how to deal with her sarcasm. Did I joke along with her or try and get her to open up to me? Maybe she was just this way naturally.

"How are the ribs?"

"They're pretty good with the right barbecue sauce. I personally like Famous Dave's."

I stopped what I was doing and stared at her. Did she really think I was talking about food?

"Uh...I meant *your* ribs. You know, the ones in your body that are broken."

She shrugged slightly. "I'm sure they would be good with barbecue sauce too, but I'm not really into cannibalism. Although, I don't think I'd be alive to eat my own ribs, so you'd have to be the taste tester."

I cleared my throat, wondering if now was the time to step away and excuse myself, then run for the goddamn hills. But I was a professional. I could handle this.

"Do you want some breakfast?"

"Sure. Do you want some help?"

"Yeah, can you make toast?"

She snapped her finger in a shucks gesture. "Damn, that's the one thing I always burn."

"You burn toast?"

"Unfortunately. I seem to be toast deficient."

"Toast deficient," I repeated slowly. "You know there's a little knob that you set to get the perfect toast, right?"

"Oh, I know that. It just never seems to work for me."

"But all you do is push the lever down."

"I know," she said incredulously. "It sounds so simple. You would think I could do it."

Looking at her strangely, I handed over the bread to her, sure she was lying to me. She shrugged and took it from me. I made sure the setting was right on the toaster and went back to making the bacon. The eggs were done and I scooped them onto some plates, then cracked a few more for her parents.

"Do you have butter for the toast?" she asked.

I pulled it out and handed it to her, then put the bacon on plates and finished up the rest of the eggs. Raegan's parents, Robert and Susan, came out just a minute later, greeting us with smiles and gave Raegan hugs. I pulled out mugs and poured coffee for everyone, setting out sugar and cream in case someone wanted some.

Setting the bacon in the center of the table, we all sat down and I frowned when I looked down at my plate. There were two slices of burnt toast. Not just partially burnt, but fully blackened toast. I looked at everyone else's plates and saw they all had black toast.

"See?" Raegan said with a shrug. "I told you it would happen."

I got up from the table and examined the toaster. The setting was where I always kept it and I didn't see anything else that was strange.

"Did you push the lever twice?"

She quirked an eyebrow at me. "No. I'm well aware how a toaster works."

"But, the setting is where I always keep it."

"I know. I don't understand it either. Toasters just don't like me."

"A toaster doesn't decide to burn toast out of hate," I said, shaking my head at her insanity.

"It's true," Susan said with a smile. "We could never figure it out either. I even stood next to her and watched exactly what she did. It still came out burnt."

They all bit into the disgusting, blackened bread, chewing as if it was normal toast.

"So...you just eat it? Like that?"

"You get used to the taste after a while." Richard wiped his mouth with a napkin and dug into the rest of his food. I glanced back at the toaster. This couldn't be right. I'd watch her the next time and find out what was really going on.

"So, what do we do now?" Raegan asked. "I mean, now that my days as a gun moll are over."

"A gun moll?"

"In my version of this story, I was on Lucky Luciano's arm and I was living the high life. It was nothing but jazz, liquor, and money."

Raegan's parents were staring at their plates, obviously not happy with the nonchalance in her tone. I wouldn't be so relaxed either if I was hearing about my daughter's involvement with gangsters.

"Well, we're going to keep you here for a while. We need to make sure that whoever was trying to kill you at the house is gone. Which leads me to my first question. Why were they trying to kill you?"

"It was probably because I overheard Xavier trying to make a deal with his supplier to take over someone else's territory. I would imagine that would be something his gang BFF's wouldn't want me to know. On the other hand, it could be this guy he was trying to outsmart. I'm sure he'd want to know everything I knew. And it's not like Xavier was the brains he thought he was. I'm sure the minute he started planning out this little takeover, his competitor knew about it."

"Who's this competitor?"

She leaned forward, resting her elbows on the table. Her eyes flared with mischief. "Would you believe me if I said the boogeyman?"

"No." My voice was flat, letting her know that I wasn't playing right now.

"I don't know." She sat back, crossing her arms over her chest in disappointment. "I've heard about him and how he controls things. I've seen some of the things he does, but I've never heard a name. I don't think he wants anyone to know who he is."

"That's kind of strange for an arms dealer. They usually want to be well known."

"All I know is that this guy is the largest weapons dealer on the east coast."

"And Xavier really thought he could pull off a takeover?"

"Xavier started getting cocky over the past two years. He thought that he was Doc Holliday or something. That's why I called my parents that day. I knew it was only a matter of time before someone shot him. Turns out, he got off easy. I don't think the other guy would have made his death quite so easy."

I sat back in my seat and watched her, waiting for her to break down over that day, but she said it all so matter of fact, like it wasn't her that had actually experienced any of it.

"I'll do some research into what you've told me and we'll take it from there."

She shrugged indifferently. "What can I do to earn my keep around here in the meantime? Clean your weapons? Polish your boots?"

"I'm not sure I want my weapons cleaned by a gun moll. And my boots have never been polished before and I'm pretty sure the guys would beat the shit out of me if I showed up with shiny boots."

"Suit yourself. Your boots would never be cleaner."

"And the weapons?" I asked, raising an eyebrow to her.

"If I had actually intended to use a gun at some point in my life, don't you think I would have shot Xavier?"

I stared at her, wondering why she hadn't used any of his guns on him. It wasn't like she didn't have access. When we walked into that house, there were guns everywhere.

"Just get better. Those broken ribs aren't going to heal if you aggravate them."

I pushed back from the table and gave a curt nod. I had to get to work since I had been at home for days.

Raegan's last words continued to bother me as I pulled into Reed Security. I just couldn't understand why she had stayed when she could have gotten her hands on a weapon. I went to Cap's office to check in, still trying to figure out the woman staying with me.

"Jackson, how's Raegan doing?"

"I don't know, Cap. She's...." I searched for a word that would describe her. Emotionally absent? Fucked up? I took a seat across from Cap and shook my head. I was going to need advice on how to handle this woman. "Something's not right with her, Cap."

"Listen, Jackson, the woman's been beaten for years. She's going to need time to adjust. I know this is going to be hard on you, and if you want to put her in a safe house, everyone will understand. You have no idea what she's been through over the years. Beatings could just be the start of it. I'm sure she's going to be scared of you for a long time, probably flinch away from you. That's to be expected and it'll be hard to deal with."

"No, Cap, she doesn't flinch away. She...she jokes."

"What do you mean?" Cap asked, studying my face in confusion.

"Like, she called herself a gun moll. She said she was going to think of it as being on Lucky Luciano's arm. Today was the first day that she came out of her room and she didn't flinch away from me or seem timid. I asked how the ribs were and she said she liked them in barbecue sauce."

"Do you think she's not all there?"

"No, she was avoiding my question, making jokes about cannibalism."

He leaned forward across his desk, "Not about being one, right?"

"No, thank God. Could you imagine having to deal with that on top of everything else? It brings a whole new meaning to watching your back."

"So, basically what you're saying is that she's dealing with everything just fine."

"But she's not, Cap. It's all a defense mechanism. She needs to talk this shit out. If she doesn't, she's never gonna deal with it."

"You can't make her want to talk about it." He shrugged his shoulders, as baffled by this as I was. "Some women just deal with things differently than others. Look at Cara. She was tortured by a psychopath for ten days, and now years later, she still has panic attacks.

Then there's Freckles, who had her fingers chopped off by a gang and she's ready to go blow up the world. I mean, who the hell knows what runs through these women's brains. It's a fucking miracle that I'm not dead after living with Freckles all these years. I'm pretty sure that I'm not going to die in battle. It's going to be because Freckles shoves a grenade down my pants in my sleep." He shrugged nonchalantly. "I've made peace with my impending death."

"Your woman has a seriously fucked up fascination with grenades."

"Tell me about it. I blame Sinner. He's the dipshit that started teaching her all this crap. If it weren't for him, she'd be a normal reporter, chasing after her stories like anyone else."

Cap was delusional if he seriously thought Freckles would ever be a normal anything. Freckles was the woman that ran toward danger, and not because she was out to save someone, but because she liked the edge. Cap could see the disbelief in his statement on my face and sighed.

"Yeah, you're right. She would still be Freckles."

"So, what do I do about Raegan?"

"Fuck if I know, Jackson. I can barely figure Freckles out, let alone someone else's woman."

"Whoa, she's not my woman. She's just staying with me."

"Yeah, right," he snorted.

"She is. I'm protecting her. That's what we do."

"Keep telling yourself that. Now, get the fuck out of here. I have work to do."

I stood, leaning on his desk as I glared at him. "I'm fucking serious. She's not my woman."

"Yeah," he nodded with a grin. "I completely believe you." He shooed me away, laughing like I was the fucking idiot.

"I'm fucking serious, Cap. It's not happening."

He burst into laughter and I clenched my jaw. I was not like everyone else. I wasn't falling for a woman I barely knew. I didn't have some white knight complex and I wasn't tripping over my feet to please her. She was just staying with me. I stormed for the door, throwing it open and turning back one last time to Cap.

"I'm just fucking protecting her. This will never be more than that. I don't want her."

Cap bent over laughing, clutching his stomach and I could see tears leaking from his eyes. The man was fucking laughing at me like I was going to turn into one of them and fall all over my feet for a woman. It wasn't happening and I would fucking prove it to them. I slammed the door behind me, shaking my head in irritation when I heard another bark of laughter from Cap.

"Yo, Jackson," Gabe said, walking up to me. "How's Raegan?"

"Fuck off! I'm not fucking falling for her. She's just staying with me!"

I walked away, ignoring the look of confusion on Gabe's face. Fuck, none of them were ever going to let this go. I should have never brought her home with me.

6 months later...

"Just stay here," I told Gabe and Chance. "I just have to grab my shit really quick."

We were going out of town in a few hours and were rounding up all our crap to take with us. The guys had been busting my balls for months now about Raegan still staying with me, but no matter how much I told them I was protecting her, they still thought it was more. Which it wasn't.

"Whoa, wait a minute," Chance grinned. "You're not going to invite us in?"

"No."

"I have to take a piss," Gabe said, stepping out of the truck with Chance following.

"Use the bushes," I shot over my shoulder.

"That's just uncivilized. We're grown men. We don't piss in bushes anymore."

"Look, her parents are here and they don't need to hear how you guys talk. When I'm at home, I watch my mouth around them."

"Aww, he's sucking up to her parents," Chance said sappily. "This is serious. He really wants them to like him."

"It's called respect, asshole."

"It's called love, loverboy," Gabe said, wrapping his arm around my neck and putting me in a headlock. He scrubbed his knuckles over my head like a brother would do and I punched him in the stomach, shoving him away from me.

"Seriously, you guys can't come in. Just stay here. I'll only be a few minutes."

"You know, I'm kind of hungry," Chance said, shoving past me for the house.

"I could eat." Gabe followed Chance. I hung my head, knowing I was about to get razzed within an inch of my life.

When I walked through the door, Chance and Gabe were already making their way to the kitchen where the most delicious smells were coming from. Raegan and Susan were excellent cooks and I had been spoiled every single day I was home with their homemade meals. I didn't need anyone else knowing about it. Soon, I would have a whole group of guys coming over to steal my food. They would make me share and Raegan would definitely give me shit if I didn't let them eat.

"What are you cooking, half pint?" Gabe asked.

Raegan punched him in the shoulder, sticking a few knuckles out to make a point. "Half pint? I'm a normal sized woman."

Gabe rubbed his shoulder playfully and then punched her back. She stumbled back from the force of his hit and I saw red. What the fuck was he thinking, hitting a woman that had been in an abusive relationship?

"Gabe," I shouted.

"What the fuck?" Raegan said. "You hit like a girl. Even Xavier hit better than that."

She shook her head and walked away, as if everything was totally normal. Chance looked over at me with a raised eyebrow. *What the fuck?* Chance mouthed. I shrugged. I didn't get it either.

"Boys!" Raegan called from the kitchen. "Dinner's almost ready. Go get cleaned up. Make sure you scrub your hands!"

"Make sure you scrub your hands," Chance mocked, shaking his head as he walked toward the guest bathroom. I went into the kitchen to see what Raegan was making and licked my lips at the feast in front of me. There was lasagna and garlic bread that was just coming out of the oven. Susan was setting the table like we were eating Christmas dinner, complete with wine glasses that I didn't even know I owned.

Chance, Gabe, and I stood around the fancy looking table, looking completely out of place. We were dressed in our tactical gear, sans the bulletproof vests. I still had my guns strapped to my thighs and my shoulder holster still in place.

"Well, sit down." Susan brought out the wine and started pouring.

"Uh, none for us. We're going to hit the road soon. We have a job to go out on."

"You boys work too hard," she scolded in a motherly tone. "You let me know when you're coming home and I'll make sure you have a nice dinner waiting for you."

"Gabe has his own family to eat with," I smirked. Gabe frowned, probably because he didn't get a whole lot of home cooked meals. Isa was a great cook, but she worked too and didn't have the time to make the kind of meals that I got.

"I don't have a family." Chance shook his head sadly, gaining the sympathy of Susan immediately. She walked over to him, pinching his cheek before pulling him in for a hug.

"You come over whenever you want. We can't let you starve."

"Uh, this is still my house," I said irritatedly.

"Oh, hush. These are your friends. Are you really going to let them go hungry?"

"Trust me, they won't starve."

"But I have nothing better to do. I could make a nice meal for you boys a couple of times a week. It's the least I can do to help out around here."

Now I just felt guilty. The woman was trying to help, and even though she was taking over my house, I didn't really feel all that angry for how she took control. She and Raegan pretty much took over taking care of my house and cooking, and Robert had taken over the upkeep of the property and house. I really didn't have a whole lot that I ever had to do.

"Now, you boys sit down and Raegan and I will get dinner on the table." She cupped her hand around her mouth, "Robert! Dinner!" And then she was rushing back into the kitchen, leaving us standing by the dinner table. Gabe and Chance were grinning at me like fools.

"Your mother-in-law is so sweet," Chance said.

"Fuck off."

"She takes such good care of you," Gabe laughed. "And you know what they say about women. If you want to know what your wife will be like when she's older, look to the mother."

"Raegan is not my wife," I bit out.

"And Susan?" Chance let out a low whistle. "She's the trifecta. She can cook, she's fucking hot, and- well, I guess I don't know for sure if she's a good fuck, but based on the way she moves those hips, I'd say you are one lucky fucker."

"Stop talking about my mother- about Susan that way!"

Gabe and Chance broke into laughter. I had walked right into that one.

"He's so fucked."

"Let's get something straight," I said to Chance. "She is not my mother-in-law and Raegan is not my wife."

"Thank God for that," Raegan said as she walked around me. "Oh, by the way, sweetie, I washed your laundry for the trip and packed your bag. I'll run out later today and get you some more underwear and socks. You're running a little low. Should I also get some more lube for you? It looks like your bottle is almost empty."

She smiled sweetly at me as Chance pressed the heels of his hands to his eyes as he roared in laughter. "Good God, woman, I think you just made my whole fucking year."

"Who's ready to eat?" Susan asked as she sat down at the table.

We all pulled out our chairs and sat down. Susan had us all hold hands, which was fucking creepy since I was sitting next to Gabe, and Susan grabbed my hand, gaining looks from both of those assholes.

After we said grace, Susan stood and started dishing out the lasagna and Raegan passed around the garlic bread.

"Do you know when you'll be home, sweetie?" Raegan asked, blinking those damn eyelashes at me. Laughter and snorts sounded around me. I threw down my fork and pushed back from the table. As I stormed away, I decided I wasn't going to let those assholes take a perfectly good meal away from me. I went back, grabbed my napkin and tucked it into the top of my shirt, then grabbed my plate and fork. I would eat in the fucking bathroom if it meant getting away from those assholes.

Chapter Three

RAEGAN

3 months later...

After all this time, Jackson still treated me like I was a delicate flower that he had to be careful around. I just wanted him to see me as a regular person. I wasn't damaged, well, not completely. Yeah, I had made some stupid choices, but that didn't mean I was irrevocably fucked up. Lately, any time I was near him, he made some excuse to get away from me. It was like it was too hard for him to be in the same room with me, afraid that I would freak out on him or start asking him to heal me. He was the only person my age that I had any contact with. It would be nice just to have someone to talk to.

I waited him out all afternoon, appearing to be reading, but really, I couldn't concentrate. I was too worried about putting my plan into motion. I just had to catch him at the right time. So, when he came home and said he was just gonna hang out downstairs and watch movies, I quickly volunteered to join him.

"Uh, you know, I'm probably gonna watch action movies."

"Perfect. I love action movies."

"Yeah, but there could be some...violence in there and I know that could be hard for you."

I stared him down, crossing my arms over my chest. "Do you really think that I'm that weak? That a movie is going to make me freak out and run screaming from the room?"

"I didn't say that-"

"I'm not going to break, Jackson. Stop treating me like I'm made of glass."

"I'm not treating-"

"Yes, you do. Do you know how many times you've backed away from me because you think I'm going to get scared of you? You do it all the time."

"It's not that I think you're going to get scared."

"So what is it then?" I threw my hands in the air, frustrated that he couldn't just give me a straight answer. "You run in the other direction. You don't joke around with me about anything, but I know you can because you do it with Chance and Gabe. Or is it that you just don't want to be associated with a woman like me?"

"It's because I fucking like you!" he shouted when my tirade was over.

We both stood there staring at each other in silence. I wasn't sure quite what to say to that. "Well...I don't get it. If you like me..."

He sighed and rubbed his hand across his face. "Yes, I like you, Raegan, but nothing can happen between us right now."

"Why?"

"Well, first of all, you're living with me and so are your parents. It would be a little weird, don't you think? And second of all, you need more time. You just got out of a bad relationship and I don't want to do anything to fuck you up."

My ears were practically steaming by the time he was done. So, he did think I was too damaged. Perfect.

"You're not going to fuck me up," I bit out. "You just told me that you back away from me because you like me and it's not because you think I'm damaged. Then you tell me that we can't hang out because you think I need more time? Which is it, Jackson? I'm not some little girl that needs her hand held."

"I hear the nightmares that you have. Do you really think that I can't hear your screams on the other side of the fucking house? Those screams don't say that you're fine."

"And what about you? Do you ever have nightmares from being in the military?" He just stared at me, clenching his jaw and refusing to answer. "So, if you have nightmares, does that make you too fucked up for dating or just hanging out with women in general? Does that mean you're too damaged?"

He didn't say anything and I was too pissed to try and change his mind any more right now. How the hell was I supposed to ever move on when the only man my age acted like I was helpless? I couldn't date and I didn't know when I was going to be able to leave. Eventually he would get tired of us being here and then what would happen? Would he send us to a safe house where I would never see anyone or have the chance to be normal?

I went and sat outside on the back deck, staring off into the distance. I had to face the fact that this was my life and I did this to myself. It wasn't his fault that I was stuck and couldn't move on with life. I just wished there was some way for me to know what the future held for me. It would be a lot easier to deal with.

The sliding door opened and Jackson stepped outside. He didn't say anything, just stared into the distance. I wasn't going to be the one to break the silence between us. He cleared his throat several times, almost like he was trying to figure out what to say. Finally, he just said, "So, do you want to watch movies with me?"

I took that as his peace offering. It was probably the best I would get for now and I could deal with that. "Yeah."

I followed him downstairs and sat down on the couch, sure to leave him plenty of space so he didn't feel like I was trying to encroach on his territory or attack him. He had a small kitchen downstairs and a living room set up with a huge tv and a couple of leather couches. I didn't come down here very often because it seemed like Jackson's sanctuary.

He made some popcorn and brought over some pop for us. Halfway through the first movie, I stretched, having given myself leg cramps because of the way I was sitting. I was trying not to disturb him. I didn't want to do anything to get me kicked out of the room.

"What are you doing?"

"I'm stretching."

"That is not stretching. You're moving like you're an old lady that might break her hip if she moves her leg too fast."

"I have leg cramps, okay? I was sitting funny and my legs fell asleep. Then when I tried to move them, my muscles started cramping up." He sighed and gave me the *come here* motion. "What?"

"Give me your legs. I'll rub the cramps out of them."

"Seriously?"

"No, I was joking. I'm really gonna chop them off."

I shifted my legs toward him and he tugged me closer, rubbing the muscles of my calves.

"For all I know, you would. Just because we live together doesn't mean I know who you are. You could be like Dexter. Maybe you're actually a serial killer in your free time."

"A serial killer. And what would lead you to believe that I could be a serial killer?"

"Oh, come on. It's so obvious. You have weapons stashed all around the house."

"I work in security."

"And you have like, twenty rolls of duct tape stashed in various places. It's like you're just preparing for any situation where you might need to tie someone up."

"Duct tape can be a quick fix for a lot of household problems. You never want to run out of that."

"And then there's that big bin with at least five large tarps. Who needs that much tarp? Serial killers."

"It's from when I painted the house. I don't like to be wasteful."

"And then you have a shovel in your shed."

"Most people do."

"You have rope in your front hall closet. Come on, even you have to admit that's weird."

"Alright, I don't remember why I have the rope, but that still doesn't mean I'm a serial killer."

"And then there's the wood chipper you have in the back yard. I'm not sure why anyone would need to have their own personal wood chipper, other than to get rid of a body. And then, you have bleach stacked up in your garage. Do you see how psycho that looks?"

"See, any normal man would see these as regular items that a man needs around a house. A woman automatically freaks out and assumes that I'm a serial killer."

"That's what a serial killer would say! And you were in the military. I'm sure you know hundreds of ways to kill someone without leaving any evidence behind."

"That's not really true. Any good medical examiner would find signs of why a person died."

"And because you know that, it makes me so much more suspicious of the wood chipper. Just throw those bodies in there and no one needs to know about all the people that have gone missing on your property."

"Well, I haven't killed you yet. Although, I am considering it now," he grumbled.

"That's because too many people know that I'm here. You can't just get rid of me without someone from your company getting suspicious."

He snorted, "Are you kidding me? A couple of well placed bullets around the house and a busted in door?" He shrugged nonchalantly, "Everyone would assume you were taken by Xavier's men."

I pursed my lips, refusing to be bested here. "Fine, then tell me what's with the door in the corner of the room over there."

"Panic room. You already know this."

"Not that door," I smiled smugly. "The other one that has a lock on it. The one you told me never to try and open."

"What exactly do you think is behind that door?"

"I don't know. Maybe it's a spare room and you have a freezer inside where you hide limbs and you know, save the meat."

"Cannibalism? You think I'm a cannibal?"

"Or maybe you have a trap door under the basement where you store dead bodies."

"You would smell them."

"Tokens from each of your killings," I guessed.

"You're right. You've got me. I can't deny it any more. I'm a serial killer, but I promise to go to SKA meetings every week until I'm reformed."

"What?"

"Serial Killers Anonymous."

"Well, as long as you try to get help," I sighed dramatically.

He shook his head and turned back to the movie, which we had now missed quite a bit of. His hands lazily continued to massage my legs. For just a few minutes, it felt like we were a real couple, just hanging out and watching some movies on a night in.

"So, why do you really have a wood chipper?"

I was starting to doze off and I probably should just go upstairs and go to bed, but this was the most time I had ever spent with Jackson. I didn't want to leave him just yet. After two movies, we started talking about our favorite movies and making fun of the ones we were watching. It was light and playful, and I got to see a side to Jackson that he never really showed me. His relaxed side. He was always so tense around me.

I struggled to keep my eyes open and every now and again, my head would dip and I would jerk upright again. After the sixth time of that happening, I felt Jackson pull me in closer to him so I could rest my head against him. My body naturally turned into him and snuggled into his warmth. He pulled a blanket over me and I drifted off to sleep.

I woke slightly several times. The first time, Jackson was playing with my hair, running his fingers through it over and over again. It felt so good that I drifted back to sleep. The next time I woke, I had just felt his lips against my cheek. I couldn't be sure that I hadn't dreamt it, but it felt so real that I sighed happily and went back to sleep.

The last time I woke up, it was the middle of the night and completely dark in the basement. The tv was off and Jackson was laying with me on the couch. My body was toward the inside of the couch and I was practically laying on top of him. My head was on his chest and his steady heartbeat thrummed under my cheek. His arm was wrapped around me, holding me close to him. I smiled, happy that things were finally starting to look up between us.

I jerked awake as Jackson practically jumped off the couch, tossing me to the floor. "Ouch," I said as my elbow hit the table in front of us. "That wasn't really how I planned on waking up."

"We fell asleep," he said, slightly panicked.

"Yeah, that's usually what happens when you're tired."

I was squinting under the harsh lighting. He had flicked on practically every light in the room.

"We shouldn't have been sleeping down here, together, I mean. It can't happen again."

"Relax, Jackson. It's not like we were fucking all night. We were just sleeping. Besides, we're both adults. It wouldn't matter if we were fucking."

Jackson looked at me almost as if he were in pain and then he shifted and I saw it. Jackson was hard and by the looks of it, very well endowed. I licked my lips, imagining what it would be like to taste Jackson, to feel his hard cock in my mouth.

"Would you stop it! I'm not a piece of meat."

"That's a piece of meat," I said, pointing to his cock. Probably not the smartest thing to do, but it was early and I was still waking up.

"There aren't going to be any more movie nights or me rubbing your muscles. No more letting you sleep on my shoulder. In fact, we're not even going to be alone in the same room together. It's not safe."

"What exactly do you think will happen? Are you going to put me in your wood chipper?"

"Do you see this?" he pointed to his cock.

"Uh, I've been staring at it for the last few minutes, so, yeah, I see it. I could help you with that-"

"No, that is never going to happen. This," he motioned to his very hard erection, "is not something that can happen again."

"Trouble getting it up?" I asked mockingly.

"I don't have any trouble getting it up. I just shouldn't be getting it up with you."

"Right, because I'm damaged and you're a serial killer," I nodded sleepily. "I'll keep that in mind. Don't fall asleep on the serial killer's lap. He might fuck me before he kills me."

"Do you take anything seriously?"

"I could seriously go for a cup of coffee right now. But if you said that you were going to tie me up naked down here to have some kind of serial killer ritual, I would probably take that seriously."

"I'm not a serial killer!"

"Fine, we'll go with your story. You're just a normal man that knows how to kill professionally, has creepy murder weapons all over the house, and the means to easily dispose of a body."

"I don't have creepy murder weapons."

"You have a sickle in your garage."

"Would you stop giving me an inventory of what I have!"

"Hey, it's not like these are things that I particularly want to know. But you try sitting around a house all day long for close to nine months. You'd be taking a mental inventory of everything too."

"We're getting off track here. Like I was saying-"

"Yeah, I remember. No movies, no fun, no erections. Got it."

"And no more snuggling together."

"Admit it, you liked that."

"I liked it as much as any serial killer likes sleeping with his victims."

"Ha! See, I knew I could get you to admit it!"

He rolled his eyes at me and stormed up the stairs. Well, it had been fun while it lasted.

Chapter Four

JACKSON

We were outnumbered with nowhere to go. Men surrounded us, their weapons trained on each of us. I didn't know how the hell we were going to get out of here, but at least all of our families were safe. I dropped my weapon to the table as instructed, even though it killed me to do it. I still had another gun on me and I always kept a knife strapped to my ankle, something I had done since I got out of the military.

I saw Becky stand and press something on her computer. I wasn't completely sure that she had activated our secondary measures, but I would bet that was what she had just done. All of our computer information would be transferred off site and as soon as that was done, the IT room would go up in flames. I just had to wait for the explosion and until then, fight like hell to survive.

As soon as Cap gave the signal, we all knew what we had to do. Unless he was incapacitated, he was the one that would make the first move. I steadied my breathing and glanced to the guy at my right. He was watching me, but he was also paying attention to his leader.

I saw Cap make his move out of the corner of my eye and took my chance. Grabbing the man's gun, I pointed it up so no one else got shot and then twisted his arm, yanking the gun from his hands. He was so shocked at what was happening, that he wasn't prepared for my attack. With a kick to the gut, he fell to his knees and I pointed the gun at his head. His eyes went wide, pleading with me not to shoot him, but he had come into our place of business and attacked. There was no mercy for someone like him. I pulled the trigger, barely watching as he fell to the ground, before I moved on to the next guy.

Men started rushing us, firing random shots, anything to take us down. I ducked down behind the conference room table and pulled my other weapon. I unloaded a clip as men continued to pour into the building. I couldn't tell where they were coming from, but they must have found another route in since only a few came from the elevator. Sensors were set to go off whenever someone was on the roof, where I was guessing they came from, but somehow, they had bypassed our security measures.

Chills raced down my spine as I felt someone's sights on me. I dove to the right, hoping I wasn't jumping into the line of fire. A bullet burned through my flesh as it pierced my arm. Rolling under the table, I quickly checked the damage, seeing it was only a superficial wound. I grabbed the knife that was strapped to my leg and shot up on the other side of the table, slamming the knife into a man that was about to fire at Cap. He crumpled to the ground and I finished him, slashing my knife across his throat.

Cazzo was right next to me, grappling with another man. A boot shot out, catching me in the side when I couldn't move fast enough. I crashed into the table, my foot catching on a chair. The man was thrown over my body, pushing me back toward the table. I couldn't get my foot untangled from the chair and my leg bent awkwardly, sending sharp pains through my leg.

I bit my lip, holding back the curses that I wanted to shout. Shoving the man off me, I slid off the table, untangling the boot lace that had caught on the chair. I ducked just as a fist flew toward my face and used his momentum to throw him over my shoulder and onto the table. I spun around and snapped his neck before he could stand up and fight back. Arms wrapped around my shoulders and neck. I was just seconds from getting my own neck snapped. I lifted my injured leg, shoving off the table and pushing us backward until we crashed to the ground. I threw my elbow back, slamming it into his face twice before I rolled off and slammed the heel of my hand up into his nose. I heard the bone in his nose snap free from the rest of his skull and watched his eyes go dead as it pierced his brain.

Over the course of five minutes, our building turned into a war zone. Men were scattered all over, some dead and some wounded. We had taken out most of the men, but some of our own were down also. Fire was still spreading through the building and if we didn't get out of here soon, we would all burn up. I limped around the room, searching for Gabe and Chance. Gabe was sitting on the floor against a wall, blood dripping from his head. I ran over to him and knelt by his side. Tearing a piece of my shirt off, I pressed it against his head, his eyes just barely opening to look at me.

"You doing okay, man?"

He tried to nod, but then winced.

"Just stay still. I'll get Hunter or Rocco."

My gaze swung around the room as I looked for one of our medics. Rocco was already patching people up and I called him over. The blood was still seeping from Gabe's head when he got to my side.

"Let me take a look," Rocco said, shoving my hand out of the way. Gabe grabbed my hand just as I was about to back up.

"Find Chance," he muttered. I nodded and stood, going around the room, trying to see where he was. Then I remembered that he had been on his way out of the conference room. He had to be over by the elevators. My leg was killing me, but I pushed through the pain. He wasn't by the elevator and as I searched the rest of the floor, I was beginning to get worried. He wasn't in the conference room or in any of the offices. The smoke was getting too thick now and my eyes burned. Everyone had started to evacuate, but I couldn't leave without Chance.

"Cap!" I shouted from down the hallway. He spun around and ran toward me. "I can't find Chance. Has he already been evacuated?"

"He was taken," he said angrily. "I couldn't stop them."

"We have to get him."

"Too many of us are injured. We need to regroup and find out where they took him. Lola said he was dragged out of here and she caught the plates of the vehicle he was taken in. We'll have Becky check camera feeds from around the town and see which direction they went. Right now, we have to make sure everyone else gets out."

I didn't like it, but he was right. We were in no shape to go after him when most of us were injured. I nodded and followed him to the conference room where it all began.

"Jackson!"

Chris was kneeling on the floor beside Ice, holding his hands to Ice's chest. He looked like he was already dead.

"We have to get him out of here," I coughed. "The whole place is going down."

"We need something to move him on." Chris didn't even look at me, all his attention on Ice and keeping him alive. I tore off my shirt, handing it to Chris to press to Ice's wound. I saw Lola and called her over.

"Help me get a door to carry Ice down on."

We quickly went to work, trying to get a door off its hinges, but it was taking too long. Spotting a desk in one of the offices, I ran in and swept everything off it and threw the table over. Lola grabbed one end and I grabbed the other. The smoke was getting too thick to see anything and we were both coughing so hard that we could barely walk. Back in the conference room, Chris had wrapped another shirt around Ice's mouth and nose to keep the smoke out of his lungs as best as possible. We quickly loaded him up and made our way to the back stairs. The elevator was no longer safe to use.

"Chris, grab the other end," Lola shouted. "I'll run ahead and get all the doors open."

Chris switched places with Lola and we headed into the stairwell. With one glance back, I made sure no one was left behind. The dead were left behind. We had no time to get them out, and even if we did, they deserved to burn in here for what they had done. When we finally made it outside, ambulances were already standing by, waiting for more people that needed to be rushed to the hospital. I helped Chris load Ice into the back of an ambulance and then he climbed inside. A coughing fit overcame me and a paramedic tried to get me to go to the hospital, but I refused.

Looking back at the building, the whole thing was on fire. It would be nothing but ashes by the end of the day. Even though the panic room wasn't attached to the main building, I still turned and ran for it. I had to get to Raegan.

Chapter Five

RAEGAN

It had been hours since we'd been brought here and I still didn't know what was going on. Not that I was alone in that. Every other spouse was here with me and all the kids. They seemed pretty cool about this, though. Like this was all just routine for them.

"Hey, you're Jackson's girl, right?"

I looked at the short woman standing next to me. Her hair was pulled in a tight bun and she wore glasses that made me think of a nerd. I wondered who she was with.

"I'm not Jackson's, but I am staying with him. I'm Raegan."

"I'm Claire. It's nice to meet you."

"So, which man do you belong to?"

"Superman," she said breathlessly.

"That's cool. I would have chosen Iron Man, but I'm still new to this whole thing."

She laughed and fanned herself. "Superman is Derek. This may sound crazy, but when I first met him, I thought he was Superman. There were just all these really strange things happening and he just happened to be there at the right time. What was I supposed to think?"

"I probably would have gone to serial killer first, but yours is more chipper."

"Have you seen one of these guys kill yet?" I shook my head. It was kind of a strange question to ask someone. "H-O-T. That's all I have to say."

"Hot."

"Oh, yeah. The first time I saw Derek kill, it was like eleven men or something. I actually watched him snap a man's neck. I swear to God, I could have jumped him right there."

"What stopped you?"

"He did. Apparently, he thought more men would be coming after us and we had to run away. Blah, blah, blah. You know how it goes. But I'm telling you, the way his muscles flexed every time he threw a punch or twisted a man's body..." She stopped talking and her eyes went wide. Then everything rushed out in a river of word vomit. "Not that I like seeing people being abused or anything. I mean, these were bad people and they deserved to die. I would never wish this on a woman. Not that all women are good. I'm sure there are some really terrible women out there that could use a good beating. But definitely not someone like you. Well, not you specifically, but a woman like you that just got wrapped up in shit unintentionally. At least, that's what I've heard from Derek and I really hope that he's not wrong because then you would break Jackson's heart and he's a really good guy. Not that he's in love with you or anything. He's just a normal guy that hates commitment and pushes people away until someone knocks him upside the head, but he could someday with the right woman. I don't know if that's you or if you're even interested in something like that after having the crap beat out of you, but Jackson would never do that. I mean, look at him. He's like, really hot, and believe me, I've seen him work out. The way sweat drips down his body makes me- I mean, any woman want to lick every drop of sweat from his body. Not that I stare. I'm a married woman after all, but we can still look. It's not like it's breaking the law or something. It's just looking, just-"

I slapped my hand over her mouth to get her to stop blabbering. "Are you always like this?"

"Mmmaahwah."

I removed my hand so she could speak.

"Not always. It's just when I get really nervous, like when I say something stupid. And then one thing leads to another and I'm shoving my foot in my mouth. Figuratively, not literally."

She went quiet as she sucked her lips between her teeth, obviously trying to hold back from saying more. She must be a riot when she's drinking.

"You don't have to worry about offending me. It takes a lot to make me lose my shit."

"I would imagine, otherwise you would have left that asshole a long time ago."

She shook her head, closing her eyes as she bit her lip in shame. I huffed out a laugh. She was right. There was no point in being offended by it.

"That's exactly what I said. You know, I stayed with him through drugs and arms dealing, but the minute he decided to take over someone else's territory, I was like, *that's crossing a line and I can't believe you're such a terrible person.*"

"Well, it could have been worse. He could have been stealing puppies and kittens, then forcing them to dress up like Anne Geddes does for her pictures."

"I know. That's truly cruel and unusual punishment, but I think she did that with babies," I said.

"That's even worse. No child should ever be dressed up like a flower unless the baby is running from the police or something."

"And you know many babies that are on the lam?"

"Hey, it could happen. Kids are dangerous. They steal your time, your body, your sanity! I'm just not sure I can do it. I like having sex with Derek too much. I mean, how could I have my superhero fantasies if there are kids all over the place? And not only that, but I wouldn't be able to watch Derek kill people. Somehow, I don't think that would be appropriate for kids to see."

"I don't know, they already have a training center for the kids here. I'm thinking that their kids seeing someone being murdered isn't that big of a deal to them."

"Hey," Becky yelled. "Jackson and Knight are here!"

Becky had gotten out of the Reed Security building soon after the fighting started. Cazzo had dragged her to the back stairs and made sure she got out. She had run over here and had been working on securing all the information and setting up a new site for everyone to meet up at later.

The doors to the panic room opened and Jackson and the Black Prince rushed in. When Jackson saw me, his shoulders sagged in relief and then he was running toward me. I wasn't really sure how to act around him. I always put up a good front, but inside, I was disappointed that he saw me as a damaged woman. He thought I wasn't ready for a relationship because I hadn't faced reality yet, and he probably had a point. But I wasn't asking for a relationship. I just wanted him to look at me like I could be something more than the woman that stayed with Xavier too long.

So, I was really surprised when he practically crashed into me, pulling my body to his and smashing his lips down on mine. I was so shocked that I didn't know what to do for a moment. But just when my brain came online and I responded, he pulled back. His eyes bored into mine, but I couldn't read him. I didn't know what he was thinking. Was it a mistake? Was he wishing he hadn't kissed me? Or maybe he was thinking about doing it again. My eyes dropped to his throat as he visibly swallowed. He took a step back, running his hand over his head. It was only then that I noticed he was favoring one leg.

"Oh my gosh! What happened to your leg?"

"It's fine. I just bent it awkwardly."

"What about everyone else? Is anyone hurt?"

His eyes cringed slightly and I knew that it was bad. "I need to talk to everyone." He turned and let out a high whistle. Everyone got quiet and Knight walked over to where he stood, his arm still wrapped around Kate's waist protectively.

"You all know we were attacked. We have a lot of injuries, but most aren't too serious."

"Most?" Claire asked stepping forward.

"I need Lucy and Lindsey to come to the hospital with me. Nobody else has life threatening injuries, so I want the rest of you to stay here."

"I want to go with Lucy," Claire said quickly, but Knight shook his head.

"For now, we need to know that everyone is safe. It's too distracting if we have more people than necessary to watch."

Jackson looked back to me and then turned away, walking out of the panic room with Knight, Lucy, and Lindsey. The women looked scared to death and they were gripping each other's hands. Neither had said a word when Jackson said their names, which was either shock or understanding.

"What's gonna happen now?" I asked Claire quietly.

"Now we go to war."

Chapter Six

JACKSON

Knight and I drove Lindsey and Lucy over to the hospital. As soon as we got in the truck, the questions started pouring out.

"What happened?" Lucy asked.

"How bad are they hurt? You said life threatening."

"Yeah, is that like a life threatening paper cut or life threatening like getting shot in the head?"

"Are we going to be able to see them?"

"I swear, if Hunter dies on me, I'm going to use his body for witch-craft rituals."

"Tell me about it. John didn't even have the courtesy to clean the hair out of the sink before he went and got himself shot or knifed or body slammed into a hard wall."

"Men are so inconsiderate. You know, this is just like Hunter to go out and make something about him. I told him I wasn't ready to start a family, so he went out and got shot so he could wield that sexy body against me. *I could be dead right now, Lucy. We should make a baby now while we still have the chance.*"

Lindsey leaned over the front seat, grabbing at my shirt. "Is this payback? Like, I scared him when I got thrown down the stairs by a burglar, so now he's going to one up me? Because I can do worse."

"I don't think—" I tried to break in, but was cut off by Lucy.

"You know, you're right! Hunter's trying to show me how upset he was when I was hurt and didn't want help. Is that it, Jackson? Is he trying to teach me a lesson? Because I will take Kate with me and we can sit outside the house all night, just like he did with Knight." She turned her steely gaze on Knight. "Did you put him up to this? Is this some kind of test?"

Knight just glanced over at me with a bored look on his face. Knight didn't put up with crazy shit like this. His woman didn't freak out like these ladies were. Then again, he watched her like a hawk, so she never had the opportunity to freak out.

"Seriously, Jackson, why aren't you talking? Why aren't you telling us what happened?"

"If you two would shut up for a minute I could get a word in!" I yelled.

The two women looked shocked and then slumped back in their seats, crying and holding each other. I closed my eyes and tried to regain my composure. I had to remember that they just found out their husbands were injured and they were still trying to process what was happening.

"That's why you don't say anything," Knight grumbled beside me.

I turned around, hating that I had to tell them what happened. "Hunter was shot in the neck. It was pretty bad, but Knight got there pretty fast and applied pressure. Rocco took over and got him out of the building and to an ambulance. I don't know anything more than that."

"But he can survive that, right?" Lucy asked, wiping the tears from her eyes.

"He can," I said hesitantly. "We just have to hope we were fast enough."

"What about John?"

"He was shot in the chest. Chris was doing everything he could for him, but there was a lot of blood."

"What does that mean?"

I looked at Lindsey, trying my best not to show my doubt. "It means that we'll have to see when we get to the hospital."

After that, it was silent the rest of the way to the hospital, apart from the sniffles that came from the back seat. As much as the girls wanted to run ahead, Knight and I made them walk between us so we could protect them. We didn't know if the threat was gone yet and we weren't taking any chances.

It was chaos in the hospital. Nurses and doctors were rushing around the emergency room and shouting to one another as they tried to handle all the men that had been brought in. I wasn't sure what the hell was going on and who else was injured. Cap was pacing the waiting area as a nurse followed him, trying to get him to sit down. His arm hung loosely at his side and he was shouting at someone on his phone.

Florrie was sitting in a chair with her head in one hand while her other arm was still in the sling. Cazzo, Sinner, Derek, Lola, Chris, and Jules all stood together, talking animatedly. It only took one look at Sinner to see he was favoring one leg, much like I was. But he had blood running down his leg, which made me wonder what the hell he was doing out here.

"Sinner!" I shouted as I walked over. He gave a chin lift but stayed where he was.

"What the hell are you doing? You have blood dripping all over the fucking floor."

Cazzo jerked Sinner around, checking where the blood was coming from. Then he smacked him upside the head.

"What the hell are you doing? You should be getting checked out," Cazzo snapped at him.

"It's just a ricochet. I'm fine."

"You have blood dripping all over the fucking place," Cazzo shot back.

Sinner rolled his eyes. "I think I can handle a little blood loss. It's not that bad."

"Let me see," Cazzo said, flicking his hand up as if to tell Sinner to raise his pant leg. Sinner took a seat and pulled up his pant leg and Cazzo grabbed his foot, placing it on his knee.

"See?" Sinner laughed. "It's just a-ow! What the fuck?"

Cazzo pressed on his wound, making more blood seep out and causing Sinner a helluva lot of pain.

"Doesn't look like just a little blood to me." Cazzo dropped Sinner's leg to the floor with a thunk.

"That's because you just shoved your fucking finger in my hole!"

I glanced to my left and laughed when I saw Cap and the look on his face. "We're at a fucking hospital. Is it possible that just once I can walk in on a conversation with you guys without feeling like a fucking pervert?"

"Not that hole," Sinner grumbled. "He shoved his finger in my bullet hole."

"Sinner..." Cap just shook his head and sighed. "I want everyone checked out. Go check in with the nurses and tell them what the fuck is going on with you. I want everyone seen by a nurse before we leave this fucking hospital."

"Does that go for you too, Cap?" Cazzo asked.

Now that Cap was closer, I could see that he wasn't too steady on his feet anymore and the amount of blood that still leaked from the hole in his shoulder said that he should be in a fucking hospital bed right now. As if on cue, his eyes fluttered and he started to tilt. I grabbed onto his arm right before he started to go down and Cazzo caught him from the front, holding him up so he didn't crash to the floor.

"Nurse!" Chris yelled. "We need a stretcher over here."

A few minutes later, Cap was plopped none too gently on the stretcher and was being wheeled off, but before the last nurse could walk away, Cazzo snagged her by the arm. "That's not all. We have one more patient refusing to be seen."

Chris hauled Sinner out of the chair and pushed him forward.

"What's wrong with this one?" the nurse asked.

"Bullet wound to the leg," Cazzo informed her. "But watch him, he's a sweet talker."

"One of those, huh?" The nurse smiled and waved over another woman. "I have just the nurse for you. Winnie loves the bad boys, really knows how to handle them, if you know what I mean."

A mean looking older nurse walked over, smiling sadistically at Sinner. "What do you have for me?"

"Nothing!" Sinner insisted, panicking at the sight of the mean woman. "It's a scratch. I'm fine."

An orderly brought over a wheelchair and shook his head with a smile as he walked away.

"Relax, sir." Chris pushed him into the chair and grinned, as the nurse leaned in and whispered. "It's not like I'm going to give you a colonoscopy." She turned to wheel him away, but then turned back to us with a grin. "Yet." She laughed maniacally as she wheeled him off, all the while Sinner tried to escape the wheelchair.

"Do you need to be seen?" Cazzo asked me. "You're limping pretty bad."

"No, I just tweaked my leg. It's just a muscle strain."

"You're sure?"

"Positive. How are Ice and Hunter?"

Cazzo looked over to where Lindsey and Lucy were sitting, waiting to hear anything about their husbands and leaned in close to whisper. "Hunter was barely alive when he was brought in. Rocco said he was shot in the neck, but there was no exit wound. He was taken into surgery immediately, but we haven't heard anything yet."

"Shit," I said, scrubbing my hand over my face. "Lucy was threatening Hunter with all kinds of shit on the way here. If he doesn't survive this..."

"I know. Ice isn't in any better condition. He was hit in the chest and..."

"Yeah, I saw. It was pretty fucking bad."

"We just have to wait for updates. Burg was brought in with wounds to his leg. Gabe has a pretty nasty concussion from what I could tell. Alec jumped in front of Florrie and took a bullet to his side. I don't think it hit anything major, but again, we have to wait and see. Rocco," Cazzo scoffed, "the asshole had a knife wound and didn't tell anyone. We didn't know he was hurt until the fucker almost passed out when we got here. The rest of us got off easy."

"Wait, where's Craig?"

"I thought he was with you."

"No, I haven't seen him since we were attacked. He came into the conference room with me, but...He was going on and on about having a bad feeling on the way to Chance's house."

Cazzo pulled out his phone and dialed, his eyes searching the room as he waited. "No answer." He dialed again. "Becky, I need anything you have on a location for Craig. Can you pull up the footage from the conference room? Okay, let us know." He pocketed his phone, swearing under his breath. "She's going to look, but she said that there wasn't very much before the cameras went offline."

We split up and went around the room asking the last time anyone had seen Craig. Nobody had seen him, everyone thinking they had seen him leaving with someone else. The hospital hadn't admitted him, at least not under his name, and there was no record of a John Doe being admitted either.

"Fuck, I hope to God we didn't leave him in the office to burn."

Bile churned in my stomach as I tried to remember where everyone was when I looked back before leaving the building. I just couldn't remember seeing anyone but our enemies lying on the ground. But that didn't mean he wasn't somewhere else I hadn't seen.

"The chances of him being left behind in the building are minuscule. None of us would have walked past him if he was injured. One of us would have grabbed him. He's gotta be somewhere else."

"But how the hell do we find him?"

"We wait and see what Becky says. Maybe he went home or..."

"Ran to the grocery store for some beer?" I said sarcastically.

Cazzo was under a lot of pressure at the moment and I didn't need to be laying my shit on him right now. It was bad enough that we had so many injured, but then Cap was down for the count and that just made it feel like we were missing a limb.

"So, what's the plan now?" I asked.

"We need someone posted outside everyone's rooms. We can't afford to take any chances right now."

We gathered everyone up and got our orders from Cazzo. "Alright, I want someone posted outside every room our men are in. Derek, you've got Sinner. Lola, you'll take Hunter when he gets out of surgery, but until then, cover Rocco. Chris, you're outside Ice's room when he gets out of surgery. Jackson, you're outside Gabe's room. Knight, you stay out here with the girls. Jules, you're on Burg. Florrie, if you're up to it, you're outside Alec's room."

"I still have one good arm. That's all I need." Florrie was so badass.

"What about Chance and Craig?" Derek asked. "What's the plan?"

"We'll wait for Cap to wake up for that. We just don't have any manpower right now. Becky's working on it and she'll call us if she finds anything. Until then, we take care of our own. Cash is on his way, but he's not gonna be here for at least a day. Our best bet is to lay low until we can figure out our next move."

Chapter Seven

CAP

"I told you that I'm fine. I don't need to stay in this fucking bed anymore," I practically yelled at the nurse. "I'll sign the waiver releasing you and the hospital from any liability. I have men waiting out there for me and I need to get out of here."

"Sir, you were shot."

"And the bullet has been removed."

"But we need to monitor–"

"I'll still be in the fucking hospital! If I collapse, I'll be just down the hall from the best medical care in town," I gritted through my teeth. The nurse didn't look too happy, but got everything taken care of so I could get back to my men. What a clusterfuck this had all been. If I was being honest with myself, I really did need to lie down for a while. I was a little dizzy and I was fucking exhausted, but there were others that were in worse condition than me. I didn't even know for sure the extent of the injuries. I couldn't just sit here and pretend none of this was going on.

"I'll make sure to look after him," Cazzo said to the nurse from the doorway. "We'll be in the waiting area and I promise to make sure he takes it easy."

The nurse gave a curt nod and scowled at me before leaving the room.

"What happened while I was out?"

"Sinner is getting his leg taken care of. Everyone else is guarding anyone who's laid up. I have Knight watching Lindsey and Lucy."

"Any word from Becky?"

"Not yet. I didn't want to call her and keep bugging her."

As we walked into the waiting area, I saw Lindsey and Lucy still waiting. They looked tired and if they would listen, I would tell them to go back to the panic room to get some sleep. Knight spotted me and came over. When Cazzo told me he was watching the girls, I was actually surprised that he was here and not in the panic room with Kate and his daughter. "Any word on the guys?"

"Rocco's fine. He's being patched up and discharged. Gabe should be released in the morning. He has a pretty nasty concussion. They want to monitor him overnight. Alec will be released soon also. They were all the lucky ones. Burg just got out of surgery a little bit ago. The bullet Lola put in him nicked his bone and was lodged in his muscle, but he should be good for the most part. Ice and Hunter are still in surgery."

"If they're in surgery that means they're not dead."

"Craig is missing," Knight said after a moment.

"What the fuck do you mean?"

"We don't know where he is," Cazzo said. "We all thought he was with someone else. Nobody saw him leave, but he hasn't been admitted to the hospital."

"I checked before we left. The only people left were Lola, Chris, and Jackson. If he was in the building, I would have seen him." I knew I hadn't left anyone behind. Everyone else got out.

"But you were out before Chris."

I narrowed my eyes at Knight, not liking his implications. "I was helping Gabe get to an ambulance. I was about to go back when they came out with Ice."

"I'm not accusing you, Cap. I'm saying that maybe he went back in. Since you were busy with Gabe, maybe nobody saw him go back in. Maybe he thought he would help get Ice out and got pinned down."

"Shit." If we left a man behind, I would never forgive myself.

"Becky's looking into the security footage, trying to see if she can find him. But there's not a whole lot before the cameras went out from the fire," Cazzo said.

"So, we have two missing men. What do you think the probability is that Chance and Craig were both taken?"

Knight leaned in closer, making sure no one else could hear us. "If this was The Broker, he would have gone after Chance because of his connection to Morgan. Why would he take Craig?"

"But if this wasn't The Broker, Chance could have just been convenient to take. He was by the elevator and unconscious. Maybe Craig was taken also," I surmised.

Knight glanced back at Lindsey and Lucy who were sitting together, staring off at nothing. "What the fuck is going on, Cap? There's no way anyone should have been able to get into the building. At least, not as fast as they did. They followed you back and were in the building in less than two hours. It's like they knew what to expect."

"They would have to have gotten access through one of us," Cazzo added.

It still didn't add up. Why give them access? "The Broker deals in information and if someone crosses him, they end up dead. But the only thing we did was rescue Morgan. It doesn't make sense that we would be attacked by his men. So, why would they be after us? What information could we have that The Broker would want?"

"Records?" Knight asked. "Is it possible he knows that we've figured out who he is?"

"Wait." Something was missing from all this. Something that none of us had thought of. "When's the last time anyone saw Storm?"

"You'd have to ask Jackson. I know he was around for a little bit after we got Morgan back, but I don't know what his plans were after that."

"What if he's the mole? He worked at the club. He was the one that called us to help. He befriended Morgan and she trusted him, so of course she would go to him for help. Then, he could make sure Chance was out of the way by telling him Morgan was with The Broker. If they were working together, they set it all up perfectly.

Chance was the only one that would have spontaneously shown up at the club. He was the only one Storm would have to worry about. They got Morgan and us out of the way. And then after we found Morgan, we invited him back to our offices. He would have seen all our security measures."

Knight shook his head. "Even if he was the mole, how did he bypass the facial scanner?"

"You set up the new measures," I said. "If you were going to break in, how would you do it? You're the hacker."

"See, that's what I don't understand. I tested all these things out for weeks. Even the most experienced hacker wouldn't have been able to get past all our sensors and into the building in less than two hours. They got past all our external sensors at the entrances. They were up on the roof and no alerts went off. I had backup systems in place in case we were hacked, but none of those systems were activated. Once they were past those, they had to get through the security measures in the elevator, at the roof access, and the back stairwell. There are five different doors they had to go through to get up the back stairs, all with different security measures. Whoever did this had to have access to our prints, and that's something you can't get on the fly. You can't just hack a person's handprint and scan it. They would need the actual hand for our sensors or the full print on a glove. Not only that, the eye scanner can be hacked, but it would take hours to reprogram the system to get in. And then there are the codes, which change daily. How did someone get the codes for the day on top of everything else?"

"We need to have Becky go through the records and see who has used the scanner over the past month and when. It might not give us anything, but we need to know if there are any abnormalities. If the information wasn't destroyed, maybe we can get whose scan was used right before we were ambushed."

"Fuck, this has to be a leak," Cazzo growled. "How else would anyone get all that information? They would have to have it weeks in advance, right?"

"To get it all done in one shot?" Knight asked. "Hell yeah. It would take a lot of practice. All the security measures are timed, so it's not like they could take their time if something went wrong. The whole system would have shut down and we would have been alerted immediately that we had intruders."

"Which means it couldn't be Storm," Cazzo surmised. "At least, it can't be just him. He would have to be working with someone."

"So, who is it then?"

Knight and I looked around the room and I knew what Knight was going to say before he opened his mouth. "It's possible Craig is the traitor. It would explain why he's not here."

"I never thought Cal would be a traitor either, but he turned on all of us. I suppose anything's possible. Fuck, I just don't want to believe it. I'd like to think I'm not such a bad judge of character that I would employ two traitors in ten years."

"I saw no signs, if it makes you feel better. But I've been fooled before."

"Let's keep this between the three of us for now," I said quietly. "We don't need any distrust right now. We're already broken. We need to regroup and find out who the fuck is behind this."

"Agreed."

"For now, we keep everyone posted outside the rooms. You said Rocco's being released?"

"Yeah. He should be out any minute now."

Commotion to my left caught my attention as Lucy and Lindsey stood and rushed to a doctor that was walking out.

"Who is it?" Lindsey said urgently.

"Family of Hunter Papa-"

"That's me," Lucy practically shouted. "How is he? Did he survive? That man is so stubborn, there's no way he didn't make it out of surgery."

"He did make it out. He's stable, but in critical condition and he's being moved to the ICU."

"What happened?" I asked calmly.

"He was shot in the neck, but the bullet didn't exit. The bullet bounced around in his chest, hitting some ribs. It's currently lodged in his shoulder, but for now, there's no need to remove it. We had to crack his chest to tie off veins and arteries. He lost a lot of blood and we had to give him multiple transfusions. He flatlined several times, and unfortunately, he's not out of the woods yet. With as many blood transfusions as he had, he's at high risk for blood clots."

"But he's going to live," Lucy said.

"We'll see how the next few days go. I'm sorry I don't have a better answer for you, but it really is up to his body right now to continue fighting."

"And what about the bullet?"Lucy asked. "You said it doesn't need to be removed, but isn't that dangerous?"

"It can be just as dangerous to remove the bullet. And he's in no condition for any more surgery. We'll keep an eye on the bullet and if it's not causing any problems, it's best to leave it in and let him recover."

Lucy swiped at her eyes and I wrapped my arm around her shoulder to show my support. "When can I see him?"

"He's being moved to the ICU right now. The nurse will get you when he's all set up. He's in a medically induced coma right now to allow his body to heal. He's on a ventilator and we'll keep him on that for a few days as he recovers."

Lucy nodded and the doctor smiled sadly as he walked away. Lucy turned to me and I wrapped my arms around her for a hug. She started making strangled noises against my chest and was flailing around. This had to be so hard on her. She shoved back from me, but she wasn't crying. She was pissed.

"What the hell is wrong with you guys? You're all a bunch of military experts, but you keep getting shot. Hunter got shot in the neck. Seriously? There's all these other areas to get shot that are larger targets and he takes one to the neck? Did he stand up taller to stretch his neck for better access? Geez, you guys talk about needing to put us in bubble wrap, but I'm beginning to think we have to take over for you. Look at all of you! You're shot in the shoulder. Hunter is on a ventilator, and John is still in surgery. Who knows how everyone else is. And Chance is missing!"

Then she spun around and grabbed Knight by the shirt, pulling him closer. "And you suck at your job. You're supposed to teach these guys how to protect themselves and half of them are in the hospital."

"Lola," I snapped as she walked out with Rocco. He looked like he had seen better days, but at least he was able to walk.

"Yeah, Cap."

"I want you posted outside Hunter's room in the ICU. Let me know if you have any issues with the staff."

"I'm on it, Cap."

She walked off with Lucy to the ICU and I looked around to assess who I still had available to help out.

"Rocco, everything good?" I asked.

"Just a scratch," he said with a shrug.

"They don't admit people for a scratch."

"Just a few stitches. I'll be good as new in no time."

I nodded, not sure I believed him, but he was a medic. He knew how far he could push himself.

"We're going to have to take shifts being on watch. I don't want anyone left unprotected."

It was sometime in the early morning before we heard anything about Ice. A tired looking doctor came out and sat next to Lindsey and I.

"Your husband was shot in the heart." Lindsey gasped and I tightened my hold on her hand, though I wasn't sure if it was for her or me. "His chest had been properly packed, so he made it into surgery and we were able to put him on bypass. The bullet hit his left ventricle, but luckily missed the aorta. We were able to repair everything, but he'll have a long recovery ahead of him. We'll keep him on bypass for a day at least."

"If you fixed everything, why does he have to stay on bypass? Are you not sure that he'll be okay?"

"It's to make sure he retains a good sinus rhythm. It's normal for heart surgery."

Since Ice was already in the ICU, the doctor led her to see him, answering the questions she continued to ask. I slumped in a chair, feeling exhaustion hit me hard. I hadn't spoken to Becky in hours, but if she had found something, she would have called. I needed sleep, but at this point, I wasn't sure what to do. I wanted to get back to the panic room and see my girls, but we had men here that were severely injured and there would be no one to watch out for them if we left. In short, we were just too beat down to do much of anything right now.

Relief and worry filled me when Becky called. She would only call me if she had found something. I slid the touch sensor to answer and held the phone to my ear.

"Bossman, I have news you're not going to like."

My eyes slipped closed as I dropped my head. "What is it?"

"Rocco's handprint was the one used on the scanner."

My head whipped up, my eyes searching for Rocco. I didn't see him anywhere and he wasn't watching anyone right now, but that didn't mean jack shit. Any one of our guys would allow him to visit with our injured men. He was one of us, at least, that's what we all thought.

"How sure are you about this?"

"One hundred percent. I don't have any other proof that he's the one that did it. I'm just saying it was his handprint."

"Do you have any way of telling if the handprint came directly from his hand?"

"No, the scanner doesn't have thermal imaging or a skin detector. There's no way for me to know if someone placed his prints on the scanner."

"Alright, thanks, Becky. Let me know if you find anything else."

I walked over to Knight, gesturing for him to follow me. When we were out of earshot of anyone that might walk by, I laid out what Becky had told me.

"What do you think?"

"I'm thinking that it sounds too much like a setup," he replied, crossing his arms over his chest.

"How do you figure? You suspect Craig and we don't have anything pointing to him."

"Craig is missing. No one's seen him and we most likely don't have any footage that will help us. To me, a missing person is more suspicious than a handprint. Given the right technology, anyone can hack a scanner."

"You said it couldn't be done."

"No, I said it couldn't be done in under two hours along with everything else. If you think about it, anyone could have gotten Rocco's handprint at some point. They might not have even targeted him. It could have been whoever was easiest to get a print from."

"So, what the hell do we do then?"

"We run his handprint against the one that was used and look for inconsistencies. The program is designed to allow minimal flaws because you might have a cut on your hand or something. If we compare the two, we should be able to see if there's anything that doesn't line up right. That should tell us if it was his handprint or a double."

I nodded, pulling out my phone to dial Becky and relay the information. This was all way too fucking complicated. We were too vulnerable right now and that led to mistakes. We needed to get out of this fucking place and back to safety before someone else got hurt.

Chapter Eight

CHANCE

My head was killing me. I vaguely remembered being tossed around in the back of a truck or van. I remembered that my hands and feet had been tied, and not being able to move, but then I passed out again. Wherever I was now, the light was bright and made my headache even worse.

I felt around my restraints, but couldn't concentrate enough to find a way out of them. It was rope, but it felt really tight. I swiveled my head and blurry images came into my view. I blinked again and again until my vision cleared slightly. There were men sitting down on sofas, but we were moving. I shook my head again, looking around the room some more. A plane. We were on a plane.

I let my head fall back to the floor. I felt so sluggish, but not like I normally felt when I had a concussion. This was different. It was like something was weighing me down, like I had something in my system. That had to be it. They must have drugged me.

"Looks like your friend is waking up," one of the men said. My head swiveled on the ground, but I still couldn't make out any faces. Everything was just too damn blurry.

"Give him another dose. We're not taking any chances until we reach our destination."

That voice, it sounded so familiar, but I couldn't place it. It must not have been one I heard often or I would recognize it right away, right? I felt my arm being jerked and the slight prick in my arm. I briefly thought that I should be fighting back, but thinking was not something that came easily right now. It didn't take long for me to slip into blackness.

I fell hard to the ground, landing in what I thought was mud. I was no longer tied, but I couldn't move my arms or legs no matter how much I tried. How much of that shit had they given me? My face was in mud, squishing against my skin and slipping inside my mouth, but I couldn't move to get it out.

"What are we supposed to do with him now?"

"Leave him here. The boss said we leave him here until he gives us further orders."

Where was here? Who was the boss?

"What does the boss have against this guy?"

"Don't know. He said he's just following orders."

Metal slammed together and then they were gone. I laid there for hours, waking up a little more every time. My body started to shake as the drugs wore off and I pulled my knees up to my chest to ward off the chill. It was only then that I realized I was stripped naked. I pushed up to my knees and hit my head when I tried to stand. The ceiling wasn't even high enough for me to sit up all the way on my knees.

The metal I had heard earlier was the sound of the door slamming. I was in a cell with a door similar to those in a prison. The door was only wide enough for one person to fit through. Even though the world was tilting in every direction, I held out my hand and tried to grip onto the bars. It took me a few tries before I connected with a bar and when I tried to push against it, I fell to the side, slamming into the ground again.

Refusing to give up, I felt along the walls to find out how wide my cell was, but came up short after just a few feet. I wouldn't even be able to stretch out all the way in here. Trying to escape was pointless right now. Even if I got out of here, I wasn't sure I would be able to walk in a semi-straight line. I huddled in the corner of the cell, trying to escape the chill of the night air as much as possible until the drugs wore off. At least the wind wasn't hitting me directly.

When my head finally felt clear enough to think, I sat up and leaned back against the wall. I was still dizzy and the events of the last however many hours were still fuzzy in my mind. From what I could piece together, I had been taken at Reed Security and then transported on a plane. Someone wanted something with me, but what exactly, I wasn't sure. What I did know was that they were going to get what they needed through torture. I wasn't just hanging around in this cell naked for no reason.

When the first light of dawn started to appear, I looked out of my cell for any sign of where I was, but all I saw were trees. Palm trees, to be exact, though I highly doubted I was in Florida. I could see a path that trailed off through the trees, but the trees were so dense that I couldn't see where it led. I sat back against the wall across from my cell door and let the cooler air wash over me. I could feel the humidity building already and I was sure as soon as the sun was up, I would be sweating profusely.

It was a few hours before anyone came to see me again. It was a man that looked vaguely familiar, but I couldn't place his face. He approached me hesitantly and squatted down to my level. Shoving a shallow metal bowl under the door, he took a step back like I was going to attack him. With what? I looked down at the bowl and grimaced at the supposed meat that was in the watery concoction. He pulled out a bottle of water and rolled it to me under the door. Interesting. Maybe bad water in the area?

The man sat back and watched me, probably trying to figure out what I would do. Since there really was nothing I could do right now, I stared back. The man was sweating, but it wasn't warm enough yet for that. And then there was the way he was squatting, perched like he was ready to run. He looked around in disgust, but none of it was directed at me, but the area in general. He didn't even have a gun strapped to him.

"Who are you?" I asked after a minute, snatching the water bottle up and guzzling half the bottle.

"You don't need to know that." His voice wasn't the strong, intimidating kind that I would have expected. In fact, he almost seemed like he didn't want to be here. I didn't want to push though and ruin my chances with him. I had to let him get to know me first.

"Do you know why I'm here?"

He shrugged. "I just do what I'm told."

"Thank you for the water," I said, lifting the bottle in a thanks gesture.

He nodded and took a step back. He looked like he wanted to say something more, but then turned and walked away. I could work on him. A guy like him didn't want to be in a place like this, doing whatever he was doing. Since I was so out of it last night, I hadn't been able to check the bars on the door for any weak spots. I quickly felt around the bars, looking for someplace to dig, but the ground was hard after just an inch. If I started digging, it would take weeks to get out and someone would notice the hole as I dug. I could try digging next to the concrete wall and hope that no one would notice, but it wasn't a guarantee. Right now, it was my only option.

Chapter Nine

RAEGAN

"Wait," I stuttered in confusion. "We go to war? Like, battlecry and swords drawn?" I asked Claire.

"No," she said with wide eyes, "but that would be so cool. We could all get in old fashioned battle gear and take those assholes down. Derek could play Mel Gibson's character in *Braveheart*. He's Irish!"

"Uh, isn't *Braveheart* based in Scotland?"

Claire shrugged. "Work with me here. None of the guys are Scottish that I know of. Derek's the closest and he's so good at playing the hero."

"Wasn't William Wallace hung, drawn, and quartered?"

Claire huffed in irritation. "You are totally ruining my fantasy here."

"You fantasize about going into battle with a sword?" I asked slowly. What had I gotten myself into with these people?

"Well, I've never had a fantasy where I was the one that rescued Derek. He's usually the superhero. I think now is the perfect time for a change in our roleplaying."

"I do often fantasize about shoving a sword into someone. Although, there is no hero, the sword is a gun, and I don't have to wear any face paint."

Claire grabbed my hand and dragged me through the panic room to a room with computers set up. There were two women looking at something on a screen and talking animatedly.

"Maggie!" Claire said excitedly. "What's the plan? Should we gear up? Strap on our armor? Sharpen our swords? Prepare the horses?"

"Well, since we don't live in Medieval times, I think guns would be more efficient."

"Yeah, but can't you just see it?" Claire said dreamily. "We'd be in those beautiful dresses and our knights would come to save us. Maybe there would be a duel in order for Derek to defend my honor!"

"I totally get what you're saying. I always hoped that when Xavier went off to sell his weapons that he would die in a duel defending my honor. That way I could leave him thinking better of him."

"You're kind of twisted, you know that?" Claire said.

"Says the woman that likes to watch her husband kill people."

"Look," Maggie interrupted. "Normally, I would be all about running off and fighting the battles for our men. Defending their honor and killing the assholes that dared threaten us. I gotta say, I would really love to throw a grenade right about now. But Sebastian would be stressed out if we ran off and that's not what he needs."

Becky placed a hand to Maggie's forehead, frowning as she pulled her hand back. "Strange. I thought for sure that you were running a high fever because there is no way that Maggie, the woman that is so impulsive no one can ever predict what she'll do, other than run into danger, would tell everyone to stand down."

"I'm trying to be a better wife and think about my husband's feelings."

"So, no swords?" Claire asked in confusion. "No gun battle at the OK Corral? No riding off into the sunset on horseback?"

"Afraid not," Maggie sighed. "We're sitting this one out, Lois."

"Damn, that just sucks." Claire plopped down in a chair and pouted. "You know, Derek wouldn't just sit by while something happened to us. And you know that Cap would be leading the charge."

"Claire, we're not going."

"Fine."

I sat down by Claire, who really looked truly devastated to not be able to go fight. It looked like we weren't going to go play Dungeons and Dragons anytime soon.

It was so irritating waiting around. I had nothing to do and no idea what was going on. Besides Jackson coming by earlier, we hadn't heard anything about what was going on. We knew some people had been injured, but that was it. I wandered around the panic room, which was a ridiculous term for what we were in. It was more of an underground mansion. There were enough rooms that every family could have someplace to sleep, along with about ten extra people. Every room was the same as mine for the most part. There were several beds with room dividers and an attached bathroom. There was a closet in every room that was filled with essentials like toothbrushes, soap, and hairdryers. They hadn't missed a thing. And every room had spare clothes of nearly every size. Did they just go shopping for everyone and have their rooms stocked with extras?

When I wandered into the kitchen, my eyes widened at the enormity of it all. It was more like an industrial kitchen with its super fancy appliances and steel countertops with special drains. I momentarily thought of a morgue with a drain on the table for autopsies and shuddered. There were two refrigerators, which seemed a little ridiculous until I thought of how many men there were, not to mention wives and kids.

There were women and children scattered all throughout the extra rooms, which could be called living rooms, but were more like mini houses. There were three of these rooms and they all held every luxury you would find in a normal house. But the most disturbing room I found was behind what looked like a pantry door. It was filled with everything from canned goods, toilet paper, and bottled water to these weird packages that said they were meals, but vacuum sealed. I tossed it back in the pile and walked out.

Hearing a single voice down one of the halls, I went to see who was there and almost choked on my own saliva. The room was like Steve Jobs's dream come true. In reality, it rivaled the tech room in the Reed

Security building. Becky was sitting in front of a computer and I almost walked in when I heard her speaking to someone on the phone.

"Well, who's currently admitted?...What about Jackson? I saw him limping around here earlier....Uh-huh....He just collapsed?... Oh my God! ...Is he going to be okay? ...How long do they think he'll make it? ...Is anyone going to tell her? ...I can't believe this..."

I couldn't listen to any more of her conversation. Jackson had collapsed and they didn't think he was going to make it? And apparently no one was going to tell me. But why would they? As far as everyone else knew, Jackson and I weren't an item. And technically we weren't. He had kissed me earlier, but that had been our first kiss. I felt something hard sink in the pit of my stomach. I couldn't believe that I would never see Jackson again. I had to at least go say goodbye to him. I had come to care for him a lot over the past year, and even though I pretended like it didn't hurt me when his friends mocked him for having a wife, deep down, I was wishing that someday that would be true.

I rushed down the hall, needing to get out of here. I had to get to the hospital. But when I got to the entryway, I realized it wasn't as simple as opening a door. I kicked the door in frustration and then hopped around on one foot from the pain I had just inflicted on myself.

"What did the door ever do to you?" Maggie asked from behind me.

I turned and glared at her. "I just found out that Jackson's in the hospital. He collapsed and they don't think he's going to make it. I have to get to him, but this stupid door won't open."

"Yeah, it's not meant to open. If just anyone could come and go as they please, it wouldn't be very safe."

I slid down the door and dropped my head into my hands. This couldn't be happening. Jackson was supposed to be mine. That was the way I had planned it since I got to know him. I mean, he hadn't come around to the same way of thinking, but it was only a matter of time before we figured things out. At least, that was what I told myself. Now I would never know what could have been.

"I can't believe I'm not going to get to say goodbye."

Maggie sat down next to me and patted my knee. "You don't know for sure that he won't make it. You just have to stay positive."

"Is that what you would do?" I looked at her sharply, begging her to deny it.

Maggie gave a look of sympathy and then checked to see if anyone else was around. "Are you serious about getting out of here?"

"Yes, I need to at least see him before...you know."

She nodded and took my hand. "Come on. We're going to have to be quick."

I didn't question her, I just followed and stayed quiet. We ran down several hallways until we were outside a room that I hadn't seen in my explorations. Maggie opened the door and followed along the wall, not turning on the light. I swore we were going to trip over something, but she seemed to know exactly where we were going. She released my hand and I had a momentary panic attack being in the dark room and having no idea what was going on around me.

"Where is it?" she grumbled. "I know it's just...ah! Here it is." I didn't know what she did, but I heard a whoosh and then saw dim lighting in the floor, but it was only in one spot. I stepped closer, but felt her hand stop me. "Be careful. This is our way out, but you don't want to just fall through the hole. Come on."

I saw her dark figure hover over the edge and then she dropped down below. I followed her lead and found myself in a tunnel that was lit with track lighting. Maggie went to the wall and hit a few buttons on the wall and the escape door closed above us. Maggie snatched something off the wall and then turned to me with a grin.

"We only have a few minutes to get out of here. Becky will have gotten an alert by now. We have to run."

She took off and I ran after her, my heart pounding the whole way. I felt like I was in some kind of female version of a spy film. It was probably the most exciting thing I had ever done in my life. About a minute later, we were in a large space that was filled with vehicles. She held up the object and pressed something. I heard the beep of the vehicle and we were running toward it and hopping inside.

"This place is seriously scary," I said as Maggie peeled out of the parking space. "Who has a panic room the size of a mansion and hidden tunnels and vehicles? The next thing you know, we're going to fly out of the bat cave!"

"Not yet. We have to drive for a while before we'll make it out of here."

"Where does it let out?"

"In the middle of nowhere. The whole point is that no one knows there's another entrance. It's completely hidden."

"Right," I said sarcastically. "I'm sure they use bushes and vines to cover the entrance, like in Robin Hood."

"You're not too far off," she grinned. "See this button here?" I looked by the center light and saw a small button that blended in with everything else. "This button opens a door on the other end, and yes, it's covered with grass, vines, twigs, basically anything that would be growing in the area at the time."

"You know, this experience has really opened my eyes to all I'm missing out on. I'm seriously the luckiest girl in the world. Who wouldn't want to have met and lived with an arms dealer, then lived with one of the hottest men ever, and ride around in secret tunnels under a panic room? This is the stuff life is made of. I tell ya what, all those girls out there that are living their normal, boring lives of going out with the man of their dreams and getting married and all that shit, they don't know what they're missing out on," I said sarcastically.

Maggie just chuckled at my sarcasm. "You get used to it."

"I'm sure. I mean, being pulled from a job to go hide in a panic room because you're trying to escape maniacs is probably second nature to all of you now."

"Well, I'll admit that a few of the ladies have gotten fired from jobs when they've had to hide out, but you just learn to roll with the punches."

She hit the button and we were creeping up higher and higher in the tunnel until the road finally emerged from the side of a hill of sorts. Looking back, I could see there was a rock wall where the door had been, along with vines to cover the rocks to look more natural.

"So, how are we going to get in the hospital without anyone seeing us? I'm sure your husband isn't going to be too happy that we left."

"He won't be. In fact, I'm pretty sure I'll be getting a phone call any minute now. I hope you know how much shit I'm going to be taking for you. I collect favors, so expect me to come to you one day when I need something."

The phone rang on cue and Maggie ignored it. "You're not going to answer it?"

"And get yelled at? Hell no. Just text him that I'm fine and I'll be back at the panic room soon enough."

"I think we can do better than that."

"Ran out for Monistat One. Terrible yeast infection," I said as I typed.

"He's going to think that's a ridiculous reason to leave."

"It doesn't matter. Men hate the subject and don't want to talk about it."

The phone rang again and I answered this time. "Maggie's phone."

"Put my wife on," he growled.

"I can't. She's currently in the bathroom."

"She suddenly developed a yeast infection and had to leave right now to get treatment?"

"Well, trust me, you would have wanted her to. She had me go into the bathroom with her back in the panic room because she couldn't see down there with her huge stomach, and trust me, you don't ever want to see what I did. There was this white, curdling liquid that looked like cottage cheese, and you don't even want to know how big her labia is. I'm surprised that she can even find her vagina right now. She was practically humping the furniture in the panic room because it itched so bad."

There was silence on the other end and Maggie was biting her lip to keep from laughing. Sebastian cleared his throat several times before answering. "Just hurry up and get back."

He hung up before I could respond and Maggie and I burst into laughter. "Oh my God, that was hilarious."

We pulled up to the hospital in no time and made our way over to the hospital entrance. Maggie was all stealthy despite her large belly, whereas I was clomping all over the place and making a ton of noise. She spoke to someone at the front desk and then we slipped into the stairwell and headed to the fourth floor.

"Why did she let us up? Isn't it too late for visitors?"

"She's a friend. Don't worry. We're covered."

Maggie peeked out the door and then let it fall closed. "Alright, I'm going to be the lookout for the guys while you go visit Jackson. I'll come get you if I see someone coming."

I nodded and headed down the hallway. There was someone outside his room, but the closer I got, the more confused I was. What the hell? I stopped just feet from him and stared. He was staring right back, looking pissed as hell.

"What the fuck are you doing here?"

"How come you're not dead?"

We both glared at each other and then Jackson spoke. "What do you mean *why am I not dead?*"

"I overheard Becky on the phone and she said that you were in the hospital and you had collapsed and they didn't know how long you were going to make it. I thought this was my last chance to see you." I sighed. "Well, I guess this was a wasted trip."

He narrowed his eyes at me. "Sorry to disappoint you."

I peeked around him to see who was in the room and gasped when I saw Gabe sleeping in the bed. He looked so pale, but still just as strong even in his sleep. I shook my head in disbelief. I didn't know these people well, but I felt like I was losing family at the same time.

I turned back to Jackson, but couldn't speak. Down the hall, a man that I recognized all too well was walking toward me. He was speaking to someone on the phone and then was practically running.

"Jackson," I whispered, taking a step back. My heart pounded in my chest as I took another step back. How had they found me? Were they looking for me or was this a coincidence? If I had led them here with my foolishness, other people could get hurt. What the hell had I been thinking? I spun around and ran down the hall, hoping like hell that I could make it out of here alive.

"Raegan!" Jackson shouted from behind me. He couldn't leave his post and I wouldn't stick around to bring hell down on him.

A man appeared at the end of the hall, dressed in black and holding a gun that could only be meant for me. So much for hospital policies about guns. I turned down another hallway, hoping to get to the other side of the hospital and a different elevator or stairwell. I followed the signs for the elevator, taking twists and turn, wondering why this hospital was such a maze. I was just about to the elevator when another man stepped out from a different hallway. I recognized him too. Spinning around, I made to run back the way I came, but there was another man rounding the corner at the other end of the hall. Maggie came out of nowhere, grabbing my hand and bursting through the door to the nearest stairwell. She was practically dragging me down the stairs, which was unbelievable.

"If only I was pregnant, I might be able to run as fast as you," I panted with each step. Bullets started pinging off the railing and Maggie moved us toward the outside of the stairs, stopping on the third floor and pushing into the door to the third floor. We saw Cap in the distance, but there was also a man standing between him and us. Suddenly, a hard arm was wrapped around my throat and pulled me backward. I stumbled and Maggie heard me. She spun around and looked back and forth between the men closing in on us and her husband who was too far away. He couldn't fire from this distance without risking hitting someone.

Maggie started slowly backing up and I wanted to yell at her to stop moving in that direction, but the arm around my neck was too tight. When Maggie bumped into the man behind her, a look of shock crossed her face and then she grinned. I almost didn't see her flick open the knife or slam it back into the guy's thigh. It must have been really good luck, because he immediately yelled and fell against the wall while blood poured down his leg. I was too stunned to do anything else, but the arm around my neck disappeared and I was being dragged off again. I barely registered that it was Jackson pulling me behind him, heading across the hospital to a different exit.

Glancing back, I could see members of Reed Security rushing around the men that had been dropped. We stopped just at the end of a hallway and Jackson pulled out a gun from the back of his pants.

"Do you know how to use this?"

"I wouldn't be a very good gun moll if I didn't."

"Point and shoot," he said firmly.

I rolled my eyes. I had just said that I knew how to use it. I held it up and checked it out, accidentally pulling the trigger when I was looking at it. The bullet pinged off the wall as Jackson threw me to the ground.

"I didn't tell you to fucking shoot a wall!" he whisper-yelled at me.

"I didn't think you would give me a gun that didn't have a safety!"

"The trigger is the safety."

"Maybe tell me that next time."

"You just said you were a gun moll," he shot back.

"Yeah, well, my training only goes as far as point and shoot."

He swore and pulled me to my feet. "Just don't point that anywhere near me. You only pull the trigger if I'm not in front of you." He turned to go, but then stopped and looked back. "Don't pull it if I'm in your peripheral either." He slightly turned and then stared at me once more. "You know, you really don't need that. How about I just take that back from you."

He took my gun, which kind of pissed me off, and started down the stairs of a different stairwell. I followed, irritated that he wasn't letting me have a gun. I wouldn't have put my finger anywhere near the trigger in the first place if he had just told me it didn't have a safety. Jackson stopped outside the next door and pulled me to his side.

"Shit, we've got company. You know any of these guys?"

I looked through the small window and nodded. "Yeah, the one yelling at everyone. He's one of the guys that used to work on transport with Xavier."

"Looks like his loyalties have changed. How many guys did you see over the years?"

"Xavier met with a lot of people at the house. I don't know all their names, but if I saw them, I could identify them."

"Looks like you just became someone they don't want around anymore."

He pulled his phone from his pocket and dialed Cap.

"Yeah, I'm boxed in. I've got Raegan with me and these assholes aren't too happy she's alive. She knows too much...Southeast stairwell... Yeah, I gotcha, Cap."

He peered through the window again and then pulled me into the corner of the stairwell. "Here's the plan. Cap's making a diversion-"

He didn't finish his thought. He spun me behind him, shoving me into the corner and firing at someone below us. Bullets pinged all around me and I screamed like a little girl. "Now would be a really good time to give me a gun!"

"Get up the stairs!"

I took off up the stairs as the large window in the stairwell exploded from gunfire. I yelled again, shielding my head from any stray bullets that could be flying around. Jackson grabbed my hand and pulled me with him as he jumped out the window that wasn't completely broken and crashed through it, dragging me with him. I screamed, wide-eyed and terrified, as we plummeted from the second story window down to the grass below.

"Roll into it!"

We landed, me awkwardly on my feet and then flying forward to my hands and knees. Jackson landed on his feet and rolled over to stand.

"I told you to roll into it!"

"Yeah, as we were jumping out the window! I don't even know what that means," I yelled. "That's something you might have explained, oh, I don't know, *before* you pulled me out a fucking window!"

Jackson fired up toward the window and then was pulling me along again. It was like I was a fucking dog on a leash. We ran through the bushes around the hospital and then streaked through the parking lot. Jackson paused at the sound of beeping and then took off in that direction. We were almost there when gunfire surrounded us. Jackson shoved me to the ground, shoving a gun into my hand.

He took off without saying anything. I stared at the gun, wondering what the hell I was supposed to do. Did he mean for me to follow him? Was I supposed to be his backup or something? If I was, I was doing a really shitty job. I sprang to my feet and ran in the same direction Jackson had gone and screamed when someone started shooting at me. I ducked behind another car and peeked under the car to see where shoes were. They were getting closer. I only had one option. I stood with my eyes closed and fired, screaming with every pull of the trigger.

I was still screaming when the sound of bullets leaving the chamber finished. I opened one eye and glanced around. There were men all over the ground, none of them moving. I took a hesitant step out and kicked the first guy I came to. He wasn't moving. The second guy was still making some gurgling noises, but wasn't making any attempts to move. The third guy sprang up just as I was getting closer and I fired, but there were no bullets left. He grinned at me and pulled his own weapon. Not knowing what else to do, I threw my gun at his head, hoping that I could knock him out or something, but he just blocked my throw and stood on wobbly feet.

I took a hesitant step back, my eyes darting around the parking lot, trying to find a way out. Where the hell was Jackson? An engine roared to the right of me and the lights practically blinded me. I stumbled back just as the truck revved and tore forward right at the man. He drew his weapon and fired at the windshield, but then was crushed between the truck and the car that was parked across from it. The man flopped backward against the car and his eyes slipped closed.

The door of the truck opened and Jackson stepped out, still limping. His eyes were burning with anger as he stepped toward me. I swallowed hard and moved away from him, but he kept coming after me.

"Do you want to tell me why you fucking shot me?"

"I didn't...what? Where?"

He pulled the ripped fabric away from his thigh where blood trickled sluggishly.

"It doesn't look that bad."

"It's not, but why the fuck were you shooting at me?"

"Because I was trying to kill the bad guys," I shouted.

"Yeah, with your fucking eyes closed! Who does that?"

"I was scared!"

"So, you closed your eyes and hoped for the best?"

"It was a gut reaction. I didn't mean to do it. It just happened!"

"And did you mean to follow me and join in the action? Because you were supposed to stay right where you fucking were while I took care of them."

"You didn't say that," I shouted incredulously. "You shoved a gun in my hand and ran away. I thought I was supposed to be your backup or something. Next time say something."

"There won't be a next time. I'm not ever giving you a gun again!"

"I'll do better next time!"

He scoffed. "Yeah, like you might keep your eyes open? Or you'll try not to shoot me?"

I scowled at him and stomped around the back of the truck and over to the passenger side of the truck, opened the door and hopped in.

"What are you doing?"

"We're leaving, aren't we?"

"Not in that truck. There's a man's innards all over the front. That's not exactly being discreet."

"Well, I didn't know that," I said, hopping out of the truck and stomping back around to his side. "You could have just said, 'Hey, Raegan, we're going to grab a different truck since I just splattered a man against this one. See how easy that is?"

"I would think the fact that there's a dead man attached to the grill would have clued you in," he scowled.

"I just thought you were going to get rid of him."

"In a hospital parking lot? Where exactly would I get rid of him?"

"The morgue?"

"Sure. I'll just walk through the hospital with a dead body and take him right down to the morgue."

"Well, that's where dead bodies go. It makes sense."

Shouting drew our attention and then Jackson was grabbing me and shoving me into the truck I had just gotten out of. Then he was backing up and peeling out of the parking lot, running over the man that had fallen from the grill.

"I thought you said we weren't taking this truck?"

"That was before more men came after us. We could have gotten a new truck if you hadn't argued with me about the dead body for so fucking long."

"Oh, so now this is my fault?"

He took a turn too fast and I was thrown across the truck into him.

"Well, let's look at this rationally. You were supposed to stay in the panic room, but instead, you came here for God knows what reason. Then all these people started shooting at you because apparently, you know a bunch of shit that's gonna get you killed. And let's not forget that you fucking shot me when you were supposed to stay hidden, and now you just keep arguing with me instead of letting me do my fucking job."

"I thought you were dead! That's why I went to the hospital. And I didn't know that people were going to show up at the hospital and try to kill me!"

"That's why I told you to stay where you were. We didn't know who would come after you."

"See? I made your job easier. Now you know."

"Yeah," he sneered. "Now I know. The only problem is, they're right on my fucking ass and I don't have any backup."

I had no idea where we were as I looked out the window. I had been too wrapped up in arguing with Jackson, but now I could see that we were going higher and higher on a large hill and the drop on my side was a little too steep for my liking.

"Can you slow down just a little? There's no guardrail on this side."

"That's a good thing. Are you buckled in?"

"Why?" I asked in panic.

"Because, these assholes are getting too close and we can't outrun them much longer."

"So, what does that mean?"

"I'm gonna roll the truck and then set the truck on fire. They'll think we're dead and we'll have enough time to get away or at least get in a defensive position."

I nodded, trying to process what he had just said.

"Raegan, are you with me here?"

"Sure. Of course. This is totally normal for me. Why not fake my death by plummeting to the bottom of a hill?"

"Raegan, buckle your goddamn seat belt now. You have five seconds and then we're going down."

I scrambled to shove the belt into the buckle. The wheel jerked and suddenly, the world was tilting around me. We were spinning in circles, my body jarring with each impact of the truck against the hill. I lost count of how many times the world spun and then we rocked once more before coming to a stop upside down. The blood was rushing to my head, but I didn't know how to get out of this situation.

"You okay?"

"Great. Ready for ice cream?" I asked.

"Stay where you are. I'm coming around to your side." I watched as he fell to the top of the truck and then scrambled to my side. He held onto my body as he instructed me to undo the belt. He caught me as I fell and then I was shoved out the window, which I hadn't realized was broken.

"Stay near me and don't stand up."

I watched as he ripped the lining out of the roof of the truck and rolled it into a tube. He went to the gas tank door and pried it open, shoving the tube of fabric inside.

"Get ready to run," he grinned right before he flicked a lighter and set the fabric on fire. He grabbed my hand and we bolted into the trees, only making it just inside the trees before the tank blew. The fire burned hot, but luckily, it had rained recently and the grass was still slick.

I stared at the fire burning, wondering what the hell we were supposed to do now. Jackson's face was dirty and the light from the flames was dancing across his face. "Now what?"

Chapter Ten

CAP

"What the hell were you thinking?" I yelled at Freckles in the hallway of the ICU. We were outside of Gabe's room as the doctors worked on him. They weren't sure what happened, but he had gone into cardiac arrest and no one knew why. He'd had a concussion, but all his films came back normal.

"Sir, you're going to have to lower your voice or I'm going to have to ask you to leave," a nurse said in a stern voice. I nodded and she walked away, scowling.

"Raegan overheard Becky talking to someone. She said Jackson was dying and this would be her last chance to see him."

"Becky wasn't talking about Jackson," I bit out. "She was talking about Ice."

Freckles stood in shock, tears threatening to spill down her cheeks. "I knew it was bad, but...Where's Lindsey?"

"She's with him now."

Alarms sounded down the hall and I took off to see what was going on. Lindsey was crying and squeezing Ice's hand as doctors rushed into the room.

"What's going on?" she cried.

"Ma'am, I'm going to have to ask you to leave."

"No! I'm not leaving!" I stepped into the room and quickly pulled her into my arms, doing my best to drag her out of the room with only one working arm. She struggled against me, yelling and crying that she couldn't leave him. I felt her tears dripping down on my forearm and I wanted to tell her he would be fine, but I didn't know that. He had taken a bullet to the heart. What were the chances that he would survive?

Outside, Chris pulled her from my arms and wrapped her in a big hug, rubbing her back and keeping her faced away from the window of the room. She didn't need to see if he died. It took me a minute to hear the second set of alarms sounding and I closed my eyes slowly. This couldn't be happening. Lola and Knight stood outside Hunter's hospital room with Lucy. Derek rushed over from down the hall where Sinner was limping behind him. The fear and desperation on Derek's face almost killed me. Hunter was practically his brother.

I shook my head in disbelief. What were the odds that all three of them would go into cardiac arrest at the same time? My head snapped up and I stormed over to Lola, dragging her away from the window.

"What happened before he went into cardiac arrest?"

Lola stood stoically in front of me, trying desperately not to let her emotions show. "Nothing. A doctor came in to check on him and about ten minutes later, he just..."

"Who was the doctor?"

"Dr. Sanchez. I checked out his credentials. He's on duty tonight on this floor."

"Let me see his profile." She handed over her phone that had Dr. Sanchez's photo and all pertinent information. "Send this to my phone."

I stormed down the hall to Chris, who was still holding Lindsey back. "Was a doctor in here before he went into cardiac arrest?"

"Yeah, maybe ten-fifteen minutes before. Why?

"Was it Dr. Sanchez?"

"Yeah. Why?"

I ignored him and went to the nurse's station. "Excuse me." I held out my phone to the nurse and showed her the picture of Dr. Sanchez. "Is this Dr. Sanchez?"

"No," she shook her head. "I've never seen that man before."

"Have you seen Dr. Sanchez tonight?"

"Um, no, but that's not unusual. I have a lot of patients to check in on. I usually see him when he's finished with his rounds, or if a patient's medications need to be updated."

"Wouldn't he be here when three patients are in cardiac arrest?" I said irritatedly.

She glanced at the ICU rooms and paled, just realizing that something was wrong with this picture.

"Get security now. The hospital needs to be placed on lockdown. Tell them Dr. Sanchez is missing. This man," I showed her the picture on my phone again, "was posing as him and visited at least two of the men before they went into cardiac arrest."

She picked up the phone and immediately started talking with the head of security. I swore silently to myself and looked to all three rooms. I didn't know what to do. Everything was falling apart and I couldn't move forward without my men, but we couldn't stay here and risk more lives either.

I pulled out my phone and dialed a number that I never thought I would have to use. I couldn't stand around and hope for the best. It was time to get to work.

I stood outside Ice's room and watched as the doctors tried to revive him. They had gotten a rhythm back, but a half hour went by and he was flatlining again. Whoever these assholes were, they had snuck into the hospital and posed as doctors, walking right the fuck past us. They had hit us hard, most likely injecting Ice, Hunter, and Gabe with something that had sent them into cardiac arrest. They had done all three hits at the same time.

The echocardiogram had been fluttering slowly to a flatline over the past five minutes and the doctors weren't having any luck reviving him, not that it would matter at this point. The doctor had already told me that a heart attack would most likely kill him at this point. Even if they got a rhythm back, he most likely wouldn't wake up.

I had let them down. I had let them all down. Every one of my guys depended on me to be their leader and I had fucked up. When shit got tough and everything went sideways, could they really depend on me? We had three men on the verge of death and three missing. This was so far beyond a clusterfuck that I was surprised any of them were still hanging on with me. Why hadn't they all gone their own way at this point?

Those were questions that plagued me as I stood there and watched the doctors do everything they could for Ice, but there were no answers that would make a difference now. I couldn't, no, wouldn't lose any more men over this. I would get everyone out and we would fight back and get these assholes that were trying to kill us. They would pay in the worst possible way. Death would be the easy way out when I was done with them.

The doctors shut down the monitors and walked out of the room, pulling off their gloves as the nurse started shutting down machines attached to Ice. He was gone. The doctor gave Lindsey a sympathetic look, but she had seen everything. She didn't need the doctor to tell her Ice was gone. As I watched Lindsey in Chris's arms, she turned to me and the look in her eyes said that I needed to move the fuck on. She didn't want me anywhere near her. I walked away and headed for Hunter's room. It was already empty of doctors and the monitors were off. Lucy was sobbing next to Hunter, begging him to come back to her. Derek was trying to pull her off him and Lola stood by, trying not to break down herself.

Jules walked up to me with Rocco, the look on his face grim. "Gabe's gone." Jules' face was set in a hard line and there was a slight mist to his eyes. "Isa didn't get to say goodbye," he said quietly.

Rocco cleared his throat. "They didn't get Burg. He had already ripped out his line and was trying to get the hell out of there. He's with Florrie right now."

"Nobody goes anywhere alone from now on. We're getting the fuck out of this hospital and getting somewhere safe."

"What about the bodies? We're not just going to leave Ice, Gabe, and Hunter here, are we?" Rocco asked.

"No, we'll take them with. We're probably breaking a helluva lot of laws, but Lucy, Lindsey, and Isa won't leave without them."

"What the hell are we going to tell their kids? We failed them," Jules said quietly.

"We can't think about that right now," I said coldly. I had to stay detached so I could get us all out of here and make sure everyone stayed alive. "Has anyone gotten ahold of Jackson yet?"

"No answer," Jules said. "His phone is out of service."

"Contact Becky and ask for his last location."

While Jules was on the phone, I walked down to Gabe's room and stared inside at his body. He didn't look dead. He just looked like Gabe, but he wasn't moving. Now I had Jackson on the run and no idea where he was or if he was still alive. I didn't have the manpower to go search for him when everyone was in danger. I didn't want to leave him behind, but losing three men just because they had been in the hospital was already a huge blow.

"Becky said that the signal went out about fifteen miles outside of town. She said that police are reporting a fire. A truck went off the road up in the hills and there was an explosion. No word yet if there are any survivors."

So what did I do? Did I take everyone back to the panic room and take...who was still up and moving? Cazzo, Knight, Jules, Lola, Derek, and Chris. That was all I had. Six people weren't injured. Did I risk the last of my men to go look for Jackson or did I pray that he got out and was following our plan? As I looked at Lucy and Lindsey crying down the hall, I knew the answer. I couldn't stand to see any more women crying and I didn't want to tell any more kids that their dad wasn't coming back.

"He's on his own then. He knew what the plan was. If he's still alive, he'll either find a way to contact us or get out to us. Get everyone together. I want everyone back at the panic room and ready to move out within the hour."

I pulled Knight away from the window outside Hunter's room. "Go get Kate. We've lost three men, but we're not leaving them behind. I want Kate over here to make sure they're transported with us properly.

I have a friend here that can make sure we can get the bodies out of here without any issues."

"Do you want me to tell Isa?"

"Not yet. She'll want to come along. Right now, we just need to get moving."

Knight disappeared through the doors of the ER, not taking anyone with him. He always did like to work alone, so I didn't expect him to take anyone along.

Lucy and Lindsey walked over to me, tears in their eyes and pain etched eternally in their features. Lindsey stepped forward, staring at me, her nostrils flaring in anger. Her hand shot out and slapped me hard across the face so fast that I didn't even try to react. She was hurting. "You were supposed to protect them. That's why you had men outside their rooms. You let this happen!"

"Lindsey, I know you're angry right now–"

"Right now? What, do you think in a few hours when I've had time to let it sink in that I'll be okay with this? What about my kids? Do they matter? Do you care at all that they won't ever see their father again?"

Maggie wrapped an arm around Lindsey's waist, pulling her in to support her. I didn't know what to say as Lindsey sobbed. What could I say right now? There was nothing I could do and the longer we stayed here, the more danger we were in. Lucy was just standing there in shock. It was like she didn't believe it was true.

"I know that you want to be angry and lash out right now, but we have to get out of here before someone else gets killed. We've already lost three and Jackson is missing. Cash should be arriving soon and he's going to protect everyone while we get to a new location. You and your kids will be safe, but we have to get moving. The longer we stay, the more danger everyone is in."

"Yeah," Lindsey scoffed. "Wouldn't want any more blood on your hands, right?"

She turned away with Maggie and Lucy, heading for the door with Cazzo, Sinner, and Derek. I rubbed a hand over my tired face and turned to those that remained.

"Okay, we leave in two groups. Burg, you go with Lola, Rocco, and

Chris. Jules, Florrie, Alec, and I will head back in another vehicle. If you suspect anything, you let me know immediately. We aren't taking any chances. We get back, we load up, and we get the fuck out of here so we can regroup."

Watching Lindsey and Lucy break down while their husbands died was awful and telling Isa was downright brutal. Cazzo agreed to come with me to tell his sister about Gabe, but she didn't need Cazzo there to soften the blow. She could see it in my eyes that Gabe was gone. She asked Maggie to watch the kids and she followed me on shaky legs into a private room.

"Just say it," she said sharply as she spun around and glared at me. "Don't try and make me feel better or whatever the hell it is you tell the wife."

"Isa," Cazzo stepped forward, wrapping his arm around her.

"No," she cried. "Don't give me those bullshit hugs. Don't tell me everything is going to be okay. What am I supposed to tell Enzo and Vittoria? We're a family. We're happy and now you're telling me one of the best things that's ever happened to me is gone?"

Cazzo rubbed her back as she broke down in his arms. I hated this. I didn't want any of this to have to touch them. They didn't deserve it.

"You didn't tell me to come to the hospital, so what happened? Did he just suddenly get worse?" My gaze flicked to Cazzo's, but Isa shoved me back. "Don't you dare lie to me or try to make this easier. Just tell me what the hell happened!"

"He just had a concussion, but some men snuck in the hospital and gave Ice, Hunter, and Gabe something through their IVs. It basically stopped their hearts. We don't know what it was or who did it, but we don't have time to figure that out right now. We have to get out of here and pull ourselves together."

She swiped at her eyes, laughing humorlessly. "You know, Gabe and Cazzo promised me that we would always be safe here. They said that this was a big family and everyone protected each other. From what I've seen, all you do is get everyone killed while you sit on your throne and toss your men aside like their lives are expendable."

Hearing that killed me. I wanted to believe that she was only speaking in anger, but maybe it was true. Maybe I was no longer the leader I had once been. And if that was the case, what the hell was I going to do now? We were injured and broken. I couldn't leave my men now just because I wasn't leading the way I needed to.

"When this is over, I'm leaving and no one from my family will ever be associated with you or your company again." She turned to Cazzo with an angry glare. "Are you going to continue to risk your life for him?"

Cazzo didn't say anything, obviously uncomfortable with where this was going.

"If you stay and work for him, I don't want to see you ever again. I don't want anything else coming back on me and my kids. This place is toxic."

"Isa-" But Isa held up a hand and cut her brother off.

"Just, don't tell the kids yet. It'll be too hard for them to make the trip knowing that he's gone."

"If that's what you want," I said quietly.

She swiped at her face and walked away. Cazzo's face was grim and I wished that I could ask him what he was thinking, but now wasn't the time for a conversation like that. Besides, he needed time to think. It was the only thing I could give him at the moment.

Chapter Eleven

JACKSON

"Move faster, Raegan. We've gotta get out of here." I was pushing her hard as we ran through the trees. We didn't have the option to move slowly.

"I am moving fast."

"Not fast enough."

"If you would just give me a break, maybe I could actually catch my breath."

I stopped suddenly and pulled her in close, holding her by the arms. "You don't get it. It won't be long until they find out that there aren't any bodies in the truck. They'll know we escaped and they'll be looking for us, and the way you're stomping through the trees, you're leaving every fucking marker possible to lead them right to us."

"Sorry, they didn't cover running stealthily through trees the day I went to super spy school. Besides, you're running just as fast. You can't tell me I'm the only one that's leaving a trail."

"You're like a fucking bulldozer going through here. I told you to step where I step!"

"In case you haven't noticed, I'm a good head shorter than you. So, unless you have some rocket boots on you, there's not a chance that I can step where you step. Besides, why can't we just wait here and then you can take them out when they come through?"

"Because we have a head start on them. As long as we keep moving, we should be able to get away from them."

"Derek took out eleven men," she muttered under her breath.

I snapped my jaw together hard. One thing I really hated was when women compared all of us, without understanding the circumstances, and just assumed that every scenario was always the same. But I didn't have the time to go through all of that with her right now.

"Look, down this hill is a creek. We're going to get to that and then we should be able to lose them. Then it's just about fifteen miles back to Reed Security."

"Just fifteen miles?" she said in shock. Then she started laughing at me.

"What?"

"I just think it's hilarious that you think I can make it fifteen miles on foot, in the middle of the night, when I'm hungry and tired."

"Would you prefer to be dead?"

She didn't say anything and actually seemed to be considering this. "Can I think about it?"

"No," I said in exasperation. I started pulling her behind me, hearing her grumble the whole way. "Watch where you step now. It's getting–"

Suddenly, we were tumbling down the hill, hitting every tree root and rock along the way. I tried to grab onto Raegan and pull her in close to me so I could protect her, but her arms kept flailing, smacking me in the face as we flipped in all different directions before finally splashing into the water at the bottom of the hill.

She groaned next to me and I was immediately on my knees, bent over her to see if she was okay. "Does it hurt anywhere?"

"Yes."

"Where?" I asked urgently.

"My arms and my legs. My stomach hurts a little too. I think I might have whiplash, and I also might have peed a little."

"Raegan," I said irritatedly, "are you injured or just sore?"

"Is there a difference?"

"Well, one means you get up and move on and the other means I leave your ass behind."

She sat up with a groan and glared at me. "Chivalry really is dead. I should have listened to my mom."

"Hey, I fake killed you. Don't tell me that wasn't chivalrous."

"You're right. What ever was I thinking?" she said in a mocking tone.

I hauled her up to her feet and threw her over my shoulder. She squealed and smacked me on the back.

"What are you doing?" she screeched.

"Would you shut that fat trap of yours? I'd like to get out of here alive."

"Just for the record, calling a woman fat in any way, even if it's about her mouth, is just not cool."

I started stomping downstream, hoping that I could get far enough that they would lose our trail.

"You know, this really isn't the most comfortable way to travel."

"File a complaint with the Better Business Bureau."

"Why are you so mean to me? You know, when I first met you, you were actually nice to me."

"You hadn't opened your mouth yet," I muttered.

"Are you implying I'm annoying?"

"No, I was flat out saying in a nice way that when your mouth is shut, you don't annoy me nearly as much."

"I don't understand you. You always seemed like the good guy. The guy that wanted to...well, it doesn't matter. You're just not what I thought you were. And why the hell would you kiss me when we were in the panic room if you didn't like me?"

I plopped her down on her feet and held her steady with my hands on her arms. "First of all, I *am* a good guy. But I can't reach you."

"I'm standing right in front of you. You're holding on to me," she smarted off.

I glowered at her and yanked her closer to me. "You know that's not what I fucking meant. I tried to get you to open up to me about what happened with that dickhead. I tried to understand, but you don't talk about anything. You don't take anything seriously. You hide behind your sarcasm and your jokes. I want someone that's going to be real with me. And that kiss was a moment of weakness, taking what I wanted for once."

"I don't hide behind anything," she snapped. "I just don't think whining about it or crying on someone's shoulder is going to make a difference. That's how I deal with shit."

"And it's all stuck in your head!"

"Would it make you feel better if I told you that I was beaten so bad sometimes that I prayed for death?" she yelled. "Or that every time I ended up in the hospital, I tried to get help, but he always had someone on his payroll? Or maybe I should tell you that I wanted to run, but I was too fucking terrified that he would catch up with me and it would be worse when he caught me. Does that help? Does that make you feel like you know me better? Because what happened in those years wasn't who I am. Those were just some shitty years where I couldn't get out. I was stupid to stay as long as I did, and then it was too late to get away. So, instead of feeling sorry for myself, I'm choosing to move on and try to have a different life, one where I'm not the weak person I was with him. So, I'm sorry if I don't fit the mold of what you think I should be acting like. This is me, take it or leave it!"

She held her hands wide and I looked at her for the first time, truly seeing the woman she was. She was exactly what she said, a woman that was moving on and letting go of the past. I threw her over my shoulder and trudged on through the river.

"What the hell?"

"Did you want to wait for them to catch up or should we keep moving?"

"That's it? That's all you have to say?"

"What should I say? I wanted you to tell me what the hell was going on in your head. Now I know. It really was that simple."

"You asshole. You've been treating me like I'm damaged goods for the past year!"

"Look, men really are pretty simple. If I ask what you're thinking, just say it straight out. I don't want a bunch of bullshit that I can't understand. I can't read feelings and I don't do flowery sentiments. If you say you feel sad, I'll comfort you. If you say you're angry, I'll give you a gun and take you to the range. If you can't fucking sleep, I'll make sure to wear you out enough that you'll sleep for a week straight."

She stilled over my shoulder and then tapped my back. "Um, are we talking sex, or like, running a marathon?"

"If I wanted to run a fucking marathon, I'd just go work out at Reed Security."

"So...is this your way of saying you like me or-"

"This is my way of saying that I want to fuck you. And yes, I fucking like you. I wouldn't offer to comfort you if you were sad if I didn't like you. And as much as I find a woman with a gun sexy, I probably wouldn't go out of my way to see you taking out a target if I didn't want to fuck you."

I trudged through the water at a much faster rate than I would have if I had to wait for her. My leg was killing me, but the cold from the water was numbing the pain. Besides, I kind of liked her over my shoulder, her ass so close to my face. I could smell the arousal coming off her and if we weren't trying to avoid being killed, I might throw her down on the ground and eat her pussy.

"Can I ask you something?"

"What?" I snapped.

"How long have you wanted to fuck me?"

"Probably since the moment you woke up and called Knight *the Black Prince*."

"I did what?" she screeched.

"You want to scream a little louder? I don't think you've given up our position yet."

"I did not call Knight that," she whisper-hissed.

I chuckled and slapped her lightly on the ass. "You were all loopy and shit, talking about him being the Black Prince and having dysentery. And then there was the whole thing about shit falling on someone's head and moths."

She gasped. "I did not."

"Yes, you did. I believe you called him hot, but then you called me gorgeous, so I wasn't too put out."

"I don't believe you. Besides, who remembers something like that? It was a year ago."

"Raegan, I remember every fucking conversation I've ever had with you. I remember you telling me about your first period; also when you were on drugs." She groaned, but it just made me grin. There was so much she had told me that week. I had enough material on her to last a lifetime. "Yeah, I gotta say, I thought it was a little weird that you just thought you sat in red paint."

"We were in a hardware store!"

"Was there paint just laying around somewhere?"

"Shut up. You have no idea what it's like to be a woman!"

"I'm pretty sure I have a pretty good idea after you told me about the first time a guy kissed you and you got wet. It's not too different from a guy getting a woody. Only difference is, we can't exactly hide it."

"I really hate you right now."

"You'll get over it. I'm gorgeous, remember?"

"No, I don't remember. For all I know, you're making all this up."

"Go ahead and ask Kate if you don't believe me."

I got out of the creek on the other side. I had traveled downstream quite a while and there was a good chance I had lost them. But my legs were fucking freezing and I needed to warm up if I was going to keep moving. When we were out of the water, I set Raegan down and grabbed her hand again. Before it was to pull her along. Now, it was just because I wanted to hold her hand.

"So, are we really going to walk fifteen miles?"

"Don't worry, babe. It gives us a lot more time for you to tell me embarrassing stories."

Chapter Twelve

RAEGAN

"I really hate you right now," I grumbled as we continued to make our way through the trees, fields, side roads, and even another creek. I was tired, cranky, and ready to kill anyone that made me mad.

"It's only another ten miles. We'll be to Reed Security by sunrise."

I groaned and plopped down on the ground in frustration.

"What are you doing? We have to keep moving."

"I need a break. In case you haven't noticed, I don't do this very often. I don't lift cars for fun or do that thing where you shoot paint at other people for fun. I'm an outdoor girl, but *this* is beyond just a hike for the day. We don't have food or water and the last time I peed was when we fell in the creek. Oh, and in case you were wondering, no, I did not eat my Wheaties for breakfast."

He knelt in front of me and ran a tired hand across the scruff of his jaw. I could see the pain on his face when he knelt down. It was obvious his leg was hurting him, but he was doing everything he could to hide it from me.

"Look, I know you're tired and you want to take a break, but we need to keep moving. The longer we stay out here, the more vulnerable we are. I promise, as soon as we get to Reed Security, you can sleep as much as you want."

"And a hot bath."

"You got it."

"And a very big breakfast."

"I'll take you out to Ihop and get you everything on the menu."

I swiped a stray tear from my face and pouted slightly. "And you promise to give me a full body massage."

His eyes twinkled in amusement. "Don't push your luck."

"Fine." I took his hand and we continued on our way. He held my hand the entire time and I did my best to keep up with him.

"So, you're an outdoor girl, huh?"

"Yeah, well, I used to be anyway."

"What changed?"

"Xavier," I said, not really wanting to talk about it.

"And Xavier didn't like the outdoors?"

"Oh, sure. We went hiking and fishing all the time," I said sarcastically.

"How did you meet him?"

"The usual way. You know, the whole running into each other. Hellos were exchanged. Flirting happened, and then dates. Just your typical girl meets boy situation."

Jackson stopped, gripping my hand tighter and wrapping his arm around my waist. "Are you ever going to answer a question seriously?"

"I am."

"You're skating the truth. I'm not judging you, Raegan."

"I didn't say you were," I said defensively.

"Do you think I don't realize that you use sarcasm so you don't have to talk about things? I see past all that bullshit. I know that you don't want to be real with me because you're ashamed of what happened."

"Wow. I didn't realize I was so transparent. I guess my illusionist skills aren't paying off."

"Cut the shit, Raegan."

"No, Jackson. You cut the shit. You think you know me so well just because we've lived together for a year? You don't know jack shit about me."

"So, tell me why you stayed then," he said angrily. "All I heard was a bunch of excuses. You were scared or he had people watching you, but you could have slipped away if you tried. Hell, all you did was call your dad and he sent us. So what is it? Was there an actual reason you couldn't leave?"

I didn't say anything. It was true. There wasn't a reason that I stayed other than just being scared. I was just a stupid girl that got stuck in something she was too scared to get out of. I wished that there was some deep, dark secret that kept me there, that didn't make me feel like such a failure in life.

"That's what I thought," he said, turning away from me. He started to walk off, but then turned back to me angrily. "You can push me away all you want, but I'm trying to get to know you. I'm not judging you or trying to throw anything in your face. I like you, Raegan. I love your sarcasm and how defiant you are. I think you're fucking beautiful and if you could just see yourself the way I do, you wouldn't see some weak woman. You'd see a woman that made some bad decisions, but got herself out of a really fucking horrible situation. Yeah, it took you a while, but you did it. You were strong when it really counted. You *will* rebuild your life and it could be great, but you have to trust someone to take you for who you really are."

I dropped my eyes to the ground and listened as he walked off. He was right, and I hated that he saw things so clearly. Still, it just wasn't who I was to sit around and talk about things like I was some poor woman that was taken advantage of.

"Look," I said, running to catch up with him. "This is just how I deal with things. I'm not like most girls when it comes to my emotions. I don't cry over every little thing and if someone tells me something sad, I get really uncomfortable and make jokes. If someone slips and falls on the ice, the first thing I do is laugh. I had a friend once tell me that she loved me. I think my reaction was *I know. I'm pretty lovable.* And then I stood there twitching uncomfortably."

"I can understand that stuff. Not everyone processes mushy feelings the same way."

"Okay, when there was flooding by my parents' house years ago, and people got stuck in the water and drowned, my first reaction was to call them stupid for trying to drive through the water. I just can't relate to those situations. I don't know what to say, so I just say whatever comes to mind."

"How can you not relate? Maybe they were trying to get to a family member."

"Can you relate to a woman having a baby and how she feels?"

"No, but that's different. I'm not a woman."

"And I'm not a touchy feely person. I don't do mushy stuff and I get uncomfortable when people try to rope me into that crap. Like I said, sarcasm is just how I respond to uncomfortable situations."

He just stared at me for a minute. "So, I shouldn't expect tears out of you every time something goes wrong." I shook my head. "And if I ever say something hurtful-"

"I'll most likely say something hurtful or sarcastic back."

Again, he just stared at me. "You were a fucking idiot for staying with Xavier as long as you did."

"And you were fucking stupid for giving me a gun so I could shoot you."

"What kind of woman continues to let a man beat up on her over and over again?"

"The same kind of woman that would leave him and then instantly be attracted to someone like you. Both seem unwise with deadly consequences."

"You're emotionally stunted," he shot back.

"You keep your house so clean, I would almost think you're a woman."

"You talk like a man."

"I fuck like one too."

He slammed his mouth down on mine and gripped my hair harshly, shoving me down on the ground and pushing himself between my legs. "Is that what you like? To be thrown around and treated like a fuck toy?"

"If you're still talking, you're not doing this right." I yanked his head back down to mine and slammed my mouth against his. He yanked my shirt up over my head and latched onto my nipple through my bra.

"Your tits are fucking amazing."

"So's my pussy. Get down there and fuck me right."

My pants were yanked down my legs, but got stuck on my shoes. Instead of pulling my shoes off, Jackson threw my legs up over his head and crawled between them before undoing his pants and showing me his massive cock. My eyes widened and he smirked right before he shoved himself inside me. The first thrust was so hard that I felt like I had rug burn against my ass. His hands slipped under my shoulders and his hands cradled the back of my head. At first I thought he was trying to protect my head, but then he gripped onto my hair and realized he was controlling me so he could kiss me anywhere he wanted. His lips sucked on my neck and he nipped at my ear, all while thrusting violently into my body.

I moaned and screamed my pleasure every time his cock impaled me. I felt like I was actually about to be split in half. I could feel the insides of my legs bruising from the force of his body slapping against mine. His hips pounded against mine harder and harder until I was clenching around him.

He rolled us into a sitting position with my legs wrapped around his back and then he was lifting me up and down, bouncing me on his dick. I wanted so badly to pull my legs apart so I could be the one to control the speed, but unless I took the time to get my shoes and pants off, that wasn't going to happen.

I jerked him to the side, our bodies crashing to the ground and splattering the mud all around us. His hips instantly started jerking into me as we lay staring at each other. He wrapped his hand around the back of my neck and pulled me in for a kiss. My hand wandered all over his body, feeling his tight abs and the thin line of hair that led down to his cock. My fingers slid between our bodies until I could feel his wet cock moving in and out of me.

His fingers moved to my hips and squeezed me right before his body pistoned against mine so fiercely he was pushing us across the muddy ground with each thrust.

"I want you to take me from behind," I moaned.

"Your legs are wrapped around me. That'd take too much time to get out of."

"Bullshit." I rolled us over again and he hovered over me, barely slowing his speed. "Crawl out from between my legs and then fuck me hard from behind."

"I'm not leaving your pussy until I'm ready to come all over your body."

"Oh God, say it again."

"I'm gonna come all over your body," he hissed. "I'm gonna pull my cock out of your tight pussy and spread my seed all over your tits and down your stomach. And when I'm done, you're gonna lick my cock clean."

My eyes rolled back in my head as another orgasm struck, wringing my body out until all I could do was lay there and pulse around his cock. He pulled out and jerked his cock twice right before he shot his cum all over my stomach. He did as promised and started spreading his cum up to my breasts, taking extra time to rub it into my nipples.

Resting his forehead against mine, he laughed slightly then pulled back to look into my eyes. He was breathing hard and staring at me like I wasn't real. I slapped his cheek lightly and grinned. "Good to know you're a decent fuck."

"If we weren't laying in the fucking mud and you didn't have such a fucking tempting body, I would have taken my time with you and done things the right way."

"Hard and fast is never wrong."

"That wasn't exactly how I saw our first time going."

"I have to agree with you there," I panted. "I never envisioned our first time with me having mud between my ass cheeks."

He chuckled and pressed a kiss to my mouth, then wiggled out from between my legs. "I think you got mud on my balls," he muttered while he tucked himself in. I cleaned the mud off my backside as best as I could and then pulled up my pants.

"Ready?" he asked, holding out a hand to me. I took his hand and got to my feet.

"Yeah, but now I really need a shower."

"Sorry about the muddy ass."

"That's not the biggest problem. If anyone sees me, they'll smell the cum that's all over my body."

He bent over and scooped up some mud, spreading it over the belly of my shirt. "There, problem solved."

I raised an eyebrow and shook my head. "Yeah, nothing covers up cum quite like mud. Why didn't I think of that?"

"Because you're a woman."

We tromped off through the mud and further through the trees. "Oh, so I couldn't have thought of that because I have a vagina?"

"No, you couldn't have thought about that because women come up with logical solutions, like wash your clothes or put another shirt over the one you have on. Men come up with whatever is right in front of them. Hence, the mud. Not logical, but still effective."

"You know, for someone that keeps his house so tidy, I really wouldn't have seen mud as your solution."

"Outdoors is a place for dirt. Inside, I want my place to be my sanctuary. How could I possibly relax in a mess? I want to be comfortable, but I'm not a pig. And you make it sound like I obsess over the cleanliness of my house."

"You do. The first month I was there, I put a cup down on your table and you put a coaster under it."

"That's because it would have left water rings. I didn't pay good money for my furniture to be ruined by stupidity."

I started huffing as I tried to keep up with him again. He seemed to have all the energy in the world, while I felt like a nap would be a great idea. "See, that's usually something a woman thinks of. And what about the books on the bookcase? You are constantly making sure the spines all line up perfectly at the edge of the shelf."

He stopped and rubbed the back of his neck. "Look, I'm gonna tell you something, but if you say a goddamn word to anyone, I'll kick you out of my house and never sleep with you again."

"Scout's honor," I said with a hidden grin.

"My mom was a library and computer teacher. I had to help her in the library every day after school and then right after school let out for summer break. I had to make sure all the books were put back in order and were perfectly shelved, all while listening to Rod Stewart. I swear to God, I joined the military just to get away from my love for Rod Stewart songs. I thought they were going to turn me gay."

I snorted and tried to hold back my laughter, and when he scowled at me, I just laughed harder.

"It's not fucking funny."

"You're right," I said solemnly. "I'm sure Rod was traumatizing to you."

"Do you know what I thought of Rod as a young boy?" I shook my head, biting my lips between my teeth. "I wished that I could be sexy like him. I wanted to have his hair and dress like him. Do you know what wearing a fucking jumpsuit would have done to me?"

"Make women look at your cock?"

"Can you imagine if I had gone into the military dressed like that? I would have been beaten to death in the first week of boot camp."

"So, how did you get out of this dangerous life you were living?" I asked mockingly.

"I hid it."

"You- I'm sorry, did you just say you 'hid it'?"

"Someday I'll show you my Rod Stewart impersonation. You'll see why I was so determined to hide that part of me from the world."

"I can't wait to see that."

He smirked at me. "I bet you can't." He pressed a kiss to my mouth and pulled me against the growing bulge in his pants. "Let's keep moving before I throw you down for another mud fucking," he murmured against my mouth.

I nodded dazedly and then ran after him when he took off without me.

Chapter Thirteen

JACKSON

We hid in the ditch just a mile from the hidden entrance to Reed Security. There was a vehicle on the side of the road with its headlights pointed right in our direction. We couldn't make it across the road without being seen as long as the vehicle was there. If I knew for sure that the vehicle was just broken down, I would have no problem getting Raegan across the street, but if these people were part of the team that had come after us, I would be leading us to our death.

Raegan was slumped beside me against the slope of the ditch, her eyes barely open. Her skin was cold from being outside all night and the dark circles under her eyes showed signs of stress. She was doing a great job of being brave for me, but everyone had their breaking point. Especially people that weren't used to this kind of stuff. Still, she rarely complained more than the occasional grumble about mud being stuck to her ass.

A man stepped out of the vehicle and stood right in front of his headlights. The lights showed his silhouette perfectly, and along with that, the gun that was clutched in his right hand.

"Fuck," I swore under my breath. Raegan came alive instantly and I had to push her back to the ground so she didn't give away our position. I heard the squawk of a radio, but couldn't understand what was being said. I saw the man turn his head to look in the distance from where we had just come from. Turning to see what he was looking at, my heart burst out of control. There were flashlights headed in our direction. If we didn't get our asses moving, we would be shot or taken in no time.

"Raegan, I need you to listen to me and do exactly as I say."

She nodded and sat up a little straighter. "What's going on?"

"We're getting boxed in. They're close on our asses and we have to make a run for it. We're about a mile from the underground entrance to Reed Security. We need to haul ass there. Can you do that?"

"Well, I might rip my ass cheeks apart because of the dried mud, but I'd prefer that over being dead."

I smirked at her and gave her a swift kiss before clutching her hand. "As soon as I say when, we're going to make a break for it. Don't slow down for anything. If anything happens to me, you haul ass until you can get someplace safe to hide."

"I have to admit, my chances are much better without you." I looked at her quizzically. "What? You're bigger than me. You make a bigger target, which I will use to my advantage. Sometimes being smaller is better."

I huffed a laugh as I looked back one last time. The guy from the vehicle was walking toward the group of men headed our way. Now was as good a time as any. "Ready? Now!"

I took off, gripping her hand in mine. She stumbled and fell, then shot up and ran with me.

"I thought I told you to be ready?" I said as we rushed across the open field. I could hear the men shouting behind us.

"You said to go on *when*! I didn't hear you say that!"

"I said, 'Ready? Now!' What part of that isn't self-explanatory?"

"Do you really want to argue about this now? I have a limited supply of oxygen and you're using it all up arguing with me," she said, huffing as she ran beside me. I chanced a glance behind me and saw we still had a good distance between us and our pursuers.

I knew we were getting close to the entrance, but I hadn't been out this way in a while. I had to focus so I didn't miss it and waste valuable time. I pointed off to our right. "There, just over by that hollowed out tree."

A gunshot fired behind us and Raegan squealed and ducked her head, putting on an extra burst of speed. I ran behind her, hoping to block her from any stray bullets headed our way. None of the bullets were close to us, which meant they didn't know exactly where we were. We would have just enough time to get inside before anyone saw us.

I grabbed her hand and pulled her into the large hollow of the tree, pulling aside some faux bark and placing my hand on the screen, then entering a code. The trap door in the floor opened and I quickly shoved Raegan down the stairs and pulled the hatch closed behind me. Against the wall was the button to secure the hatch and I slammed my hand against it, then raced down the stairs after Raegan. Grabbing her hand again, I pulled her along behind me as we ran down the tunnel, guided only by the track lighting on the walls.

"We're here!" Raegan said in excitement. "I'll get a bath and a soft bed to sleep in."

"Let's hope so," I muttered. We slowed as we approached the doors to the panic room, but when we got to the outer door, I already knew that something was wrong. The light was blinking in a sequence and then repeating itself. It was morse code. I watched it over and over, my morse code skills severely lacking at the moment. But after a few minutes, I was able to decipher the message.

"They already moved on." I punched in the code and entered the panic room slowly.

"What do you mean they left?"

"I don't know for sure. They must have decided to move on when those men showed up at the hospital."

"They just left you behind?" Her face morphed into a comical state of disbelief and I had to force myself not to laugh.

"Raegan, I'm far from helpless. If they left, it's because they felt there was too much danger and they had to get out right away."

"Sure, that makes sense. There's so much danger that they figured, hell, Jackson can deal with this on his own. He's practically superhuman. Plus, that Raegan sure does know how to handle a man."

"Relax. We have everything we need here to sneak out and get to our next location. It'll take some time to make sure we aren't followed, but we'll be fine. Besides, as a former gun moll, I'm sure you know a thing or two about being on the run."

"So, does this mean that I don't get a bath or a full night's sleep before we leave?"

"Afraid not. It's best if we don't hang around too long. We should just load up and go."

She sighed and jerked her head in the universal signal for *let's go.* "Come on, if I'm not getting any sleep, I'm gonna need a gun for sure."

"Why's that?"

"Let's just say I don't deal well with a lack of sleep."

She walked off toward the bedrooms and I wondered what the hell I had gotten myself into with this woman. She definitely wasn't the wilting flower I took her for.

I gathered up weapons and grabbed a burner phone, putting everything in the SUV. Raegan went through the closet in the room she had been staying in and put together a bag of clothes and toiletries for herself and then did the same for me. Within a half hour, we were in the SUV and driving through the tunnel. Unfortunately, I had no idea if anyone was in the area. The tunnel let out a mile from the property, but that didn't guarantee that the men that were after us weren't lying in wait somewhere close by.

"So, how sure are you that we're going to leave this tunnel and nobody will be waiting for us?" Raegan asked.

I weighed my options and our chances, considering what I really wanted to tell her. "I'd say ninety-ten."

"Ninety percent chance we're good?"

"About, well, maybe more eighty-twenty, if we're lucky."

"Wait, how can it be an eighty percent chance, but only if we're lucky? I want to know what our actual odds are."

"Fine, honest to God odds?" She nodded at me. "Ten, no, probably more like seven. Yeah, seven percent."

"You're giving us a seven percent chance of sneaking out of here?"

"More or less."

She turned in her seat, staring at me like I was crazy. "If there's such a little chance of us sneaking by, why don't we just go out with our hands up? At least they might not try to kill us."

I snorted at her. "You're funny. Yeah, I'm never going to just walk out with my hands up and surrender. That's just not who I am."

"Then why are you driving?"

"Because I'm a man."

"Whew, that's good to know, because I was scared that you were really a woman and that hair growing out of your face was just a really bad waxing job. I was actually about to suggest that you go to a new salon!"

"You need to relax. I'm a really good getaway driver."

"And that's really great for you, but if they start shooting, who's going to fire back at them? Keep in mind that I already shot you, and as fun as that was, I don't think the odds are very good of me doing something like that when I mean to."

"I can shoot and drive at the same time."

"I'm sure you can, but wouldn't it make more sense if I drove?"

"Not if we want to live," I muttered. I pulled to a stop in front of the exit and sighed. "What do you want to do? You want to drive?"

"Well, I don't think giving me the gun is the answer."

"Can you handle driving with bullets flying at you?" She cringed. "What about another vehicle trying to ram into you? Can you hold steady?"

She thought for a moment and then gave a curt nod. "I can do it. I swear, I won't screw this up."

"Fine." I put the SUV in park and got out, walking around to her side. I shifted all my weapons from where I had placed them to the passenger side and in the back seat to where I could easily access anything I might need. "Okay, here's the plan. When I open the door, you're going to pull out like everything is totally normal. Do not do anything to draw attention to us."

"I can do that."

"Good."

I pulled the remote down from the visor and entered the code to open the door. Slowly, Raegan pulled out of the hidden tunnel and crept toward the road. We had gone about a mile at this slow pace when I'd finally had it.

"A little faster, Raegan. At this pace we'll-"

I didn't get to finish the sentence as bullets pinged off the side of the SUV. Raegan squealed and continued to creep along.

"What the fuck are you doing? Drive!"

She slammed her foot down on the gas. "You said not to draw attention!"

"They already know we're here," I yelled, rolling down the window and firing out the window in the general direction the bullets were coming from. They were staying hidden, but they wouldn't for long. Raegan turned the SUV violently to the left and we were out on the road. Within minutes, another vehicle was behind us, coming up fast and slamming into our rear bumper. We jolted forward and Raegan went faster. Driving erratically, swerving from side to side and making it impossible for me to get a shot off.

"Stop fucking swerving!" I shouted, climbing into the back seat to get into the trunk. There was a small window at the bottom of the back window that could be opened to fire from. "I can't get a shot off if you keep swerving."

"I'm trying to avoid being hit again. Unless you *wanted* to be run off the road."

I opened the small window, took aim, and fired, but then was slammed against the wall of the driver's side when Raegan turned at the last minute.

"What the fuck? I told you to stop swerving!"

"I'm so sorry, oh wise one! Next time I'll let us get hit by the second truck that's joined in the race to see who could kill us fastest," she yelled back.

I shook my head and got into position to fire again. Sure enough, there was a truck that was further back, but another truck that was almost to the side of us. I couldn't get a shot off at this angle and quickly started digging around in the trunk for something else I could use.

"I need a minute! Buy me some time."

After getting the case at the base of the floor opened, I pulled out a sniper rifle and quickly loaded it, but then went back and grabbed a few grenades. If they got close enough, I could just use those on them.

Another jerk of the wheel sent me flying around the back of the SUV, feeling like a ping pong ball. The grenades I had pulled out were no longer in my hands and the rifles were sliding across the floor. "Just so you know, I have weapons back here that I really don't want to shoot myself with!"

"I'm sorry. I mistook you for someone that knew how to safely handle a gun!"

That damn woman was so fucking sassy that I wanted to smack her. Or kiss her. Either way, she loved busting my balls.

"Do you still need a minute?" she asked.

I looked out the window and ducked just as someone leaned out the window and shot at me. The glass above me shattered. I scrambled to grab the grenades. I almost caught one that was rolling around, but was thrown against the trunk door. This woman was a terrible driver. Whatever road she had taken us on was full of potholes and I could barely straighten up to look out the busted out back window.

"Uh, if I were you, I'd hurry up and do whatever it is you're going to do," she said nervously.

"I'm working on it!" I snatched up a grenade and pulled the pin. I almost released it. I almost threw it out the fucking window, but then I saw all the cows around us. Fucking cows. And she was slowing down. I quickly looked to the front and saw a whole fucking group of cows right in front of us. Looking out the back window again, I saw one of the trucks was stuck in mud and the other was coming up behind that truck, giving me a minute to get into a new position.

"What the fuck are you doing? Getaway by cows? I almost threw a fucking grenade! I would have killed us!" I shoved the pin back in the grenade and pulled out my sniper rifle as she came to a stop in the middle of a fucking grazing pasture. I snatched up as many weapons as I could, shoving the grenades into the pockets of my tactical pants, and climbed over the back seat.

"What are you doing? You have to shoot them!" she screeched.

"They outnumber us and being in the trunk is no longer feasible." I grabbed her hand and pulled her out the passenger side of the SUV. Shoving a rifle in her hands, I quickly showed her how to use it.

"Safety off. Butt of the gun against your shoulder. Point and shoot."

I took aim and fired off a few shots to keep them back. She just stared at me in shock.

"You want me to do what?"

"Just fire the fucking gun. I need you to keep them off my ass so I can take them out!"

"But I don't know how to use this!"

"I just showed you." I took a few more shots, hitting one of the men, but there were still at least three more over there.

"I'm not shooting anyone. The last time I ended up shooting you."

"Then don't fucking point it at me!"

I pulled her down behind the engine block as they continued to fire at us. Popping up, I took a few more shots, wondering how the hell I would get us out of this when Raegan kept arguing with me about using the fucking gun.

"There's got to be another way," she said as she leaned against the grill.

"Sure, let's just invite them over to share a bottle of vodka with us. We'll get them drunk and make our getaway."

She sneered at me and then her face went bright. "I've got it! Cover me."

"What?" She darted away from the truck and I quickly laid down fire to keep her from getting shot. She ran up to a cow and slapped it on the ass. It didn't move.

"What the fuck are you doing?"

"Causing a stampede!"

"It's a fucking cow. It's not going to run away unless you piss it off."

I kept firing, running lower on bullets the longer she stayed out there and I had to lay down cover fire.

"How do I piss it off?"

"Keep talking and I'm sure it'll run away from you just so it doesn't have to hear your ridiculous ideas!"

"Asshole."

"Get your ass back over here. A cow isn't going to protect you."

She peeked out from behind the cow and ran back in my direction, pointing the gun toward the sky as she tried to cover her face. I rolled my eyes and prayed I stayed alive long enough to yell at her for being an idiot.

"Next time, point your weapon at the people that are actually shooting at us."

"Can't you do your kung fu, badass shooting and take these guys out? I'm hungry and tired and I don't have the patience for this shit any more."

I hadn't wanted to resort to using a grenade unless I had to. There were animals around and we were on someone else's property, but this standoff would only last so long before either I would run out of bullets or they would overtake us.

"Enough of this shit." I pulled out a grenade, pulled the pin, and tossed it at the first truck. I threw Raegan to the ground and covered her body with mine. The ground shook and as soon as the shrapnel was done flying, I pulled out a second grenade and tossed it at the second truck, falling back on top of Raegan as it exploded.

Silence surrounded us and I slowly got to my feet, my gun at the ready. I motioned for Raegan to stay down and waited for the dust to clear. I didn't see any movement from where I was and I couldn't take the chance that someone was waiting for us. I moved forward, slipping quietly around the first burnt up truck, checking for survivors. All I saw were bloody, charred remains. After clearing the second vehicle, I walked back to the SUV and motioned for Raegan to get back inside. She didn't say anything and neither did I.

When we were in the middle of escaping, it hadn't hit me that Raegan was in danger. She had handled it so well, but now that we were out of danger, I was practically shaking internally when I thought of how that could have gone wrong.

Chapter Fourteen

RAEGAN

Jackson had been quiet since we got back in the SUV. He drove for about an hour and then pulled into a used car lot. He told me to wait for him and then returned twenty minutes later with keys to a pickup truck. He pulled it up along the SUV and quickly transferred everything into the truck. The silence was starting to get to me. I wasn't used to this side of Jackson, and for the first time, I wasn't really sure if I should break the silence. After another twenty minutes, I couldn't take it anymore.

"Did I do something to piss you off?"

"Why would you think that?" he said, almost angrily.

"Um, well, you're being really quiet and I'm not sure why."

He huffed out a laugh and drummed his thumbs on the steering wheel.

"I'm sensing some passive aggressive behavior here. I find that it's always best to just blurt it out. Just get it off your chest."

"If I say what I want to say, I'm just gonna piss you off. And then we'll be fighting, and of course, I won't win because there's no winning when you're arguing with a woman. Then I'll be spending the rest of this goddamn trip trying to make you happy again so that I don't have to worry about you chopping off my dick in the middle of the night."

"Okay, so, what I've gathered so far is that you're angry with me."

"You gathered that, huh?"

"Yeah, I used the whole right side of my brain to gather that little nugget of information. What I don't know is *why* you're mad."

"Why don't you use the other half of your brain to think back to what just happened," he sneered.

"Well, I remember me driving an SUV to escape a bunch of mad men while you fucked around in the back of the truck. I remember me being the one that tried to come up with some clever ideas to get us out of the predicament we were in."

"I couldn't do anything because you were throwing me around the back of the truck with your crazy driving. And trying to start a stampede with a fucking cow wasn't a solution. It was just plain idiotic and you could have gotten yourself killed."

"If you look on the bright side, you wouldn't have to watch out for me anymore or worry about getting shot. I'd say you actually could have done better."

He jerked the wheel, steering the truck to the side of the road. "You think I'd prefer you not be around?"

"Well, I'm not sure what to think. You seem pretty pissed at me."

"Because you could have gotten yourself killed. You were acting like this was some kind of game. It's not fucking paintball. If you take a bullet because you're running around tipping cows, it could be the last thing you ever do. I can't fucking do anything if you don't stay right by my fucking side and use some common sense."

"I was helping!" I said indignantly.

"You were a fucking liability. Do you have any sense of danger? I swear to God, you stayed with that fucker even though he was beating the shit out of you and then you dart out into a dark parking lot to try and save me. Then, you go running through a pasture to slap a fucking cow! You're gonna get yourself killed."

I wasn't trying to be a pain in the ass or get us killed. I just wasn't going to sit down and take it. Better to die trying than to sit around like I had with Xavier and wait for someone to save me. I opened the door to the truck and hopped out, turning back to face him.

"I'm not your fucking problem, and I don't need you to protect me. I was trying to help. I'm sorry if I was wrong."

I slammed the door and walked off through the field, not really knowing where I was going. But if I didn't know where I was going, neither would anyone else. I could just disappear. I could find work and get paid under the table. I'd just lay low for a while, maybe move to some small town in the middle of Montana. Who would look for me there?

Jackson grabbed my arm and swung me around, crushing his lips to mine. His tongue pushed inside my mouth and his hands roamed the curves of my body. When he jerked back, I was left dizzy from his kiss and craved more.

"See, this is why men don't talk to women. I wasn't fucking saying that you were a problem. I was saying that...that you were in danger. And I didn't fucking like that. I want to protect you, but I can't if you're running around like a fucking lunatic."

"You started out so good, and then you crashed and burned." I turned to go, but he grabbed my arm and spun me back around.

"I know I'm saying all the wrong shit. Just fucking listen to me for a minute." I waited for him to say something, but he just kept staring at me, his mouth moving like he was going to say something, but nothing came out.

"Yeah, I agree. That was a very compelling argument."

"Shut up. I like you. A lot. And I...I think over the past year I may have even started...well, you know. It's just that I always see you as this woman that...hell, I don't know why I thought that, but...you see what I'm saying?"

I looked at him in confusion. "Yes, that was crystal clear. Now that you've said that, I want nothing more than to fall to my knees and suck your cock."

"I'm trying to say that I think I love you!" he shouted.

"You think you do, or you know you do?"

"Uh...I'm not sure. Well, I mean, I think I...but it's confusing because I'm not sure if...and then I don't know if you're even...it's just all very confusing."

"So is this conversation," I muttered. "Look, I don't need you to tell me you like me or love me, whichever it is. Frankly, I'd rather you not say something like that unless you're sure that you actually feel that way."

"Wouldn't you rather know how I'm feeling?" he asked.

"If you asked me if I like having sex with you and I said, *I think I do. Maybe I really like it, but...it's confusing. I'm not sure.* Would that be a good answer for you? Would you be happy to hear that I may or may not like having sex with you, but I just hadn't decided?"

"See, this is why I don't talk to women. I don't know how to do it and now I see why this is so fucking hard for everyone else. They all help each other out and I never fucking understood it. It can't be that hard, right? But it fucking is. Talking with a woman is like trying to pull your own fucking teeth. It's painful and unnecessary."

"You know, you're doing a great job at convincing me that you like me. I'm thinking maybe you should seek advice from those other guys before you say anything else."

He pulled at his short hair as he screamed in frustration. "Fuck it, let's just hit the road. We have a long way to go before we get to safety. Neither of us has slept in a long time and we need some fucking food. Can we please just get on the road and talk about this later?"

I was hungry and the lack of sleep was really getting to me. I supposed that neither of us was at our best right now. "Fine, but please try your best not to give me any more compliments. Next thing, you'll be telling me that you want to have kids...sort of, but you're not sure if my womb is good enough to house your sperm."

I got back in the truck as he stood in place, trying to get himself under control. Good, I was glad I wasn't the only one that was having trouble navigating this odd turn of events.

"Are you really going to make me stay in a no-tell motel?"

Jackson put the truck in park and glared at me. "Look, I can't use my credit card because whoever is after you would be able to track us. I don't really want to stay in a place that's seen more venereal diseases than a hooker, but this is our only option if you want to get some sleep."

"Ugh, fine. Let's go."

I got out of the truck and grabbed my bag, following him to our motel room door. It was one of those motels that looked like a strip mall. When we got to ours, Jackson put the key in, but it opened before he even turned the knob. That was just fucking peachy.

"Well, I suppose being murdered in my sleep is preferable to being executed from behind on my knees."

"You always see the silver lining," he said mockingly. "Do you want sleep first or food?"

"Food. As much as I want to sleep, I don't think I'd be able to without some food in my stomach."

"There's a diner across the street. We can just walk there. My leg is all cramped up from sitting so long."

"Are you sure that you're okay?" I asked as he limped heavily toward the door. "How did you even run away from those guys, let alone walk fifteen miles?"

"I just pushed through. We needed to get somewhere, so I just shoved it to the back of my mind. I can rest it when we're at the safe house."

We walked across the street to the diner that had seen better days. There were bikes lined up in front of the restaurant and a few cars toward the back of the lot. Jackson pushed the door open, his eyes taking in everything as we walked through to the counter. I took a hesitant seat on the stool and refused to rest my arms on the counter. There was something sticky on it and I didn't need to touch the counter to know it was there.

A woman with her hair pinned up and a pencil shoved through it came up to us, smacking her gum and staring at us with a bored expression. "What can I get for you folks today?"

"What do you have that won't give me food poisoning?" I asked before I could think better of it.

Jackson grabbed my hand quickly and gave me a tight squeeze, telling me to shut the fuck up. "What she's saying is that she's very sensitive to foods. She'll end up in the hospital if everything isn't cooked thoroughly."

The woman raised an eyebrow in disbelief, but didn't call us out. "I'll make sure everything is cooked well."

"Thank you," Jackson said before I could tell her to shove it up her ass. He placed an order of burger and fries for both of us and I scowled when she said it would take about ten minutes. I was hangry and dealing with a shitty motel room and bad food wasn't exactly what I had thought of when Jackson promised me food and a good night's sleep. As the waitress walked away, Jackson glanced around the diner and then leaned in to whisper in my ear. "Let's try not to piss off the locals."

"I'm not trying to. I'm just very grouchy and I feel like I haven't bathed in a month."

"You look worse than that," he muttered, obviously not understanding that pointing out the obvious was not something I wanted to hear right now.

Our food arrived ten minutes later as promised. It actually didn't look that bad, but when I went to take a bite into my burger, beady eyes stared back at me. I screamed and threw my burger back on my plate, quickly backing away from the counter and tripping over the stool.

"What the hell's going on?" Jackson asked me.

I pointed frantically at my plate from the floor. "There's...in there and it...eww!"

Jackson picked up my burger and sighed, throwing some money down on the counter. He held out his hand to help me up and then pulled me toward the door. The bikers sitting around the diner were all looking at us with pissed off expressions and Jackson ushered me faster out the door.

"You just had to open your mouth," he grumbled.

"I'm sorry. I'm starving and tired."

"You really pissed her off. I've never seen someone actually put a mouse in someone's burger before."

"Who says they put it in there? That place was disgusting. For all you know, the thing was already dead in the kitchen and just got tossed in by accident." He dragged me by the elbow across the street and back to the motel. "What are we going to do about food? I'm starving."

"I think that's the least of our problems right now."

"What do you mean?"

"I mean, they're following us. We need to grab our shit and move out."

"So, no bed tonight then."

"Like you were actually going to sleep in that bed anyway."

He shoved the door in and quickly grabbed his bag while I grabbed mine. We were just getting in the truck when the bikers blocked us in from behind. Some were on their bikes and others were just standing there glaring at us.

"I suppose this would be the wrong time to apologize to you."

"I'm not the one that needs an apology," Jackson said. "Stay in the truck."

He hopped out and I scooted over to his side, rolling down the window so I could hear what was being said.

"What can I do for you?" Jackson asked genially.

"You can get the fuck out of our town and never come back," one biker said.

"That was the plan. As you can see, we're packed and ready to get on our way."

"Not just yet," the biker sneered. "You don't get to walk away so easily. See, that was my sister in there and your woman insulted her. I don't take too kindly to people treating my family like shit."

"Look, I'm very sorry. We've been up for two days and we haven't eaten in a very long time. She's just hungry."

"That doesn't excuse poor manners," the biker said, cracking his knuckles. I swallowed hard. There had to be at least ten bikers here and if they came at us, what good would I be?

"We're leaving, so if you'll just move your bikes, we'll be on our way."

"Not just yet." The biker advanced quickly on Jackson and threw the first punch, but Jackson was ready and quickly ducked out of the way and threw two punches of his own right into the man's kidneys. I cringed as the man double over and Jackson grabbed the man by the head and kneed him in the face. Two other men ran at him and Jackson did all this kung fu crap, kicking and punching, bobbing and weaving. I stood by the truck and moved along with him, as if I was in the fight. He was amazing. He barely took any hits.

When one man grabbed him from behind, he pushed off the ground, slamming the man into the truck, which I quickly moved out of the way of, and then kicked the other guy in the face.

"Yeah!" I cheered. "Punch him, kick him!" All of the other bikers were involved now and Jackson was starting to take a few hits here and there. "Don't take that crap from him, Jackson. Kill him! Break his fucking neck!"

Jackson threw an elbow at one biker and punched another in the nose. Blood spurted from the man's nose and Jackson used the opportunity to wrap him in a choke hold. "You want to calm the fuck down, Raegan? Seriously? You want me to kill him?"

"Sorry," I said sheepishly. "I was just really getting into the whole fighting thing."

"We're in the middle of town," Jackson said incredulously as he kicked an approaching man in the stomach. "Not exactly the best place to break someone's neck."

Another biker swung what looked like a tire iron, hitting Jackson in the head before I had the chance to warn him. Jackson slumped to the ground and then they were kicking him in the chest and back. I cringed and tried to figure out what to do when Jackson started fighting back. He grabbed one guy's foot and twisted it violently. He hit another guy in the nuts and kicked another one in the face with his boot. But still, he was getting the shit kicked out of him.

I had to do something. This was all my fault. And then it hit me. "I'll get the grenades!" I ran to the truck and dug through the bag of weapons, yanking out a grenade. I spun around and held the grenade high. "Let him go right the fuck now or I'll take you all out!"

One of the bikers smirked at me. "Nice try, bitch. You still have the pin in."

I looked at the grenade and yanked the pin out, holding it high in the air once more. Jackson was struggling to stand with a man's arm wrapped around his neck, using him as cover. "Let him go, or I swear to God, I'll throw this at you."

"Raegan, what the fuck are you doing?" Jackson swore.

"I'm getting us out of here."

"With a fucking grenade?"

"Well, I thought about using a gun, but I'm not the best shot. I'd probably take out you along with all of them. Does an automatic rifle stop on its own or do I have to release the trigger?" I said stupidly, hoping it would deter the bikers from trying anything else.

"Put the pin back in," one man yelled at me.

"So, how does this thing work exactly? Do I just release this little lever and throw?"

"Lady, you're holding live fucking ammo. Put the fucking pin back in."

"I'm not putting the pin back in until you hand him over. Either we drive away or all of us get splattered on the concrete."

"You're fucking crazy," one of them said.

"She's not going to do it," another one said. "She would die too."

"Yeah, see the thing is, I've got arms dealers that want to kill me, so if they get me, I'll probably be tortured to death. This would actually be the faster way to go. So...what's it going to be?"

The man holding Jackson slowly released him and shoved him my way. Jackson stumbled over to the truck and got in, wincing as he stepped up.

"Now, move your bikes so that we can leave and don't follow us. I have plenty of weapons in here that I can use."

The bikers' faces all went hard, but they walked away and got on their bikes, roaring out of the parking lot. I hopped in the truck and blew out a harsh breath.

"You want to hand over the grenade?"

"What?" I asked, still trying to process what had just happened.

"The pin is still out of the grenade and your hands are shaking. It would be a shame to get us out of that only to die because you didn't actually put the pin back in."

I nodded, handing the grenade and pin over to him slowly. He replaced the pin and then put it in the bag in the back seat.

"How about you just stay away from grenades from now on?"

"Well, I wouldn't have had to use them if you had fought them a little harder. You know, Claire told me that Derek took out like fifteen men."

"I wouldn't have had to try and take out ten bikers if you had just kept your mouth shut. And Derek didn't take out fifteen men at once."

"I'm just saying, maybe you're a little off your game."

"Really? You mean that maybe after battling men at Reed Security, running away with you, walking fifteen miles, and then driving for a few hours without sleep or food, I might be a little off my game?"

"Hey, you don't have to yell at me. It was just an observation."

He grumbled to himself about women and crazy ideas. I turned toward the window and laughed, needing to get just one more dig in. "I bet Knight could have done it."

Chapter Fifteen

JACKSON

We went through the drive-thru for food, seeing as how Raegan was a grouch and would probably offend anyone she came in contact with. I paid for another motel room a couple hundred miles from the last one and finally sank down onto a bed. I was exhausted and needed a shit ton of sleep. It also wouldn't hurt my sore body to get some rest.

"Oh, crap, that hurts."

Raegan walked over to my side of the bed and started undoing my shoes and then pulled them off. "Do you want your pants off too?"

"I'm not in the mood for sex," I groaned, thinking that was probably the only time in my life I had ever thought that.

"I wasn't offering. I'm not exactly in the mood either. Besides, I still have mud in my ass crack. That's definitely not something you need to see while you're fucking me."

"So, there will be more fucking. Good to know."

"As long as I get some more food after we wake up."

She undid the belt on my pants and pulled down the zipper. I couldn't get hard if I wanted to right now. I lifted my ass so she could pull the pants off me, but that was all I could muster up to help out with. As soon as she put my feet on the bed, I was drifting off to sleep.

"Do we have to get up at a certain time?"

"I'm not going anywhere," I mumbled. I felt her snuggle under the covers and her hand brushed against mine. I didn't have the energy to pull her into me, so I intertwined our fingers and drifted off to sleep. When I woke again, it was night and Raegan wasn't in bed with me. Figuring that she was in the bathroom, I laid back and waited, but after ten minutes, she still wasn't out.

"Raegan?" I called out, but got no answer. Flinging off the covers, I grabbed my pants off the floor and quickly pulled them on. I flicked on the bathroom light, but there was no one there. I shoved my feet in my shoes and grabbed my keys. When I looked outside, there was no sign of her. She couldn't have gone far and there was no way I would have slept through someone breaking into our room, but that didn't mean that no one snatched her off the streets. I got in my truck and drove, searching for any sign of her.

The more I drove, the more nervous I got. It seemed like I had been falling for Raegan since the day I pulled her from that shit hole she called a house. She had been bloodied and beaten to hell, but I still felt a connection to her. I wanted her and not just for a night or until I got bored. I wanted her to be mine. I had taken things slowly because of my mistaken idea that she needed time to heal, and it was probably for the best that I had given her that time. But maybe I had given her too much time. When I said I thought I was in love with her when we were walking last night, I meant it. I really did think that, but I was a bumbling fool and screwed the whole thing up. And it hadn't escaped my notice that she hadn't said anything in return. That was why I hadn't pushed the issue. What if I never knew now? What if I never found her and had the chance to tell her how I really felt?

My worry morphed to anger the longer I looked for her. She was being reckless and we couldn't afford that when we were on the run from arms dealers and a biker gang that would rather see us dead for something as simple as a stupid comment. Who would be after us next? With Raegan, it was very possible she was out pissing people off right this very moment. Did she even stop to think that I wouldn't know where she was? Did she think about what it would do to me to wake up and see that she was gone?

I gripped the steering wheel tighter and took deep breaths to keep from pulling over and beating the shit out of someone in the hopes of getting some fucking answers. I turned the truck around and headed back to the motel. And that's when I saw her. A man was gripping her shoulder and then he shoved her to the ground and landed between her spread legs. Murder flowed through my veins as I drove the truck up on the sidewalk and slammed on the brakes, barely shifting into park before I was out of the truck and yanking the man off her.

"Motherfucker! What the fuck do you think you're doing?"

I threw him to the ground as Raegan scrambled to her knees. "Jackson, don't!" Her hand shot out to grab my fist before I could slam it into his face. That's when I saw that the guy was at least sixty. "Fucking disgusting piece of shit!"

Raegan quickly moved to his side and felt at his neck, then started pumping his chest.

"What the fuck are you doing? Let the asshole die. He was trying to attack you!"

"He wasn't attacking me," She said between breaths. "He said he didn't feel good and collapsed into me. I couldn't catch him because he's heavier than me."

I quickly pulled out my phone and dialed 9-1-1. Raegan continued to perform CPR, but I took over after I got off the phone. The ambulance was fast and they quickly took over, loaded him up on a stretcher, and drove away.

As we stood there watching the ambulance drive away, I scratched the back of my head and then pulled my hair as I tried to let the anger leech from my body. I couldn't take feeling this way, like I was constantly on edge and needing to kill anyone that got close to her. I glanced over at her, but she was glaring at me with her arms crossed over her chest and her foot was tapping out an erratic rhythm. Shit. I knew what was coming. Deciding to get ahead of the inevitable beat-down I was about to receive, I grabbed her by the elbow and hauled her up into the truck.

"What the hell are you doing?"

"Getting your ass back to the motel."

"I have bags," she protested.

I looked around, seeing the bags scattered on the ground nearby. I had only missed them because I was insane with rage. I put everything in the bed of the truck and got in, slamming the door behind me. I drove back in silence and when she tried to yell at me, I just held up my hand to silence her. Her eyebrows shot high and her mouth gaped, but she didn't say anything.

I took the bags back in the room and tried to ignore the slamming of the bathroom door. Digging through the bags to see what she had risked her life for in the middle of the night, I pulled out muscle reliever, ice packs, Tylenol, and a wrap that I could use for my bruised ribs. Well, now I felt like an asshole.

But instead of apologizing like I should, I took it to the next level, because she shouldn't have risked anything to take care of me. I was supposed to be doing that for her. I went over to the bathroom door and knocked, but when she didn't answer, I simply kicked in the door.

"What the fuck? Am I not allowed to piss in private?"

"You're not pissing. You're hiding from me."

"Yeah, because you're acting like a psycho."

"Do you know what could have happened out there? You could have been raped and murdered. You could have been taken by the gang of bikers you pissed off. Hell, you could have been found by those arms dealers. And I didn't even fucking know where you had gone. You just fucking left!"

"I didn't just leave. I left a note for you."

"No, you didn't. I would have seen it."

She stormed past me out of the bathroom and over to the night-stand table where a piece of paper sat next to the phone. She handed it over to me and I quickly read it.

Jackson,

I went down to the corner store to get some supplies. You look like you're in a lot of pain even in your sleep. Be back soon.

Raegan

. . .

"You still shouldn't have left. I woke up and I was fucking terrified that something had happened to you. You can't just walk out on me. We're supposed to be a fucking team!"

"Are we? I wasn't aware that we were a team. You just boss me around and yell at me."

"Because I'm protecting you. I can't do that if you're constantly doing what you're not supposed to."

"So, instead of thanking me for looking after you and trying to take care of you, you just yell at me and act like I'm an idiot."

"You are a fucking idiot! Anyone could have taken you."

"I took your gun with me." She pulled the gun out of the back of her jeans and set it on the table. "I made sure to watch my surroundings the whole time and I would have only been gone fifteen minutes if that guy hadn't had a heart attack on me. And I'll pretend that you didn't just call me a fucking idiot because that's just plain rude."

"Raegan, I can't deal with this. The way you just ran out of here is not how I protect you."

"And watching you try to sleep on the bed when you're obviously in pain isn't something I could just sit by and watch."

"Just listen," I began, but she cut me off.

"No, you just listen. I know that you're trying to protect me and I appreciate that very much, but you were in pain. Every time you moved, you groaned. Your face was twisted in pain the whole time, and I'm sure as soon as you finally sit down again, you're going to feel every bit of pain again. Maybe you're used to women that are delicate and need to be taken care of, but it's a two way street with me. We take care of each other. That's the way this goes."

"The way what goes?" I asked hesitantly.

"This," she said, pointing to the two of us. "We just fucked last night and maybe that didn't mean anything to you, but you sort of told me you loved me and I took that to mean that this was more than just a flyby fucking."

"It was," I said angrily. "I don't just go out and fuck anyone in the middle of a field, in the mud, while I'm on the run. That was special just for you and me."

"Well, it was special to me too! It's not every day a man fucks me with twigs and mud all around, stabbing me in the back."

"And there's no *sort of* about me loving you. I've been fucked up over you since I got you out of that house and I've been falling deeper every day. I'm just an asshole who doesn't know the right words to say because I've never been in love before."

"Well, I love you too," she shouted, "and if you hadn't stumbled over your words so much, I would have told you last night."

"Well, you're telling me now!"

"That's right. I am, so stop fucking yelling at me and kiss me!"

"If you would shut your damn mouth for five seconds, I would." I pulled her into me and crushed my mouth to hers. My hand slipped into her hair and immediately got tangled in the web of caked on dirt and leaves. "You're so fucking dirty."

"You haven't seen anything yet," she said as she yanked my pants off me.

"No," I said around kissing her. "You have dirt caked into your hair." I picked her up by the ass and walked with her into the shower, turning it on without even removing our clothes. The water sluiced over our bodies, mud sliding down and caking the bottom of the tub. I ripped her shirt in two, dropping it to the floor of the shower and then got to work on her pants.

"Yes, get it off me," she groaned. They were sticking to her legs, so she got down on the floor of the tub and put her legs in the air. "Rip them off."

I tugged and tugged, but they were practically glued to her. "They won't come off."

"Jackson, I don't give a shit what you have to do. Get these fucking pants off me!"

I slipped out of the shower and grabbed my bag, pulling a blade that I always kept handy. "I've never had to use this for the removal of a woman's pants before."

"What do you normally use it for?" she asked.

"Gouging out eyes, stabbing someone in the neck, cutting ties, opening packages."

"I like how you started with the worst and ended with opening packages."

I grinned down at her as I ripped the pants to shreds. When they were finally off, I helped her to her feet and ripped the panties from her body. She spun around and shoved her ass toward me. "Get some soap. I need your fingers between my legs."

I quickly obliged her, pouring liquid soap into my hands and then rubbing her pussy. She moaned and moved so her ass hole was right by my fingers. I took that as a sign and slowly started rubbing her tight hole.

"Oh," she groaned. "That's it. Clean me. Get that mud off me." I rubbed the soap around her cheeks some more, taking extra care to make sure there was no mud stuck in any crevices. I got down on my knees and made sure the little patch of hair between her legs was extra clean and then I started on her legs, rubbing my hands up and down her soft skin. "Jackson," she gasped. "I've never had someone clean me the way you do. I need more!"

I practically started laughing at her orgasmic clean talk. "You want more of that? You want me to soap up your body and make sure it's clean?"

"Yes! Please, clean me. Wash my hair and shave my armpits."

"God, I love it when you talk dirty," I groaned as I lifted her in the air and slammed her against the shower wall, taking a washcloth and rubbing it vigorously against her armpits.

"You want some too?"

Before I could answer, she poured shampoo on my head and started running it through my hair. Then she dug her nails into my scalp, massaging away the headache that had been pounding for the last day. I groaned in pleasure and ran the washcloth over her nipples and down her stomach.

"God, your hair is cleaning all the dirt out from under my nails. It feels so good."

My breathing was hard and labored as I struggled to keep her up against the shower wall. I lowered her to her feet and then pressed on her shoulders, telling her what I needed. She took my dick in her hand and then her fingers were massaging the dirt out of my pubic hair.

"God, that feels fucking fantastic." Her hands moved to my balls and back to my ass, a place I didn't even know I had gotten dirt. Her hand jerked my dick hard, rubbing the soap all over until I was filthy clean.

I shut the water off and grabbed a towel, wiping every drip of water from her body. Wrapping a towel around my waist, I carried her back to the bed and laid her down under the covers. Getting in bed, I laid next to her and stared at the ceiling, panting hard and satisfied.

"Was it as good for you as it was for me?"

"I've never had better."

We pulled up to the gates of Knight's safe house and waited to be let in. Cap came out to meet us, along with Derek and Cazzo. When I stepped out of the truck, I groaned and did my best to stretch, but Raegan came around to my side and put her arm around me, trying to hold me up in case I fell. I didn't need her help to walk, but I'd let her think that she was helping just so I could have her in my arms.

"We weren't sure if you were going to make it," Cap said, slapping me on the shoulder. "We just got here ourselves about an hour ago. We're not even settled in yet."

"What happened that you had to take off?"

"That's something we need to talk about, but we're still waiting on an arrival."

I nodded and we started toward the house. Each step was a little more painful and I was starting to regret how hard I had taken Raegan after our shower yesterday. My ribs were aching and my whole body was sore from sitting so long.

"I don't suppose you've had any contact from Craig," Cap said.

"No, we've been running since we left the hospital."

"What happened exactly?" Cap asked, staring at my bruised face.

"Let's just say that this one causes trouble when she's hungry," I said, jerking my thumb in Raegan's direction. She glared at me, but there was no heat behind it. We walked inside the massive house after

Cap went through the ten different security measures Knight had in place. "So, how are Ice and Hunter? Who's with them at the hospital?"

Cazzo and Derek wouldn't look at me and Cap's face was grim.

"They didn't make it," Cap finally said after a minute. "Neither did Gabe."

I was just standing there staring, my heart slowing to an almost deadly pace. Air wouldn't fill my lungs and it wasn't until Raegan slipped her hand into mine that I finally took a breath. "But..." I shook my head, unable to find the right words. When I spoke again, my voice was strangled. "Gabe just had a head injury. It was just a concussion. And Hunter and Ice were doing better. They survived the surgery. How...I don't understand what the hell happened."

"Those men that were after Raegan, one of them posed as a doctor. He injected all of them with something to send them into cardiac arrest. The only reason Burg made it out was because he was so anxious to get out of the bed, he had already taken out his IV. The doctors did everything they could, but it was too late. The dose was too high. The real doctor was found unconscious in the basement."

"No, this has to be a mistake. I saw that doctor. I would have-"

"You had already gone after Raegan," Cap cut in.

I narrowed my eyes at him. "Are you saying this is my fault?"

"No, I'm saying that you couldn't have known anything because you weren't there when the guy poisoned Gabe. The guy got past all of us."

My eyes dropped to the ground as I tried to make my way through the muddled thoughts in my brain. It wasn't right. This had to be some kind of sick joke. "Where's his body?" I asked quietly.

"Jackson-"

"I want to see his fucking body!"

"Don't do this," Cap shook his head. "Don't go down this road."

"I wasn't there." I looked at Derek, who was still avoiding eye contact with me. "Were you there?" Derek nodded. "You saw it? You saw them die?"

"I was outside Hunter's room. He-" Derek cleared his throat, "They tried, but they couldn't get a rhythm back."

I turned to Cazzo, hoping for a different answer. "Believe me, my sister is torn up over this. I would give anything to change what happened, but I can't. They're gone, Jackson."

"Knight and Kate had to stay behind to get the bodies processed for transport. They'll be arriving in a few days. Some of Cash's men stayed behind to help protect them."

"To help them protect dead bodies?" I laughed humorlessly.

"They're still our family, dead or alive," Cap bit out.

I felt tears burning behind my eyes and had to get out of there before I lost it in front of everyone. I cleared my throat and shoved past them. "What rooms are still available?"

"There's one down the hall," Cazzo pointed off to the left. "Second door on the right."

I nodded and headed that way, clenching my jaw to keep my emotions under control. Every step was painful and squeezed my chest tighter and tighter. I found the door to the bedroom and slammed it behind me. I stumbled to the bathroom, sure I was going to lose whatever was left in my stomach. I made it to the toilet just in time to retch and then the first tear fell. I flipped on the water in the shower and sat down on the fancy tiled floor.

It was bad enough that Ice and Hunter were gone, but Chance was missing and now Gabe...I would never work with him again. Now I had no one. My sanity was unraveling one strand at a time until all I could think about was smashing everything in sight. I yelled as loud as I could, unleashing the pain in my chest. Raegan appeared before me and went to wrap her arms around me, but I couldn't do it. I couldn't take her in my arms right now and allow myself to be comforted by her. Had this been my fault? I had gone after Raegan when I was posted outside Gabe's room.

I shoved Raegan back, not wanting her near me, but she didn't let up. She kept pushing her way through my battling arms until she could finally wrap herself around my body. I cried into her shoulder as she ran her hand up and down my back.

"It's my fucking fault. I left him."

"It's not your fault," Raegan assured me. "You didn't poison him. You didn't kill him."

"I walked away. I went after you," I said angrily. "He's dead because

I made a choice. He was already injured and he couldn't fight back. I did this to him," I yelled.

"By that logic, it's my fault that he's dead. I'm the one that came to the hospital when I shouldn't have."

I shook my head, not wanting to do this right now with her. I didn't blame her. She was right, it wasn't my fault or even hers, but the guilt was overwhelming and I just couldn't take the comfort. "Fuck, I can't do this with you right now. I'm not trying to hurt you, but I can't be with you right now. I need some space."

I swiped the water from my face and pulled back from her. I could see the hurt on her face and I felt horrible for it, but it was all too much to deal with. And then my eyes slid closed when I realized that I was being a total jackass. I wasn't the only one hurting. I had to go see Isa.

After pulling myself together and changing into some dry clothes, I finally worked up the courage to go see Isa. I had grown closer with her and the kids since Gabe had gotten together with her. There were many nights that I would go over for a beer after work and Isa would ask me to stay for dinner. Those kids had become like my own niece and nephew.

I found Isa outside on the back deck with Cazzo. He had his arm around her back, but she wasn't leaning into him or taking any comfort. This had to be killing her. I approached slowly and cleared my throat as I stepped in front of her.

"Isa, I just wanted to tell you how sorry I am." When her eyes met mine, her expression was vacant. The only thing I saw was a dead soul, or what I imagined it would look like. "Gabe was..." I couldn't think of what to say and trying to come up with something comforting on the spot was impossible. What did I say about a man that had been there for me through everything?

"Gabe was what?" she asked with just a hint of anger. "Surely, you have something you can say about him."

"Fuck, Isa, there's so much I could say about him, but this is all too much. I just found out and I don't even know what to say."

Isa stood and shrugged Cazzo's arm off her. "How about sorry? It was you that was supposed to be watching him, right? You were supposed to have his back, but you didn't. You took off and went after Raegan."

I glanced at Cazzo and he hung his head, scrubbing a hand over his face.

"You're right. I shouldn't have left and I'll hate myself every day for the rest of my life for that choice. Those kids-"

"Don't you dare stand there and pretend that you know anything about what those kids are going through." Her voice quivered and the few tears that slipped free were quickly swiped from her face. "So much for brotherhood or whatever the fuck you call this."

"Isa," Cazzo said standing. "This wasn't his fault. What happened-"

"No!" she shouted, cutting him off. "I would think you of all people would be happy. You never wanted me with him to begin with. He wasn't good enough for me, right? He was going to break my heart. Turns out that my own brother and Gabe's best friend are responsible for that." She shook her head and then looked back to me. "You had one job."

When she stormed away, I didn't know quite what to do. I was so fucking lost and I didn't know how to make any of this right.

"She's hurting right now," Cazzo said, trying to make me feel better.

"She'll always be hurting. I can't blame her. Everything she said was true. I was supposed to be there and I failed."

"Gabe, the doctor that did that, he got past all of us. His credentials were spot-on. There was nothing that would make any of us think he wasn't a doctor at that hospital."

"But if I had stayed-"

"He still would be dead." Cazzo placed his hand on my shoulder and gave me a firm squeeze. "It's not your fault and beating yourself up about it isn't going to help anything."

"What am I supposed to do now?" I asked quietly. "My team is gone."

"Chance is gone, but we don't know if he's alive or dead. You have to keep things in check if you want to help find him. Spiraling out of control isn't going to help you any."

He walked away and I stood there wondering where the hell I went from here.

Chapter Sixteen

JACKSON

I couldn't just sit around anymore. I'd been here for a day and no one was doing anything. Chance and Craig were missing. Three of our men were dead. We had no idea where Morgan was. This shit had to stop.

"Cap." I motioned for him to meet me in one of the empty rooms. He followed me in and shut the door. "What the fuck is going on? Do we have any leads on Chance?"

"Becky's been looking, but she doesn't have much. We know that he was put on a plane, but she can't find a flight plan or who owns the plane. There's no information about someone renting it or who was on the plane. Everything is gone."

"How is that possible? How can someone just erase a flight plan?"

"Whoever it is has the right connections. She's still digging and Rob is looking into Morgan's disappearance, but it's not looking good."

"What the hell do we do then? I can't just sit here and hide out. I need to do something. I need to get the fuck out there and look for him."

"Jackson, you have to calm down," Cap said in a stern voice. "Going out and getting yourself killed isn't going to help. We're short on men and too many of us are injured. And don't give me that bullshit about going out right now. You're limping around and I can see the pain on your face when you move."

"What about Cash? He was supposed to come out here."

"He met up with us and helped us get here, but he has his own jobs right now. With nothing to go on, I can't ask him to just stick around in case. We need information and a plan."

"What about Raegan? If those men in the hospital were after her, what are the chances they're connected to The Broker?"

His face morphed in confusion. "I've already talked to Raegan. Haven't you talked to her?"

"Not today," I said hesitantly. I didn't want to tell Cap that I couldn't be around her right now.

"She's with Becky going over photos of men that we know are involved. Raegan said that she saw a man in the hospital and recognized him, but she didn't have a name to put with the face. The problem is, we don't have a whole hell of a lot of pictures for her to go through. She said that she never really got a lot of names, but she has addresses that we can check out. We just need to know how everything fits together. It's possible that the addresses she has are completely useless."

"What about Storm? Have you heard anything from him?"

"Not a word."

"Okay, then Chief. Maybe he has-"

Cap held up his hand. "Look, I get that you need to do something, but we've covered all of these things. Trust me, Becky, Rob, and Maggie are digging into this and trying to find any leads on Chance and Craig. Look, we'll have a meeting as soon as we find something out. I need you to let Becky and Rob do their jobs. And you know Maggie, she doesn't let anything go until she's gone after every lead."

I couldn't fight Cap any more on this. I didn't have any other ideas to check out. I stormed out of the room, heading for anywhere that no one else was. I didn't want to see anyone or talk to anyone. I didn't want the pitying gazes from the other guys. They were all going through this, the same as me, but they had the support of their teams. I had no one left. And the shitty part was, it was all my fault.

"Jackson!" I cringed at the sound of Raegan's voice. She wanted to talk. She always wanted to fucking talk. Ever since yesterday, she had hunted me down several times just to check in. I turned to her with a cold expression, hoping she would get the hint to leave me alone for now. She didn't.

"How are you?"

"Same as yesterday and this morning when you asked."

"Jackson, I know this is hard for you and you need some space, but sometimes talking it out helps."

"Really? Is that why I haven't heard a fucking word about anything you went through with Xavier?"

She took a step back, her face filling with sadness. "It's not the same. No one close to me died."

"It doesn't matter, Raegan. Something shitty happened to you and you don't want to talk about it any more than I do."

"But I could–"

"No," I cut her off. "You can't do anything. I don't want you to sit there and hold my fucking hand. And I don't want you to tell me it's not my fault when I know goddamn well that it is my fault. I went after you. I left him alone. He's dead because I walked away."

"And what about Chris and Lola? Are they responsible too? Because they were watching Hunter and Ice and that didn't stop someone from killing them."

"It's not the same. They stuck to their posts. I fucking left! That's the difference. I went after you, and you weren't even supposed to be there," I laughed mockingly. "Isn't that the shit kicker of the whole thing? I left to go after you when you were supposed to keep your fucking ass at the safe house."

"So, this is my fault?" she asked incredulously. "Are we just blaming anyone that walks by now? I'm sure we could blame the hospital staff and the janitor. Maybe if he would have waxed the hallways, the fake doctor would have slipped and fell and thwarted the whole plan!"

"Can't you just fucking stop? Just stop! I don't want your help. I need to be in this place right now because there's no one else to blame. I can't go after those assholes and kill them because I don't even know who they fucking are. So, let me be pissed at myself and just leave me the fuck alone."

I turned and walked away before she could say anything else. I really didn't want to be a dick, but I didn't want her to keep coming to me. I just needed some goddamn space to work through this and get my head on straight, no matter how long that took.

Finding a place to be by myself proved difficult. Everywhere I turned, someone was there, crying over the loss of a loved one or trying to entertain the kids. Since everyone was brought to the panic room, all the men and women that trained and protected the kids were there also. They had come with us and were looking after the kids for the most part, trying to keep them focused on something other than what was happening around them. Lindsey and Isa weren't really up to taking care of their kids right now, and in reality, the kids didn't want to sit with their crying mothers. Very little had been said to the kids about what happened. I didn't know for sure they had even been told yet.

I wandered out to one of the trails around the house. The property Knight had was massive and he had sensors, cameras, and electric fencing set up everywhere because there was no way to secure the grounds otherwise. Still, it made me feel like I was doing something if I walked the trails and could at least tell myself that I was looking for threats. Lola must have been thinking the same thing because she was headed toward me. I was hoping she wouldn't stop to talk, but I wasn't that lucky.

"Trying to clear your head?" she asked.

I shrugged, not really wanting to talk. "Just..."

"Yeah, it fucks with your head. Ryan doesn't really understand it. He keeps telling me it's not my fault, that it's the men that attacked us."

I scoffed, feeling like everyone was telling me the same fucking thing. "Yeah, well, at least you didn't leave Hunter. I left Gabe and I don't know if I can ever forgive myself for that."

"Raegan was also your job though. It's not like you could just stay behind when you knew she was in trouble."

"She wasn't supposed to be there. Why is it that they never listen? It's our job to protect people, but the people we protect always do whatever the hell they want. It just makes me wonder..."

We walked in silence for a moment and Lola waited for me to continue, but I wasn't sure I wanted to. If I said it, I felt like it was a decision I was making.

"It makes you wonder if you should be doing this," she finished after a minute. "I felt the same thing. When I freaked out on the job, I wondered if I should be doing this. I mean, I told myself that I was strong and I had been doing it for years with no issues, but I couldn't make myself face everyone. I could feel the judgement coming off everyone before I even entered Reed Security."

"No one judged you. I think we were all wondering if we would have handled it as well as you did for so long."

"Yeah, that was the problem, I wasn't handling it. I was hiding and making excuses. When Cap made me take leave, I kept thinking back to all the times I might have gotten someone killed because I might have flipped out. I felt like I had made a string of bad choices."

"But you're okay now."

"Yeah," she smiled. "Because I've learned to deal with it and I have Ryan. I know that you don't want to need Raegan right now, but I can see that you really like her, possibly love her. You know, it's not a bad thing to let someone in."

"You know, sometimes I miss fierce, kickass Lola."

A loud chuckle burst from her lips and the most beautiful smile lit her face. "Yeah, me too, but I think this version is so much better. I'm kickass when I need to be, but Ryan completes me."

"If you start singing *I'll Be There,* I'm gonna have your head checked."

She shoved me, knocking me off balance. The woman still had the ability to kick anyone's ass.

"So, what does Ryan think about all this?"

"Well, he's not exactly thrilled that he was basically kidnapped with Piper and Ryder."

Piper had to be a little over three now and Ryder was probably six months or so. I didn't really keep track of that shit. For all I knew, they were twice as old.

"How does that work with his business?"

"Well, Logan, his business partner, takes over most everything, but there are other people that can fill in. When Ryan's first wife died, he took off like six months and someone filled in then. I think they still have whoever it was working there."

"He must feel a little odd being the only man here."

"He's not," she laughed.

"Well, he's the only man that doesn't..."

"Kill people? Yeah, I think he's okay with that. Ryan's definitely not the type to want to get involved in this stuff."

"Isn't his group of friends a little wild?"

"I guess. Not really like us. I mean, they play paintball, but that's about the extent of how crazy they are now. Plus, they're all getting older and settling down. The last time they played paintball was a little pathetic. Ryan's kind of the gentle one of the group."

"Don't let him hear you say that. No guy wants to be referred to as gentle."

"He doesn't care. It's true. He's just not like his friends. I mean, in some ways he's just like them, but he was always the one that wanted the family and the house. And since his first wife died, he's definitely more emotional, from what his friends tell me. I think everything just hits him harder."

"Who would have thought you would end up with a guy like that?" I grinned. "I always pictured you running off with Hunter."

"There was a time I might have, but it would have never worked. We were together for the wrong reasons. And by together, I mean fucking. It was never more than that. I guess maybe that's why I feel so guilty about what happened. He tried for years to help me in any way he could, and when he needed me, I let him down."

"You don't seem like you feel guilty." And I didn't mean that as an insult. She looked at peace with herself.

"Remember what I said about having someone like Ryan? It really does help to lean on someone. He knows all about guilt and I'm sure Raegan does too, but you have to give her the chance to help."

"What does Raegan have to feel guilty about?"

She laughed lightly, rolling her eyes at me. "I swear, some guys are so stupid."

"Hey!"

"It's true. Think about it. She was living with Xavier for years and had no contact with her parents. They must have been so worried about her. Then she had to go into hiding and her parents had to do the same. They had to give up everything. They don't work and they don't really have a purpose right now. Imagine if you were her father, sitting around someone else's house and just doing what you could to help out. Wouldn't that make you feel pretty useless?"

"I guess."

"And when do they get their lives back? Right now, they're hanging out here, just following Raegan wherever she has to go. And if they do get their lives back, where do they go from there? They'll be starting over. And Raegan knows that it's all because of her choices."

I stopped walking, taking in everything Lola was saying. She was right. Even though Raegan didn't talk about it, it had to be eating her up inside.

"So, what you're saying is that I kind of fucked things up with Raegan."

She grinned at me. "I'm not one to point fingers. But if you want to hang onto her, you need to let her in."

"She doesn't let me in," I grumbled.

"Yeah, and if both of you are so damn stubborn all the time, you're both going to end up alone."

"I'm not alone," I pouted. "I have all of you. You're my family and I know you're always there, no matter how badly I fuck up."

"Yeah, but we won't fuck you," she laughed as she walked away. Okay, well, she had a point.

Chapter Seventeen

RAEGAN

I was bored. Again. There was nothing to do around here and it was driving me insane. There were only so many walks I could take and watching tv was not my thing right now. What I wanted was to talk to Jackson, but he didn't want to talk to me.

Walking into the kitchen, I smiled when I saw my mom cooking. Over the past year I had come to appreciate my mom so much more because I hadn't had her in my life for years. Now, I spent as much time with her as I could, learning to cook and just laughing about old times.

"What are you making?"

She smiled at me and went back to peeling apples. "I wanted to make apple pie. I wanted to make some comfort food for everyone, and what's more comforting than apple pie?"

I picked up an apple and pulled out a knife to help her peel them. "I'd have to agree, but how many pies are you making?"

"Well, I figure that I'll have to make at least ten pies."

"Ten? That seems like an awful lot. Aren't there eight slices to a pie?"

"Yes, but remember, men eat a lot more than women, and then there are all the kids. I would rather have too much than too little."

"But how did you even get this many apples?"

"I made a list," she grinned, "and sent the boys into town. At first they didn't want any part of it, but when I told them what I was making, they ran out of here to get me everything I needed."

"What else were you planning to make?"

"Beef tenderloin, mashed potatoes, chicken pot pie, rice...Hmm, I know there was more, but I've already forgotten. I'll have to check my list again."

"Well, I'm here to help, so put me to work."

Together, we put together all the apple pies and she showed me how to make the sauce on the stove. I may have burnt it to the bottom of the pan, but she was used to me burning things. When that was done, she put me to work on chopping potatoes for her.

"I haven't seen Jackson around lately," she said knowingly.

"He's not dealing well with his friend dying and he won't let me help him."

"Typical men. They always want to fix our problems, but they never want us to be there for them."

"So, what do I do?"

"Ignore him. I mean, don't intentionally ignore him, but you have to give him space to work things through. A person will only accept help if they want it."

"But, he's hurting and I don't like knowing that he's dealing with that alone."

She looked at me with a raised eyebrow. "And just what do you think he's been dealing with when it comes to you? That man has been head over heels in love with you since the beginning. He might not have known it, but I could see it clear as day."

"He had a funny way of showing it," I grumbled.

"One thing I could never accuse your father of was showing love. That didn't really happen until you were born. You had your father wrapped around your little pinky. He was so in love with you and it was only then that he started showing me that same love."

"So, why did you marry him if he couldn't show you how he felt? Wasn't that hard?"

"I knew how he felt. I figured that I could be with the man I wanted, knowing his limitations, or I could leave and hope for something just as good to come along. And you know what they say, there are no guarantees in life."

"So I need to be patient and wait for him to come back to me."

"Honey, he will come back to you. Don't you worry about it. A mother knows these things."

I smiled uncertainly. She may be confident, but I wasn't and I worried that the more time I spent away from Jackson, the more he would push me away.

I walked around trying to find Jackson. He hadn't come to bed last night or any of the other nights for the past week and I was beginning to wonder if he needed more than just space from me. Deep down I knew that losing his best friend was really hard on him, but my girly brain couldn't help but tell myself that this was all over. That he blamed me. To make matters worse, everywhere I went, people were sad and caught up in their grief. I didn't know any of them and didn't feel comfortable just striking up conversation with them. So, again, I was alone.

I walked outside, needing some fresh air and to get away from everyone for a while. I was on a trail that meandered through the trees when I saw a gazebo in the distance. I made my way over there, but stopped when I heard voices. I was just about to turn and head back when I heard my name called.

"Raegan! Don't be shy. Get your ass over here!"

I sighed and headed in that direction, wondering what I was getting myself into. When I got to the gazebo, I wanted to turn and run. Isa, Lindsey, Lucy, and Claire were all drinking what looked like shots. This was very bad. When people drank, what they really felt came out. Isa was probably pissed at me for my role in her husband's death.

"We don't bite," Lucy said, downing a shot and then laughing when it spilled down her chin instead of going into her mouth.

"It looks like the party has already started." I cringed at my idiotic words as I sat down, but then Isa raised a shot glass as Claire handed me one of my own.

"This is a party, to celebrate the idiocy of our husbands. A bunch of hot security men," she said with a snorted laugh, "that are so lethal, they allowed themselves to get a lethal injection!"

The girls all burst out into laughter, and I found myself joining in. Sometimes when everything was going to shit, you just had to laugh or you would break down and cry.

"Seriously," Lucy laughed, "how can they all be so stupid? I've seen almost every one of them kill with their bare hands and yet they get severely injured by a few men with guns."

"I thought it was more than a few?" I said in confusion.

Claire waved her hand, but ended up falling toward the side of her chair. "Derek killed fifty men with his bare hands when I was with him," she slurred. "Any one of those guys could have taken them out with only their pinky fingers. I've seen it. They're all superhuman!"

"How would you kill someone with your pinky?"

"There's a pointy thing under your neck that you press." Claire nodded vigorously as she pointed her pinky toward her neck. "Yup, it's somewhere over here," she said, waving at her whole neck. "And you press it and the person just falls over and drops dead."

"If you could kill someone with your pinky, couldn't you save them too?" Lucy asked. "Like, why didn't Hunter just shove his pinky in the hole in his neck? Problem solved."

"Hunter's a medic. Shouldn't he have known that?" Lindsey pondered.

"Maybe they don't use the pinky technique in the military," Claire suggested. "Maybe it's new technology."

"Right," Lindsey announced excitedly. "We just invented a new technology! We should definitely let someone know."

"Yeah, but, who do we know that's a doctor?" Isa asked.

We all sat around trying to think of someone, but came up with nothing. "Maybe there's a hotline we could call," Lucy suggested. "A doctoring hotline."

"Or, we could just write our own medical journal," Lindsey

suggested. "We could call it *How to kill someone using your pinky or save someone by shoving your pinky in their neck.*"

"I don't like it," Isa shook her head. "It's too...."

"Long?" I added.

"No, that's not it." Isa frowned as she tried to think about what was wrong with it. "We need something catchy that men will want to read."

"Just put the word *sex* in and every man will read it," Lindsey shrugged.

"Yes," Claire fist pumped. "We could call it *Pinky Sex.*"

"Maybe if the guys had read our manuscript, they'd still be alive," Lucy grumbled.

"Come on, even Knight isn't indestructible," Isa said, stumbling as she stood to grab another bottle of alcohol. "Remember when he took a bullet to the chest-"

"No, it was a saber," Lucy interjected.

"It was not," Claire cut in. "It was a grenade!"

"Anyway, he was dead! Dead, I tell you. He was burned alive in a building and a year later," Isa snapped her fingers once, "he came back. Just like that."

"So, Knight is indestructible," I surmised, trying to make sense of their ramblings.

"No," Claire said, leaning toward me conspiratorially. "That's just it. Nobody knows for sure who Knight is. He's some kind of big secret among the guys. I think he's really a Greek warrior that's come back from the dead to lead our men into battle."

"Like Achilles!" Lindsey shouted. "He's Achilles and Kate is his heel."

"No, she's the arrow," Isa shook her head.

"No, no, no," Claire shook her head wildly. "Achilles loved his foot so much that he took Kate to protect his arrow."

The other women nodded sagely. I shook my head in confusion, wondering how many shots these women had already. I discreetly got up and walked over to the makeshift bar and found two empty bottles of vodka on the floor. How were they still standing?

"Do you know what the saddest part about all this is?" Lucy sniffed. "I never hunted Stalker or Knight." The other girls nodded in agreement. "I mean, what's with that? They're always around us following and protecting." Her shot sloshed over the side as she waved her arms in the air. "And just once, I wanted to be the creepy psychopath."

Isa leaned forward, waving us all in toward her. "You know, frankly, it's probably for the best." *Yep, been there, felt that way.* "Do you know how many times Enzo has pissed on my walls? Like, a bajillion. And it's all his fault. He just had to be that guy. You know, the guy that teaches kids to pee through their peniseses."

Lindsey pointed at her, like a revelation had just washed over her. "You know, John is the same way! Do you know, he taught..." She looked off into space for a moment, her eyes glassing over. "What's my kid's name?"

"Katie," Lucy piped up.

"No, it's...it's Matilda!" Claire said.

"It is not," Lindsey waved her off. "I would never name my kid Matilda. It doesn't go with Ice. Could you imagine John walking up to someone, all big badassed and saying, *this is my kid, Matilda?*"

"Not that he would now," Isa said offhand. "Cuz he's dead. Just like Gabe and Hunter. Dead, dead, dead. All because they were stupid and just laid there while someone killed them. Did they think they were getting an alcoholic injection?"

"Seriously," Lindsey slurred. "What's my kid's name?"

"Isn't it Zoe?" I asked.

Lindsey thought hard on that and then her face lit up. "Cade! That's it. My son's name is Cade."

"And Zoe," I clarified.

"Nah, that doesn't sound right. Zo-eee. Zzzo-eeee."

Everyone else chimed in, sounding out the name Zoe. They all sounded like they were chanting or something. "Zzzzz-oooo-eeeeee."

I took another shot. These ladies were so much fun to hang out with and it made me realize that I had really missed out on a lot when I was with Xavier. By the end of my first hour out there, I was feeling just as good as everyone else.

"If you were to come back," Claire said, whispering to me, "what would you be?"

"A porcupine. That way I'd have all the pricks." I burst into laughter, but no one else did. "Because they have pokey things on them," I explained. "You know, those pokey things that stick out of them and they poke you."

"Oh!" Isa jumped up, pointing at me like she'd figured out the answer. "They have the pokey things!"

"Right," I shouted. "And they poke you."

"What do you think the guys are doing right this very minute?" Lindsey asked.

"Probably planning and stragertizing," Isa said. "You would think they would have planned on this. Like, what to do when I get myself killed. I bet they all had plans, but it was just what to do with their weapons."

"Yeah," Lucy sighed. "Unfortunately, I think Stalker is going to come back and hunt me with Knight. Do you think he'll like, hang out like a cloud in the house?"

"Or maybe he'll be like Patrick Swayze in *Ghost*," Claire sputtered. "He'll come back to save you and then you'll kiss one of us when he jumps into our body to be with you one last time."

"Do we have a choice who does this?" Lucy asked. "Cuz, I think I want to test you out first. I mean, if he's gonna come back and plant one last smacker on me, it better be with someone who knows how to use tongue."

"Come on," Claire laughed. "It's Hunter. He'll probably want sex. And how are we gonna make that happen? I mean, Derek and I are adventurous, but we don't use strap-ons."

We all looked to Isa, having heard about Gabe before.

"What?"

"Oh, come on. We all know that Gabe was just a tad too into men. I mean, Hunter practically ran in the other direction when he was around," Lucy laughed.

"He wasn't gay! He liked watching people have sex."

Lindsey started laughing hysterically, tears running down her face as she bent over holding her stomach. "Hunter's going to come back to fuck Lucy one last time and Gabe's going to jump into another one of us to watch with Isa!"

Chapter Eighteen

CAP

A whole fucking week of hearing the women crying and watching my men spiral out of control. There was nothing I could do about it, but that was coming to an end now. We had to stay together and fight together. If we turned on each other, we would break apart before we even had a chance to heal. The problem was, some of the girls were drunk out of their minds. But I had already taken the steps I needed to and I couldn't put it off.

"Hey, bossman, can I talk to you for a minute?" Becky looked around for anyone listening and at my nod continued. "I finished checking the scan of Rocco's handprint. I did a scan with my computer program after I tweaked some of the limitations, which came back affirmative. But then I enlarged the image and the one we have on file and compared them. There are differences, but they're so slight, the computer would have missed them."

"What kind of differences?"

"It's the curve of some of the lines of the handprint. They don't line up."

"But anyone's handprint would be slightly off depending on how they placed their hand on the scanner."

"Right, and I thought of that, so I used my own handprint and then used my handprint on a glove. I compared how the lines change depending on how I placed my hand on the scanner. Overall, my handprint was the same when I used my hand, but when I used the glove, the print came out just a little off. Lines were closer together or further apart. Just slightly, but when I compared it to the print that's supposedly Rocco's, the lines move in the same way."

"So, you're saying that you're one hundred percent sure that it's not Rocco."

"I can't say one hundred percent, but I would bet that he's not the mole. There are just too many inconsistencies on the print, in my opinion."

"Alright, Becky. Thanks, and let's keep this between us. I don't want everyone panicking."

"Sure, bossman."

Well, at least that was one less thing I had to worry about now. I trusted Becky's opinion and deep down, I never really thought that Rocco was the mole. But I had to be sure. I hated that I suspected him and so would everyone else, but the fact was, we did have a mole and until we figured out who that was, I was going to continue to be suspicious of anyone that had the means or motive to betray us.

It wasn't even an hour later when Knight showed up with Kate. I asked everyone to join me in the main room because it was the only place that all of us could fit. Getting the women in there was interesting and Derek had to carry Claire, while Knight carried Lucy because they were too drunk to walk.

Everyone was staring at me, trying to figure out what I was up to. There was no easy way to do this. "I need the men to go outside and help Knight and Kate. They're here with Ice, Gabe, and Hunter."

"You brought their bodies here?" Freckles shouted. "What's wrong with you?"

Before I could respond, Lucy chimed in, laughing and yanking on Lindsey. "It's happening already. They're going to bring them in and we'll need to wave their spirits on."

Rocco shook his head and walked out with every other guy in the place, none of them missing out on the chance to say goodbye to a friend. When they walked back in, most of them looked pissed. Knight wheeled Ice in on a stretcher and Chris wheeled in Hunter. Isa and Lindsey ran over immediately.

"Go to the light," Lucy shouted. "It's okay."

"Shoo! Go find peace," Lindsey laughed, waving her arms toward the ceiling. A hand shot out and suddenly Lindsey wasn't laughing any more. She looked down at Ice and let out a shrill scream, yanking at Ice's arm to get his hand off her. "Why is the spirit alive? Oh my God, get it off me! Get it off me!"

Lucy started shouting also when Hunter's head popped up and then flopped back to the table with a groan. "You were supposed to come back as a spirit! You were supposed to go into a body and kiss me! This is not what happened in *Ghost*!"

And to make everything that much more fucked up, Gabe walked in the door with a big smile on his face, thinking he was going to be greeted by his wife. Isa walked over to him and slapped him across the face. "You ruined my fantasy!"

"Uh..." Gabe looked around the room, trying to find his bearings in this new environment. I pressed my thumb and forefinger into the bridge of my nose, sighing at the mess I now had to untangle.

"What the fuck did you put in my drip?" Hunter asked.

"It was a sedative," Kate offered. "It was to keep the trip comfortable for you."

Ice was still gripping onto Lindsey's arm and she was just staring at him like a deer in the headlights. Everyone was silent around the room until Knight scoffed. "What? Like you've never seen anyone come back from the dead before?"

"Cap," Chris said angrily, "You want to explain what the fuck is going on here?"

"First, let's get Hunter and Ice settled. They're not completely out of the woods yet and they need their rest."

The guys nodded grudgingly and Kate directed everyone to what she needed and had others bring in medical supplies and help her set up the rooms. After about a half hour, the two of them were settled and everyone was back in the main room waiting on me to explain.

"So, after Ice and Hunter came out of surgery, they were doing okay for what they had been through. We had everyone on watch, but someone slipped in posing as a doctor. He had all the credentials and was able to slip past everyone undetected."

"We already know all this," Jules said irritably.

"Right, so, they were injected with something to make them go into cardiac arrest. The doctors were actually able to get a rhythm again, but there were no guarantees with everything else they had been through. I have a friend at the hospital and asked him to help me make it appear that they died. I figured that none of us were safe if we stayed there, and I couldn't just leave the three of them there unprotected. I needed everyone to think that they died, including all of you. If any one of us didn't play it right, whoever those guys were would know that they had failed. I guess I figured that if it looked like we were three men down, we appeared weaker, and those guys would feel like they were tearing us apart."

"But you did tear us apart," Cazzo said angrily. "You let Isa, Lindsey, and Lucy think that their husbands died. You let us believe that our teammates died."

"Why didn't you tell us when we got here?" Derek asked. "It's been a week."

"Kate and Knight flew with them to a small hospital about an hour from here. I paid a lot to have them kept anonymous and I flew in a cardiologist to look after them. When they were cleared by the cardiologist, I had them brought here. I didn't want to get anyone's hopes up until we knew for sure they would be alright."

"But what about Gabe," Jackson snarled. "You let me think my whole fucking team was gone. I blamed myself for his death!"

"Jackson, I know you're mad, but I couldn't bring one of them back without raising suspicions about Hunter and Ice. What if they didn't make it? Was I supposed to get Isa and Lindsey's hopes up when they were already grieving?"

The whole room was silent, just staring at me. Even Freckles was looking at me with disappointment. But, I did what I had to do and I would do it again. It fucking sucked and I knew that they were going to be pissed at me for a long time, but with everything that was going on, I had to take control of the situation fast before we lost anyone else.

Lucy raised her hand hesitantly in question. "Does this mean that none of the girls are going to kiss me?"

I didn't know if I should be pissed or happy. They were alive and that was all that really mattered. And with time, I knew that I would see the logic in what Cap had done, but right now, all I could see was what he had taken from me. It was more than my friends, it was the feeling of self-worth. It was knowing that no matter what, I was doing the right thing and could always count on my gut instincts to guide me. Basically, he had taken away my trust in myself, and I didn't know how to get past that now. There was too much doubt swirling around in my head.

"Look, we have bigger things to worry about right now than why I lied to you about the three of them. We have two missing team members and no leads on where they are. Morgan is also missing and is most likely with The Broker. We don't know exactly who attacked us yet, and it now appears that whoever was after Raegan is also involved with The Broker or the man that's in charge of the trafficking ring."

Cap looked over to Knight and everyone noticed. There was something more that we didn't know yet.

"I'm also concerned about one other thing. Storm is missing. He was last seen at our facility, but no one can pinpoint the last time he was seen. The camera feed doesn't show enough to let us know if he was there."

"Cap, are you thinking Storm is an inside man?" Sinner asked.

"No, I don't think he's the inside man." Cap looked warily at us. "I think our inside man might be Craig."

"What the fuck are you talking about?" Alec growled. "I've been working with him for years. There's no way he's a traitor."

"Yeah, he was the one that had a bad feeling about the whole thing with Morgan," I added.

"Exactly," Cap said. "He just happened to have a feeling that something was wrong and warned you to get to Chance's house."

"To what end? We didn't save Morgan. All that happened was the house burned down."

"And then Chance went after Agent Finley. It got several of you out of the way and there was a team there to take out Finley, and possibly you."

"Craig was with them," I argued. "He would have risked getting killed also."

"Could have been a change of heart," Knight cut in. "Maybe he was feeling guilty for getting involved and wanted to try and make things right."

"But none of that is evidence or even close to it. What makes you think that he's the one involved?" Florrie asked.

"Nobody has seen Craig since the attack at Reed Security. We have no idea if he made it out or if he's missing–"

"So, you automatically assume that he's a traitor?" Alec snarled.

"I'm keeping all possibilities open. Someone told those men how to get into our facility. They needed fingerprints, facial recognition, knowledge about our sensors, and the codes for the day," Cap said calmly. "Now, I've talked with Knight about all the security measures. We've figured that if it was The Broker, he could have gotten prints from Chance's house, but that doesn't explain everything else. There were only a few hours between when Chance's house was burned down and when we were attacked. Knight assures me that there is no way someone could have broken through all those security measures in that time frame. Which means that we have a mole. Craig is missing."

"So is Chance," Florrie said, challenging Cap to correct her.

"He is, but we saw him taken."

"And that couldn't be staged?" Florrie shot back. "You faked Knight's death-"

"Florrie," Cap said harshly. Not everyone in the room knew the details of who Knight was exactly.

"What? Everyone knows that we all assumed he was dead. Now he's back. It's not like that's new information. I'm just saying, resurrections seem to happen around this place."

Her glare didn't go unnoticed by anyone, and the thing was, no one seemed to disagree with her. Silence hung thick in the air and I wasn't sure what was going to happen from here. After a minute of tension, it was Chris that finally broke the silence.

"You did what you had to do," he said to Cap, "and while I might not like that I was kept out of the loop, I think what you did was right."

"Are you fucking crazy?" Alec spat. "He's accusing one of our own of turning on us."

"It's happened before," Chris said wearily. "Look, I don't like it any more than you do, but Cap has never done anything to make me lose faith in him, and you know damn well that he would put his life on the line for any one of us. I think we should listen to him and check out his theory about Craig. If anything, it might help us find him. We know someone gave us up."

"Yeah, and if it's not him, do we start looking into each other?" Burg asked. "Or maybe we just look into the ones that weren't hurt. Is this how it's gonna be from here on out? We're going to turn on each other?"

"No, we need to look into who had the most to gain from attacking us," Cazzo said, "and it wasn't Craig. We should look into the connection while we look for him, but I think we're looking in the wrong direction. We're missing something here. If The Broker only works in information, what would he have to gain from attacking us? He already had Morgan. So, let's set him aside for now. Whoever runs the trafficking ring, what would they gain from taking us out?"

"Maybe that's all they wanted, to take us out," Sinner suggested.

"They didn't try and go for any information. They were there to kill us. Maybe The Broker is working with the head honcho. Let's say the leader of this trafficking ring wanted us dead, it would most likely be because we were getting too close, we knew too much."

"And why take Chance?" Derek asked.

"To keep Morgan in line," I answered. "If The Broker wants Morgan to do as he says, he needs leverage. He wants to keep her from trying to escape. We already know that Morgan cares about Chance. She wouldn't do anything to get him killed."

"Are you sure about that?" Cap asked. "Her daughter is missing." I tried to follow his train of thought, but I was missing something.

"If The Broker wants to keep Morgan in line, he would probably be able to find out where Payton is in just a matter of days. That would be enough to keep Morgan in line. So, why would The Broker have Chance taken by the trafficking ring?"

"There's got to be a different connection," Cap said. "The Broker wouldn't need two insurance policies and the leader of the trafficking ring wouldn't want to hang on to witnesses. So, the new question is, why was Chance taken to begin with?"

Gabe was laying down in his room when I found him. His eyes were closed, but I could tell he wasn't sleeping based on the way his fingers twitched beside his gun.

"Don't shoot," I said as I walked into his room. He opened one eye and shrugged.

"Not worth the bullet."

"Really? Is that how you see your best friend?"

"You seriously believed that I was dead?" He scoffed, waving me off. "Come on, you should know that I'm not that easy to kill. That's not the way I would go. Maybe in a hail of bullets or something cool like death by fire ants."

"Really? Wouldn't that be painful?"

"Do you know how many cases of death by fire ants there are per year? It's like thirty and I think that's from all species of ants. I would definitely go down in the history books."

"At least go for something really cool, like dying in a reenactment of a famous sword fight. Or maybe get eaten by a hippo."

"Where would I find a hippo?"

I shrugged. "The zoo? People fall in those enclosures all the time. And if you think about it, it would probably be a quick death. You know, because hippos are so big."

"Yeah," he nodded. "Not because one would eat me."

I walked over to the window and looked outside. It was so normal with him back here, but for a while, I had thought he was dead. And now we were talking, just like it was old times.

"So, tell me, did you cry over me?"

I scoffed, but a lump caught in my throat. I didn't want to think about that night in the shower when I felt like I had lost everything.

"How's Isa?" he asked quietly.

"You mean besides the fact that she got drunk with everyone today and is now passed out in the living room?"

"She never drinks like that. At least, not to that point."

"Yeah, well, you were dead. She was…"

"I hate that I did that to her."

"You can thank Cap. I'm pretty sure she gave him quite the beat-down over what happened. Cazzo told me that she said he had to choose."

He sat up at that, swinging his legs over the side of the bed. "Shit. She's gonna ask me to leave Reed Security."

"Who knows, it could all be different now that you're back from the dead."

"Do you think if I got her flowers it would help?"

I turned and smirked at him. "Considering she was about to pick out flowers for your funeral, I would say no."

"Hmmm, this is one of those times Ice was talking about. I need something more, like diamonds."

"Maybe you could give her an actual wedding, you know, since technically Hunter and Lucy married you to them."

"Yeah, maybe that wasn't the most romantic moment."

"It could have been worse, you could have proposed to her with lollipops."

He burst out laughing, holding his hand to his head as he grimaced. "You have to admit, Sinner definitely has a way with the ladies. Only Sinner could pull off a proposal like that."

"So, how's the head?"

"You know, I've had worse."

"That's vague."

"How's the leg?" he asked knowingly.

"Feeling better every day."

"I'll bet. Did you get in Raegan's pants yet?" I grimaced. "Shit, don't tell me it was that bad."

"No, it was fucking great, but I'm pretty sure I fucked that up."

"How do you fuck up fucking?"

"Mud fucking."

"Do I want to know what mud fucking is?"

"Imagine mud, sticks, leaves, basically the dirtiest fucking you can think of."

"Well, my idea of dirty fucking has nothing to do with the wilderness."

"Everyone has their thing," I said with a shrug.

"So, I take it she didn't like mud fucking."

"Oh, no. She definitely enjoyed it," I grinned. "It might have been slightly unfortunate that *that* was our first time."

He burst out laughing. "Was there at least dinner first?"

"There wasn't dinner before or for a very long time after. In fact, we didn't even shower for almost a day."

"So, that's the part where you fucked up. Yeah, they like to shower afterwards. I mean, I don't mind being dirty for a while, but women get weird about that shit."

"No, that wasn't what I fucked up either." He looked around the room expectantly and I followed his gaze. "What are you looking for?"

"Sorry, I was just expecting some of the guys to walk in at some point. Usually this kind of shit is witnessed by at least three of us."

I scoffed, "Yeah, that's not going to happen."

"So, if that's not the part where you fucked up, what exactly happened?"

"There was this moment and I wanted to tell her how I felt, but I really fucked it up. It went something like, *I think I love you. Maybe.*"

"You're such a dumbass," he chuckled. "I knew you loved her. Why'd you lie about it?"

"It wasn't a lie. I swear to God, I just got nervous and freaked out. But that wasn't the worst of it."

"Of course it wasn't."

"No, that would be the part where she tried to help me after you 'died' and I basically told her to get the fuck away from me."

He started a slow clap, grinning at me as he shook his head in disbelief. "And who else have you told about this?"

"No one. Do you think I want everyone to hassle me the way they did with you?"

"I think that would be getting off easy. You're such a dumbass. You need to fix this before you lose her."

"Yeah, I just don't know how to do that."

"Beg, my man. Beg like your life depended on it."

I spent a good hour trying to come up with the perfect thing to say to Raegan. So far I had come up with *Raegan, I'm sorry I'm an asshole. I really do love you.* The problem was, every time I said that in my head, I always wanted to say *I think.* It wasn't that I doubted that I loved Raegan, it was more that I had never been in love before and I was worried that I was going to royally fuck this up. Probably by saying something stupid like *I think.* What if I was saying it too soon and then there were all these expectations that I couldn't live up to? We had only ever lived together and always under the threat of danger. What if she didn't like me for who I was when this was all over? What if I didn't like who she became?

She walked in the back door and I wiped my hands nervously on my pants. I was sweating my ass off like a teenager with a crush on the hot cheerleader. Fuck, this was hard. I strode toward her so she couldn't run away, but practically plowed her over instead of being cool and casual. She stepped back in surprise and then turned to walk away.

"Raegan, wait. I need to talk to you."

She turned and raised an eyebrow at me. Her look was so scalding hot that I could hardly think, let alone swallow the horse balls that were stuck in my throat. I wiped my hands some more and tried not to melt under her stare. It was like standing in front of a firing squad. I don't think I'd ever been this terrified in all my life.

"Yes?" she said after a minute of me staring at her awkwardly.

"Uh...I thought we should talk."

"You mentioned that," she said with a sardonic nod.

"Uh..." I cleared my throat and wiped my hands some more.

"Do you need to wash your hands?"

"No, uh...see, the thing is...when it comes to..." I scratched my temple as I tried to remember those brilliant, short words I was going to say to her.

She started tapping her foot and sighed irritatedly. I licked my dry lips and shifted from my good leg to my bad leg. Maybe if I faked a terrible leg cramp I could get out of this disaster of a conversation.

"The thing is..." she prompted.

"Right, the thing is...the other day, when I, you know..."

"Said that you wanted me to get the fuck away from you?"

I cleared my throat again and wiped the sweat that started trickling down the side of my face. "I didn't mean that, I mean, I did at the time, but that was only because I was..."

"Hurting?"

"Being an asshole," I corrected. "Although, yeah, it probably had something to do with...you." Her eyes widened slightly and I rushed on. "Not with you because of you, but with you because of how I felt about you."

"Nice, so you were an asshole to me because you told me that you loved me?"

"No! No, it was...that's not accurate."

"The loving me part?"

"Uh...wait, I'm getting confused."

"So am I. It would help if you would string together an intelligible sentence."

"I like you, that wasn't a lie."

"But you don't love me." She crossed her arms over her chest, almost like she was protecting herself.

"That's not what I meant."

"Then what did you mean?"

I took a deep breath, determined to plow through this and get my point across without making myself a bigger asshole. "I mean that I do love you, but I've never been in love before and... I'm just worried that all of this between us is because of circumstance. We've never been out on a date. So, I know that I love spending time with you, and I love your sarcastic nature. I love the way you feel wrapped in my arms. There's no doubt in my mind that I would take a bullet for you. I love the way you take care of me just because you know I'm tired when I come home after a long day." I swallowed hard, staring at the ground. "And I love that you were there for me when I didn't know I needed it. I pushed you away and you still came back, trying to comfort me. I've never had anyone do something like that for me. And I know I fucked up because I should have apologized sooner for the way I spoke to you. But I'm hoping that you'll forgive me and give me a second chance to prove that I'm not really an asshole."

She stared at me with the slightest sheen of tears in her eyes, but she was careful not to let any tears slip free. I hoped to God that they were good tears and not tears of *I hate you and I never want to see you again.*

"That was fucking beautiful," a deep voice said from behind me. I groaned and turned around to see Sinner standing in the doorway with Cazzo, both of them pretending to wipe tears from their eyes.

"Fuck off," I bit out.

"Seriously, man. I think you should start writing Hallmark cards," Sinner said.

"No, he should be writing apology cards for men. He could make a whole business out of it. That was some Grade A shit right there."

"See, I knew there was something different about him," Sinner said.

"You know, from the start, he just wasn't quite as warped as the rest of us."

"He never had issues with his cock," Cazzo grinned.

"Yeah, well, he never got drunk and tried to kill himself either," Sinner shot back.

"He's never proposed to someone with lollipops." Cazzo crossed his arms over his chest and stared Sinner down.

"He never went traveling around the country, sleeping on the ground, to find himself." Sinner used quotes on the last part. I glanced at Raegan, wondering what she was thinking about all this. She just shrugged.

"At least I didn't pretend I was having an affair with Maggie just to piss Cap off."

"At least I know what my own fucking nickname means," Sinner replied.

"I've never seen Maggie's vagina up close and personal," Cazzo said with a grin.

Sinner held his hands up in defeat. "You've got me there. There's no coming back from that one."

"Are you two done?" I asked when it appeared their fight was over.

"Seriously, you should definitely give him another chance," Cazzo told Raegan. "That wasn't just some speech. Jackson's a good guy."

"Plus, I've seen him in the locker room. Trust me, it's impressive," Sinner threw in with a grin.

Raegan flushed bright red. "That's...I'm not sure I want to know why you were staring at him...down there."

"Whoa," Sinner held up his hands in a defensive gesture, "no one said anything about staring. I mean, there has been staring, but it's not solely on his dick. And it wasn't necessarily him. Once it was Hunter, and another time it was Gabe. Who am I missing?"

"Ice?" Cazzo asked.

"I can't remember, but Jules had his legs waxed by Chris and Ice," Sinner added thoughtfully. He laughed a little, rubbing his hand across his chin. "You know, we've had some good times at work."

"Can I just say," Raegan cut in, "that I find it not only weird that you all seem to stare at each others' junk and do weird things with wax, but also quite disturbing that you consider that a good time."

Sinner puffed out his chest, trying to appear more manly. "I don't personally check out the other guys-"

"Yes, you do, asshole." Cazzo slapped him upside the head. "You were the first to check out Hunter's wax job."

"It was so I could help him. It's not like I was inspecting it and thinking about...you know, doing stuff to it."

"Do you get a wax job?" Raegan asked Cazzo.

"Why?" he said with suspicion.

"I'm just wondering if this is something that you all do as a sort of ritual or male bonding experience. You all seem...very close. It's good, really. I think it's great that you're all so...comfortable," she took a step back as she smirked at us, "sharing all of this with each other. It's really very special."

She turned and walked out of the room with a snort. I looked to the guys, confused by the turn of events.

"I'm lost. Does that mean that she's giving me another chance?"

"Do we spend too much time together?" Sinner asked, completely ignoring my question. Then his eyes flicked to my groin. "Do you wax?"

"And you wonder why she thinks we're all too comfortable with each other," I muttered as I walked away.

Chapter Twenty

REED SECURITY

Gabe

I laid staring at the ceiling in the bedroom I was sharing with Isa, my hands resting under my head. The kids were in a room across the hall, but they were sleeping now. Isa had been passed out for hours and as much as I wanted to either bring her in here or go sit with her, I was under strict doctor's orders to lay down and take it easy for a few days.

After all that had happened at the hospital, my body felt like a train wreck. I still had phantom pains in my chest from being shocked back to life. It was odd because I didn't remember anything from my time in the hospital, but I could swear that I remembered the feeling of being shocked.

I had woken up in some small town hospital in a completely different state. I wasn't even allowed to know any details while we were there in case I muttered something in my sleep. Cap hadn't been able to come see us, as he was dealing with the rest of Reed Security, but Kate and Knight were with Hunter, Ice, and me the entire time. They had sectioned off a couple of rooms for us, and no one but hand-picked doctors were allowed to enter. Knight told me later that a few of the guys from OPS had come along and were stationed outside our rooms and around the hospital. I hadn't seen them the entire time and I wasn't sure they were even aware of who they were guarding.

The first few days I was there, I was mostly in a fog, not really sure what was going on. I had multiple tests because of my head injury and I slept most of the rest of the time. When I started to stay awake longer, I took some time to visit with Hunter and Ice, but Ice was mostly sleeping. Hunter was doing a lot better, but was also under orders to stay in bed because of the severity of his injury. Apparently, he had almost bled out on the table. Ice was recovering from heart surgery and from what Kate told me, the doctors almost weren't able to save him after he had gone into cardiac arrest when he was drugged.

So, when Ice was well enough to travel, we were transported to Knight's safe house. I hadn't been expecting Isa to slap me, but then again, I hadn't realized how much it had hurt her that I was gone. A shadow crossed my doorway and I glanced over, sitting up when I saw Isa standing in there staring at me. The look on her face was filled with skepticism, as if she thought that I was just part of her imagination. I slowly got up and walked over to her, but she ducked her head, refusing to look at me.

"Isa," I murmured, reaching out to grip her hand. She let me take her hand, but she didn't grip mine back. I pulled her into me and wrapped my arms around her. I could feel her heart thumping against mine and then I felt the wetness on my shirt. She finally wrapped her arms around me, gripping me to her body like I would disappear.

"I thought you were dead. I couldn't understand why I was so happy and then it was all ripped away."

"Shit, Isa, I never wanted to hurt you."

"It wasn't you. Sebastian should have told us what was going on."

I pulled back, holding her at arm's length so I could look into her eyes. "You understand that he couldn't, right? Everyone's lives were at risk. It wasn't just about me or Ice and Hunter. He was trying to keep everyone safe, and with the clusterfuck we've landed in, he did what he had to do."

"He let me believe you were dead."

"Yeah, but I'm not. See?" I grinned. "Alive and well."

"Is that supposed to be funny?"

My smile faltered and I wasn't sure how to answer that. "No?"

"What? You're not sure?"

"Uh...You know, I was not really prepared for this."

"And what were you expecting?"

I rubbed a hand across the back of my neck, unsure how to deal with this. I always fucked up when I tried to make things right with Isa. I needed something positive that we could grip onto. Something she could look forward to in the future. I grinned and snaked my arms around her waist, pulling her in close to me and pressing my growing cock against her.

"I'm thinking we need a little reunion to get reacquainted."

"You want to have sex?" she said incredulously. "I just found out that you're not actually dead-"

"And I ruined your fantasy," I remind her, "which you still haven't told me about."

"And you expect me to just jump aboard the Gabe train and ride you into the station?"

"I was actually thinking that I would be parking my train in your station and letting the passengers get off."

Her face morphed into disgust. "Did you just suggest that you get me pregnant with a train analogy? Is that really the way we're going to talk about having future children?"

"*You* said the train analogy," I sputtered. "I just went with it. It sounded good at the time."

"Yeah, next time think that through in your head and then think about how I might react to it."

"You don't react well to anything I say."

"Maybe you should take a hint."

I gripped my hair, frustrated with the way this conversation was going, but then instantly regretted it when pain shot through my head. I grimaced and held my head in my hands as I took deep breaths to work through the ping pong ball that was bouncing around in my head.

"Way to go, genius."

"You know, I had a different scenario of how this would all play out. I would come back. You would fall into my arms and tell me how much you loved me. You would give me a blow job and then nurse me back to health in a naughty nurse costume. This," I said, making a circle motion with my finger, "is definitely not any of that."

"Welcome to the club, jackass. I didn't see myself running with my kids after my husband died, only to have him come back from the dead and act as if he didn't just tear my world apart!"

"Do the kids know?"

"That you're dead?" I nodded. "No, but I'm about to tell them."

"But, I'm alive," I said in confusion.

"Not for long," she said as she turned and walked out the door.

Yeah, that could have gone better.

Ice

I woke groggy and completely fucked up in the head. I didn't know where I was and nothing around me looked like anything I had seen over the past week. It felt like it took all my energy to look around the room, but I smiled when I saw Lindsey sleeping in a chair in the corner of the room. She looked uncomfortable though, and I just couldn't deal with that.

"Princess," I croaked, my throat dry from sleeping so long. I cleared it and tried again. "Princess."

She jerked awake and sat up, rushing over to my side, tears spilling down her cheeks. "Oh my God. I thought you were dead. I thought I was going to have to kiss someone else to see you one last time."

Okay, either my mind was way more fucked up than I thought or that just didn't make any sense. "What?"

"Nothing, it's not important. How are you feeling?"

"I'd feel better if you were laying in bed beside me."

"No way. Kate said that you need a lot of time to recover. I don't want to do anything to set you back."

"You know what would set me back? Not having you in my bed. It's a fucking king size bed. You'll fit." She eyed me hesitantly, but then started to climb into bed with me. I shook my head. "Take off your clothes."

"I don't need to be naked to lay in bed with you."

"I want to feel your skin against me."

She eyed my naked chest and the large bandage that ran down the center of it. They had cracked my chest open to perform surgery on me. I was fucking lucky to be alive right now, and knowing that, I wasn't wasting any more time without Lindsey by my side.

"Princess, just do it," I said softly.

She pulled off her clothes and laid down next to me on my right side, careful to keep space between us, but I wasn't having it. I raised my arm up, which hurt like a bitch, and pulled her into me. She was still hesitant to be this close to me, but eventually, she relaxed and drifted off to sleep. It didn't take too much longer before I followed her into a peaceful sleep.

When I woke, she was laying on her side, her ass snuggled against my dick. The doctor told me if I couldn't sleep on my back, that laying on my right side was okay, but it might be uncomfortable. It was a little uncomfortable, but I naturally rolled toward Lindsey in my sleep. And now I was going to pay for that. My dick was coming back to life, something I was assured wouldn't happen for at least a few weeks after surgery. *You won't even think about sex,* Kate had said. *You'll be too uncomfortable to want sex,* she said. *You'll be too tired.*

Fuck, that's what the doc said, but try telling that to my dick right now. Closing my eyes, I could feel my dick sliding through her ass cheeks and my eyes flew open, a reminder of our first time running through my mind.

"Shit, not again."

I groaned and tried to shift away from her, but having my chest cracked open didn't make moving that easy. And even though they wired me back together, I was still fucking sore. I gripped onto her hip, hoping that I could push off her to help roll myself over, but then she fucking moaned and my dick twitched, right into her fucking pussy. She was wet. Good God, this shouldn't happen, not only a week after surgery, but it felt so right. The heat spreading through her pussy to my dick was too much and then she fucking pushed back against me. Just. Like. Before.

This was not my fault. I couldn't be blamed for my dick being in her pussy. Well, if you discounted the fact that I made her get undressed because I was so sure that I wouldn't be in any mood for fucking. She moaned and then pushed back further. My fingers squeezed her hip harder, but this time, I was pulling her back against me harder. I slipped further inside her and then slid my hand up to cup her breast. Her nipples were so fucking hard and I could almost taste them in my mouth right now. Fuck, I couldn't wait until I could move around more.

She gasped and tried to shift away from me, but I held her tighter. Luckily, she didn't pull too hard, probably because she was afraid to hurt me. "John, what the hell? We're not supposed to be doing this!"

"Stop fucking talking," I gritted out through clenched teeth.

"John-"

"No! I'm inside you now and this is happening."

"I'll hurt you!"

"Fuck, help me roll onto my back. You can ride me."

"Are you insane? You must be insane if you think I'm going to-"

I squeezed her breast hard and she instantly stopped talking. "Just fucking do it."

She huffed and pulled away from me, slowly helping me roll to my back. I groaned and she looked hesitant to climb on me, but then she saw how hard my dick was and slowly spread her legs, straddling my cock. Watching her sink down on me was pure torture. She threw her head back and she slowly rode me, her tits bouncing just slightly and those nipples begging me to suck them.

My hands skimmed up her waist to her breasts. I thought I was never going to feel these magnificent tits again. "Faster," I panted. She sped up and her pussy squeezed me. I was going to come. I wasn't an asshole, though. I ran my fingers across her clit, spreading her juices around and around until she was clenching hard around me.

"Fuck!" I shouted as I came, holding her down on me as I pulsed inside her.

The door flew open and Kate stood in the doorway, her eyes wide in shock as she stared at Lindsey on top of me. Lindsey shrieked and covered her breasts. Kate shook her head and walked over, tossing a blanket at Lindsey on her way.

"What the hell were you thinking? You're supposed to be taking it easy. You just had heart surgery!"

"It was an accident!"

"Fucking her was an accident?" Kate asked.

"Excuse me?" Lindsey chimed in. "We are not going back to accidental fucking! You shoved your cock in me and begged me to fuck you!"

"But it was an accident. You were naked and-"

"So this is my fault?" Lindsey practically shouted, getting off me without bothering to make sure I was covered up. Luckily, Kate had the decency to pull up the blanket over my dick. "You were the one that told me to get in bed naked, that you needed to feel me against you!"

"You said that I wouldn't want sex," I accused Kate.

"I also didn't tell you to test out that theory."

She started checking my vitals and then my bandage, all the while Lindsey glared at me.

"Princess-"

"Don't you *Princess* me. You just made it sound like you didn't actually want to fuck me. And I'm not on birth control! I swear to God, if you just got me pregnant, I'm going to make sure there is never a chance for accidental fucking again!"

She stormed out of the room and Kate finished checking me over. "Well, the good news is that you don't appear to have done any damage."

"And the bad news?"

"It doesn't look like you'll need to worry about when you can have sex again."

Hunter

I was bored out of my fucking mind. How long was I expected to just lay here? I mean, sure, I almost bled out all over the floor and then went into cardiac arrest, but that was a week ago. I was fine now. So, I had my chest cracked open while the doctors pumped thirty-two pints of blood into me while they tried to save my life. Weren't you supposed to live life to the fullest after you almost died?

I was lying to myself. I wasn't okay, not really. The doctors told me I had been lucky. They said the bullet passed through my neck and then pinged around in my chest. When they cracked me open, they said they were working overtime to tie off veins and arteries to get the hemorrhaging under control. I was fucking lucky that those doctors were available and not in another surgery or I would have been fucked. They had worked relentlessly to save my life and that wasn't something I could just wash under the bridge. But knowing how close I was to dying, I just wanted to get out of bed and do something.

When Kate knocked on my door and saw the irritation on my face, she grinned and came over to check me over.

"I take it the patient is ready to get out of here?"

"More than ready, doc. Can't I get up and move around a little?"

"I think you're ready to, but not by yourself, and you have to take it easy. No superhero stuff."

"That's my job," Derek said from the doorway. "Don't try and steal that from me."

"I don't know, I did just survive a bullet to the neck. I think that firmly places me first in line for the title of Superman."

"Don't let Claire hear you say that. So, what's the word, doc? Is he superhuman or just a lucky asshole?"

"Well, if I had to pick, which I find highly strange, I would say he's more like Iron Man. Lucky to be alive with metal still in your chest? I think that one describes you best."

"Really? You're giving him Iron Man?" Derek said in disbelief.

"Just relax. The only reason I even know who Iron Man is, is because Robert Downey Junior is hot."

"Yeah, I wouldn't let Knight hear you say that," I grinned.

"He can have his fantasies and I can have mine."

Derek started laughing and Kate looked at him in confusion. "What?"

"Do you really think Knight has fantasies about anyone other than you?" Derek looked to me and I shrugged. "It's been like twenty years and the man still looks at you the same way he did when he first started stalking you."

"It hasn't been twenty years," Kate scoffed, "and if anything–"

"If anything, his obsession with you has grown," I cut in. "Don't fool yourself, Kate. It doesn't matter what you do, Knight will always look at you like he wants to devour you."

She blushed, putting back some of her medical supplies and pretended like this conversation wasn't happening. "Anyway, your body is still pretty weak and I know you're anxious to get moving again, but you have to take it easy. As long as you do that, I'd be alright with you getting up and moving around."

"I can do that," I said with a grin.

"Also, you're going to be exhausted pretty fast, so don't overdo it or you won't be able to get back to your bed without one of your friends carrying you."

I grimaced, not liking the idea of one of my friends having to carry me around. "No problem, doc. Have you seen Lucy? I was expecting her to be out of her drunken stupor by now."

"I think they were starting to wake up. I'll go get her for you."

"Thanks, Kate. I really appreciate you looking after me," I said genuinely. She really had gone the extra mile for all of us. The door shoved open again and Knight came in the room.

"You better not be hitting on my woman."

"See?" Derek grumbled under his breath to Kate.

"If you mean by thanking her, you've got nothing to worry about. Not sure I could get it up right now anyway."

Knight's eyes darkened and he growled at me. "Just because you're the only friend I have doesn't mean I won't shoot you."

"I'm hurt," Derek held his hand to his chest with a wounded look.

"Why? You're still standing," Knight stared him down. "I'd take that as a compliment."

"You're just all sunshine and roses, aren't you Knight?" He turned to Kate with a grin. "So, tell us, what was it about Knight that first drew you in? Was it his charming personality? His zest for life? That killer smile?"

"Actually, it was his darkness," she said, staring at Knight with fire in her eyes. "He was a force of evil for the greater good. If that's not a superhero, I don't know what is."

"Holy shit, man. You two really were made for each other," I laughed.

"You'd better watch it," Knight threatened. "I could always do with one less friend."

I laughed, shaking my head at him. "Sure, Hud, you keep telling yourself that."

"You don't think I'm serious?" he asked in a deadly tone.

"I think that if you shot me, you'd have to do all those new recruit trainings on your own and that would be just too much for you to take. Nah, I think you benefit more from me being alive."

Kate rolled her eyes and walked toward the door. "I'll go find Lucy."

When she left, Knight walked over to the chair and sat down. He appeared calm and relaxed, but I could tell that he was anything but. He just stared at me and it had me a little worried. But he wouldn't say anything until he was ready, so there was no point in trying to get it out of him.

"I'm surprised you're not following Kate around everywhere you go."

"I'm always watching her." He held up his arm, showing me the watch that was strapped to his wrist. "It has an LED screen. I can see where she is at all times."

"So, the cameras just follow her around?" Derek asked.

"Not exactly. I have a tracker on her and Raven. The cameras are programmed to watch them at all times, anywhere they go."

"Does Kate know that?" I smirked.

His lips twitched slightly. "She knows she's safe."

"That's vague. So," I said, waiting for him to tell me what the hell was on his mind. He just stared at me for a minute, but I didn't give up. I could do this all day, or at least until I wore myself out and fell back asleep.

He leaned back in his chair, fiddling with his wedding band. "This isn't going to turn out the way we want."

Derek was leaning against the wall, staring at Knight with a mixture of suspicion and question. "What exactly do you mean?"

"Chance being taken, it's ...I can't figure out the reasoning behind it. None of it makes any fucking sense. I think he'll be dead before we get to him."

"Give me specifics," Derek pressed.

Knight's jaw clenched, but he continued. "Morgan's gone, most likely with The Broker. He probably knows where her daughter is. She's the leverage. Chance is just a pawn in this game. There's no reason to keep him alive. If they want information out of him, they'll torture him, but he'll never give in. And if he doesn't die from being tortured, they'll just kill him."

"And if it's not information?" I asked.

He stared at me knowingly. "You know as well as I do that it's not information. They've already proven that they can break into our facility without us knowing. If they wanted information, they could have taken it the day they attacked us."

"So, he's dead anyway."

He nodded and silence hung between us. Lucy opened the door and Knight immediately stood. "I was beginning to think I was going to have to sit outside your house again."

"Why's that?" Lucy asked Knight.

He looked to me and nodded. "Good to have you back." Then he turned and walked out of my room, leaving me with Lucy and Derek.

"What did he mean by that?"

"Nothing," I said, trying to cover up his real meaning, that I had almost died and Knight would have been looking out for her. "He's just giving me shit about old times."

Derek pushed off the wall and walked over to me, holding out his hand. I took it, knowing that if Lucy weren't here, he'd probably be giving me a manly hug right now. "I'll leave you to get reacquainted. Don't take any shit from him, Lucy. The bandage is all an act." Derek smirked at me before walking out the door.

"So," she said after a moment, "I've been thinking that we should look into your idea of starting a family."

"I thought you wanted to wait."

She stepped forward and ran her hand up my leg until her fingers rested over my cock. "Why wait?"

"Well, you didn't seem too thrilled about it when I brought it up."

"Are you trying to get out of having sex with me?" She cocked her head to the side as she flashed me a sexy smile. Her hand was now rubbing my cock and I was growing harder by the second.

"I'm supposed to take it easy. Doctor's orders."

"Don't worry. I won't be too hard on you." She winked and walked away from me, shedding her clothes with every step. I quickly started pulling down my pants until I realized that something wasn't right about this.

"Wait, tell me first why you want to have kids now."

She huffed and threw her hands to her hips, standing completely nude in front of me. It was hard to concentrate on her face when her body was tempting me like that. "You almost died," she said sharply.

"I know."

"So, I was thinking, if you stay in this line of work, it's pretty likely that at some point, you're going to get maimed or killed." She shrugged lightly. "I figure I need to take you now while I still have you."

"So, you want my sperm," I said slowly.

"Well, how else am I supposed to have a piece of you?"

"You know, I feel a little used right now."

"Not as used as you're going to feel when I'm done with you," she said saucily.

I held out my hand, stopping her from coming up on the bed. I couldn't believe I was doing this. "I think we should wait."

"What?"

"I just think that this is moving kind of fast and-"

"Are you fucking kidding me? Oh my gosh, it's just like when you asked me to stay with you and then you freaked out. Only now it's over kids."

She picked up her clothes and started yanking them on.

"That's not-"

"Don't! Don't even start with me. The least you could give me after what you just put me through is a child to remember you by after the next time you go and get yourself blown up."

She slammed the door as she walked out of the room and I looked after her like an idiot. I wasn't sure what had just happened, but it didn't end with me getting laid.

Chapter Twenty-One

JACKSON

I was still looking for Raegan hours later. She had walked away after our weird confrontation with Sinner and Cazzo and I hadn't seen her since. Gabe was walking out of his room grumbling about something.

"Have you seen Raegan?"

"No, you know what else I haven't seen? My loving wife."

"Uh-oh, trouble in paradise?"

He shook his head in disgust. "You know, you would think she would have been grateful," he mumbled.

"Hey," Hunter shouted from inside his room. I walked in there, seeing him laying on the bed and grumpy as hell. "Get over here and give me a hand. Kate said I could do some walking, but I had to be with someone."

I went over to him and helped him sit up and then stand. His sharp intake of breath had me second guessing this little excursion. "Are you sure you're up for this?"

"I need to get out of this fucking room. I'm bored as fuck and since I'm pretty sure Lucy won't be coming back to see me anytime soon, I need some company."

"Where are we headed?"

"Ice's room. Kate wanted him to take it easy today because of all the moving and the drugs that were injected. I'm sure he's going fucking crazy."

"So, why isn't Lucy talking to you?" I asked as we wandered down the hall to Ice's room.

"Fuck if I know."

I opened the door to Ice's room, banging it against the wall. You know, just to make sure he was awake. He was halfway sitting up with pillows shoved behind his back, and he was scowling, though I didn't think it was because we were all here.

"What crawled up your ass?" I helped Hunter lower himself into a chair and then leaned back against the wall, leaving the other chair for Gabe.

"Is it just me or are the women acting really weird since we got back?" Ice snarled.

"It's not just you," Gabe said, shaking his head. "Do you know that Isa is pissed at me because I suggested we start trying for a kid?"

"No shit?" Hunter said curiously. "Lucy's pissed at me because I said we should wait."

Ice snorted and then grimaced slightly. "Lindsey's pissed at me because I fucked her and she's not on birth control."

"Wait," I laughed. "So, all of you are up shit's creek because of babies? Oh, this is too good. Thank God I don't have to deal with that shit."

"I wouldn't be laughing if I were you." Gabe shot me a dirty look. "Mr. Mud Fucker."

"What does that mean?" Hunter asked.

"He fucked Raegan for the first time in the mud. He's a real charmer, huh? And then, the idiot told her he loved her. Maybe."

I shot Gabe a death glare. "That's behind us. We talked things out and it's all good now."

"She just forgave you after you wobbled on *I love you*?" Ice shook his head. "Take it from me, she didn't just forgive you. Remember, I'm the king of fucking up a relationship."

"No, she did," I confirmed. "We were talking and then...and then Sinner and Cazzo walked in..."

"And everything went to hell. She never actually said the words, did she?"

I looked to Hunter as I thought over my conversation with Raegan again. "Shit, you're right."

"Of course, I'm right. And you're not the king of fucking up," he said to Ice. "Remember, I'm the one that couldn't commit and then stalked Lucy."

"Yeah, so how is it that you wanted a kid and now you're telling her to wait?" I asked.

"She was just using me for my sperm. Can you believe that the only reason she wanted to fuck me was because she wanted to get pregnant in case I got myself blown up? I'm not a piece of meat," Hunter said defensively.

"Do you hear yourself?" Gabe asked. "You're refusing sex because she wants to use your body? When did you turn into a chick?"

"I'm not a chick, but...I thought it would be special. I thought that...you know, we'd light some candles and make love. I didn't want it to be our normal hard fucking. I wanted her to want it with me, not because I might die."

The room was silent as we all weighed what he was saying, but then Ice started chuckling and Gabe and I joined in.

"What? What the fuck are you all laughing at?"

"I wanted it to be special," Ice said in a girly voice. "I wanted to make love."

"What guy, who isn't part of a romantic comedy, actually lights fucking candles?" I asked. "Do you know how much that wax would burn if you were fucking her and the candle tipped over on you?"

"Brings new meaning to the term *wax job*," Gabe laughed.

"Fuck off," Hunter snarled. "I'm a changed man. I'm more in touch with my woman-"

"You mean your feminine side," I snorted.

"No, with Lucy. I want to give her everything she deserves and-"

We all burst into laughter again.

"And that includes a special night-" he said loudly over our laughter.

"Oh, fuck," Gabe laughed, bent in half and holding his side. "Stop it. You're killing me."

"A special night of romance," Hunter finished, but we were all still laughing. "You're all a bunch of fuckheads. At least I didn't jump my woman as soon as she found out I was alive." He jerked his head at Gabe. "You tried to impregnate Isa as soon as she walked in the room and you fucked Lindsey without thinking about the fact that you might get her pregnant. Who's the thoughtful and insightful husband now?"

"You know, he's right," I said stoically. "He is the thoughtful and insightful one. You should all take lessons from him."

"Thank you," Hunter said, throwing his arms in the air.

"Yeah, if you don't ever want to get laid again, listen to the man that traded in his balls for a skirt."

"You know, you're one to talk," Hunter smirked. "You've had a thing for Raegan since she moved in with you and you *just* made a move."

"I was being respectful."

"You were being a douche," Gabe threw at me. "She's been practically begging you to fuck her for almost six months and you've been holding off because you were so fucking worried about her."

"Only you saw her, Gabe. The rest of you didn't see her when I brought her to my house. You didn't see how beaten up she was."

"Yeah, but she doesn't seem nearly as affected by it as you do. Seems to me that she wants to move on and you just don't have the balls to man up," Gabe smirked.

"There's nothing wrong with showing sensitivity in certain situations."

"See?" Hunter practically exploded. "He was trying to show his gentler side."

"Not gentler side, logical side. I don't have a fucking gentle side."

Hunter shook his head, smirking at me with a knowing look. "You say that all you want, but you really like this chick and you knew that you had to tread lightly with her because you didn't want to scare her. Because you like her. If you didn't, you would have sent her to a safe house. You're not being logical, you're thinking with your dick, and the quickest way to get your dick in her pussy and keep it there."

"You're so crass. How can you be so sensitive one minute and such a dick the next?"

"Did you just call me crass? Pull down your pants," Hunter commanded.

"What? I'm not showing you my dick."

"I'm not looking for your dick. I'm looking to see if you wear Granny panties." He shrugged lightly. "Just wondering when you turned into an eighty year old woman."

"Look, I think we can all agree that being sensitive to a woman is just part of the whole *keeping her happy* thing. If you want to get laid, you have to play to their needs."

"You know, they're always bashing us for being insensitive and shit, but I'm starting to think we're not the problem," Gabe said. "All I wanted was to make Isa feel better. She was all sad when she saw me. It was like she didn't believe it was me. I couldn't stand to see the look on her face, so I tried cheering her up. Now, you tell me what's happier than coming inside her pussy so she can shove a baby out in nine months."

"Exactly," Ice nodded. "So what if I knocked Lindsey up. I'm her husband, the love of her life. The man that listens about her freaky OCD shit. If I want to put a baby in her belly, goddammit that's my right as her husband."

"And it was special because it was your first time making love since almost being killed," Hunter added.

Ice looked a little sheepish. "Not exactly. I mean, technically I hadn't meant to have sex with her. She was snuggled up to me and...it was another accidental fucking." He raised his hands defensively, his eyebrows shooting up as he tried to back what happened. "Hey, shit happens, but that doesn't take away from the fact that despite being shot in the fucking heart, I still wanted her so badly that my dick found its way into her pussy. It knows where home is."

"She could have stopped it," I shrugged. "If she didn't want to get pregnant, she could have just gotten off you before you blew."

"That's not the only reason she's pissed," Ice said hesitantly. "Kate walked in and she was fucking pissed that I was exerting myself. I didn't know what to say, so I told her it was an accident, because it was. But Lindsey got all worked up about it because she said it sounded like I didn't want to fuck her. Which, obviously I did or I wouldn't have been hard. She took it all the wrong way."

"That's because women overreact," Gabe said. "You would think Isa would be happy that I wanted to have a kid with her, but instead, she got all worked up over the way I said it. Don't they always say it's the thought that counts?"

"What exactly did you say?"

Gabe scratched the back of his neck, squinting like it hurt to actually say the words. "Uh, she said something about not jumping on my train and riding it into the station as soon as she found out I was alive. And I told her that I wanted to put my train in her station and let the passengers off."

"That's why she's pissed," Hunter said. "Making a baby is a special thing that needs to be taken seriously. You have to use finesse and-"

"Holy shit," I groaned. "What the hell happened to you? It's like you almost died and you turned into some sentimental pussy."

"Really?" he asked. "Does everyone feel this way?" He looked to Ice and Gabe, but they just stared at him like he was delusional. "Oh, God. They messed me up somehow. Do you think they gave me a personality transplant or some shit when they operated on me?"

"They didn't operate on your brain, asshole." Gabe tapped his head near his injury. "Maybe if you had hit your head you could claim that."

"So, what is this then? It's gotta be some really bad side effect. Maybe it's the drugs talking. Yeah, that's gotta be it."

"Yeah," I mockingly nodded at him. "That's definitely gotta be it."

"Do you think you could take me back to my room? I'm feeling a little faint."

I really tried not to laugh at him, but he looked like he had been struck dumb. I grabbed his arm and helped him up.

"You'll be fine, big guy. You just gotta get back on the horse and ride that woman until you're yourself again."

He nodded as we walked into the hallway. Lucy was walking down the hall, but when she saw us, she turned in the other direction.

"Wait!" Hunter yelled. "I'm ready to fuck you hard, baby. I'll put so many little Hunter's inside you, your pussy's gonna have to acquire more land to let them all settle."

Lucy turned back around and stared at him incredulously. She looked around quickly to see if anyone else had heard that, then ran off. Hunter looked down dejectedly.

"Come on, big guy. Let's get you back to your room so you can lay down. I think you might have actually hit your head and the doctors didn't notice."

He nodded as we walked to his room and when I lowered him to his bed, he looked up at me in confusion. "Did I just refer to Lucy's pussy as land where my hunters would settle?" I winced and nodded. He paled and laid down on the bed. I started to walk away, but he grabbed onto my hand and squeezed tightly. "Get Kate for me. I think I need my head examined."

"At least you didn't say that your hunters were going to roam the plains of her pussy."

"Cap, someone's coming up the road," Knight said as he walked into the room. "They're still about five miles out."

"Does anyone else come up here?" Cap asked.

"No."

I followed Cap out of the room Becky was using as an IT room and out the front door of the house. Some of the other guys must have already been alerted because Chris, Jules, Florrie, Sinner, Derek, and Cazzo were already headed out to the gate. A few minutes later, a beat up pickup came barreling down the road. All of us had our weapons drawn and aimed at the truck. It skidded to a stop in front of the gate, and slowly, someone stepped out of the passenger side of the truck.

It was hard to tell who it was at first. He looked like he had been through hell. His face was mottled with bruises and there was no hiding the way he nursed his ribs, favoring the right side of his body. But as he stepped closer, there was no denying that it was Craig.

Florrie went to run toward the gate, but Cap put his arm out, stopping her from running forward. All of us still had our guns pointed at Craig and the closer he got, the more the grin slipped from his face.

"Who's with you?" Cap yelled.

Craig glanced back at the truck to the man sitting in the passenger seat and then back to us. "Storm. You want to let us in?"

None of us dropped our weapons, except Florrie. She took a few steps forward, against Cap's orders, and moved to the gate. "Craig, we just need some answers first. Someone gave away information on how to breech Reed Security. We're just trying to figure out who that was."

"And you think it was me?" He took a slight step back, his hand poised to reach to his back and grab his weapon. He didn't stand a chance if he pulled it.

"I don't think you did," Florrie insisted, "but everyone else wants answers. You disappeared after we were attacked. No one saw you leave and we just need to be sure."

His gaze was chilling and his whole body was flexed to run. "Good to know that my own teammates think I could turn on them, especially after everything we've been through."

"Craig," Florrie stepped forward, but he was already walking away, not bothering to keep his eyes on us.

"If you think I'm a traitor, shoot me in the fucking back," he shouted, right before he got in his truck. He stared at us for a moment through his windshield before the truck spewed gravel as it shot backwards and then took off down the road.

Florrie whirled around on us, glaring at each of us with disgust. "Are you happy now? He looks like he's been beaten to hell and he came to us for help. And you all pointed your weapons at him like he was some kind of rabid dog you had to put down."

"Florrie-" Cap started, but she just shook her head and walked away.

"Do you think he'll come back?" I asked.

"Not very likely," Sinner said. "If I thought my family didn't trust me, I wouldn't come back."

I noticed he looked at Cap when he said that and was reminded how there was a time that Cap and Sinner were at odds. Sinner had moved across the country instead of staying and trying to work things out. Now I understood why. If one of your teammates didn't trust you, where did you go from there?

"Shit," Cap swore, running his fingers through his hair. "Knight, tell Becky to find out where the fuck he went. Give her the plates."

Knight nodded swiftly and then he was gone.

"You're not gonna be able to sweet talk your way out of this one, Cap. That shit hurts," Sinner said, slapping him on the back.

"What worked with you?"

"Well, you did admit that you were an asshole. That went a long way to soothe my bruised ego. And then you apologized. If I remember correctly, you got a little teary-eyed and told me you loved me."

Cap shoved Sinner as he laughed, shaking his head and walking inside.

"Why did you forgive him?" I asked Sinner as we walked inside.

"You know, when I was taken, all I could think about was Cara, and when I was rescued, I just wanted what I had before, you know, all of it. I wanted Cara, my job, and my friends back. I could tell that Cap was sincere when he apologized and it was his own insecurity about Freckles that was making him act the way he did. Sometimes you just have to forgive and forget. Nothing changed between us, but I knew it would take a while for us to be back to the level of trust we had before. But it still came. And then before I knew it, I was delivering Maggie's baby on the side of the road and that was way more than I ever wanted to see. I'm pretty sure after that, Cap didn't have any more reservations about me."

"So, we need to find Craig a woman and have Cap help deliver his baby," I surmised.

Chapter Twenty-Two

JACKSON

We were sitting in our makeshift conference room, trying to come up with our next move. Everyone was there except for Ice and Hunter, who were taking it easy. They weren't up to strategizing or making any big decisions right now. And Florrie and Alec were nowhere to be seen, but considering what had happened earlier, their disappearance wasn't unusual. So far, we hadn't come up with anything new to go on for finding Chance or Morgan.

"I think we should head back to Reed Security and start rebuilding. We can't stay on the run forever and we can't let them intimidate us," Cazzo said.

"But if we go back and we're not prepared, we put all of our families in danger. At least here we can protect them and not worry about leaving them to go to work. We can head up everything from here," Knight said, emphasizing his point by tapping his finger on the table. "Hell, we could rebuild here. No one knows where this place is. There's enough acreage to build as many escape routes as we could ever want."

"And move away from our families?" Cazzo asked. "Maybe that doesn't matter to you, but some of us have ties to the community back home. We'd be leaving people behind."

"I agree," Sinner said. "Cara's brother lives there. He's always helped us out, but I'm not sure he'd be willing to leave his job and move with us. And then Kate's cousin is there. They've gotten really close over the years. Are you telling me your wife would be fine with leaving him behind?" Sinner said pointedly to Knight.

"My main concern right now is making sure everyone is safe. We've already lost a team member and several others were severely injured. How many more do we need to lose?" Knight snapped.

"I didn't realize you cared," I said calmly. "You always act like none of us matter to you."

"This is my fucking home," Knight yelled. "This company is what saved my life and I'll be damned if I'm going to let anyone take that from me."

"I think we can all agree that we can't go home right now." Cap stood and walked over to the tablet, pulling up aerial footage of the Reed Security property. "Sean sent this over this morning. The building is gone. The detached training center wasn't touched by the fire, but the structure of the main building isn't stable. We're talking a complete tear down and rebuild. We need to use this opportunity to redesign the building and make it exactly how we need it. In order to do that, we have to figure out how those fuckers got into our security system. If Craig wasn't the leak, then they managed to get past us some other way and we're not rebuilding until we can be sure that we'll never be breached and attacked like that again."

"So, we stay here for the time being?" Burg asked.

"That's our only option at this point. If you don't want to stay out here, I can't stop you from going home, but I can tell you that there's no way I'm sending my family back home with those fuckers still out there. If they came after us in the hospital, that can only mean that they want to wipe us out."

"Yeah, but is it The Broker or the head of this trafficking ring that's trying to get rid of us?" I asked. "We don't even know who we're supposed to be fighting."

"The Broker has to know that we know who he is. My money is on him. He's too powerful to leave loose ends," Sinner said.

"But Agent Finley was killed when we found out he was part of the ring. The way those guys moved in the alley, the gear they wore,"

Derek added, "it was the same as the men that attacked us at Reed Security. If the ring sends a team to wipe us out and they don't succeed, I would guess they'd keep coming after us until we're taken care of."

"Fuck, we're just going around in circles here," Knight snapped. "We need something more than our fucking guesses."

"Maybe these guys can help us out with that." We all turned to see Florrie and Alec standing in the doorway with Craig and Storm.

Cap pressed a button on the phone and Becky came over the line. "Becky, will you please join us in the conference room?"

"Is it alright if we come in or are we also traitors because we went to get Craig?" Alec asked. He looked calm and collected on the outside, but Alec was known to really lose his shit when he got pissed. You never quite knew when he would snap. In fact, he kind of reminded me of Knight, and based on the way they were staring each other down, I would guess that they were more alike than I had ever realized.

"Take a seat," Cap said without any preamble.

They all walked in the room, nobody saying anything as they took their seats, but the anger in the room was bordering on a lit fuse. Becky walked in with her laptop, sensing the tension and immediately took a seat. It got uncomfortably quiet as we all sat around the table, waiting for someone to say something.

Sinner stood and all eyes went to him. "Look, I'm just gonna put it out there. I have an issue with one of you in this room." Craig visibly tensed and Storm looked like he was ready to bolt. "Now, I don't want to name names, but one of you took my box of Wheaties out of the break room back home. Now, since the building has now burned to the ground, I can't do any fingerprint analysis, but I know who you are. Crumbs don't lie." He pointed his finger around the room at all of us. "Watch your back."

The tension broke and Cap walked behind Sinner, slapping him across the back of the head. "Let's get back to work. Storm, The Broker went radio silent. Any idea where he would go if he didn't want to be found?"

"If he's not at one of his properties, I don't have a fucking clue. The guy never said anything when he came to the club. However, I do have some information you may want." He tilted his head to the side and eyed Cap as he spoke. "That is, if Sinner doesn't decide to accuse me of stealing his Kit Kat."

Sinner jumped to his feet, slamming his fist on the table. "I knew that was you!"

Cap gave a slight nod to Storm and he continued. "I was on my way to Reed Security the day of the attack, hoping you had information on Morgan. The building was already on fire and I could see it from down the road. For some reason, I pulled over to the side of the road. Something just felt off. Anyway, I pulled out my scope and saw vehicles all around the building and they weren't ones I had seen before. I saw Craig being dragged out of the building and hauled into a vehicle. I got the plates and took off before they could see me."

"Why did you leave the day before?" Cap asked.

"I had a contact that I wanted to get in touch with. He was in New York, so I met him halfway."

"Care to share any more about that meeting?" Chris asked, looking up at Storm from under his cowboy hat.

"Let's just say that he works in intelligence now. He's got some pretty lofty contacts, but it'll take him a while to get back to me. He has to tread lightly while he's digging."

"How did you find Craig?" I asked.

"A friend of a friend."

"You have a lot of friends," Alec pointed out.

"Yeah, well, I was in the military too. I just so happen to have friends that made some interesting career choices after they left the service. Anyway, he was able to track the vehicle to an abandoned property close to the Ohio border. They had too many men surrounding the building, so I couldn't get him out on my own. I called the hospital to find out about how many men were brought in with injuries and it was pretty clear that there really weren't that many of you that were battle ready. I called up some men I served with to help me, but it took a few days to get everyone together."

"What did they want with you?" Cap asked Craig.

"They wanted to know what Finley told us."

"He didn't tell us anything," Cazzo said. "In fact, he was pretty adamant that he didn't even know who Chief was."

"They all say shit like that," I pointed out.

"I'm not so sure," Cazzo shook his head. "The look on this guy's face was pretty convincing. I'm not sure that he was lying to us."

"We may never know now," Cap sighed. "All the evidence says that he was involved. What else did they say?"

"Not a whole lot. It was different ways of asking the same question. The last thing the guy said to me was something about praying at the altar. And then he tried scaring me with the whole...." Craig drew a line across his neck, like someone was cutting off his head.

"Bossman, that's not a whole lot to go on." Becky was looking over her notes, tapping her fingers on her keyboard. "I'm not sure what exactly you want me to look for."

"I might have something that will help." Storm slid his cell phone across the table to Becky. "There are pictures on there of the dead men. Maybe we can identify them and we'll get lucky."

"Alright. I'll download the photos and get to work on identifications."

"That's it for now," Cap said. "Rocco, check Craig out. Make sure he doesn't need any medical care."

"I'm fine." Craig was still pissed and it didn't look like he was going to let that go any time soon. Cap just stared him down, but finally gave in and nodded.

"I want everyone that's healthy enough down in the gym and training. We're weak enough as it is. Knight, you're in charge. Also, talk with your wife and see what she needs for PT."

The meeting was over and I started to head over to Craig, but Alec and Florrie immediately formed a barrier by him and glared at all of us. The message was clear, they weren't ready to let anyone near their teammate right now.

Chapter Twenty-Three

RAEGAN

I had been waiting for Jackson to say those words to me for days. I knew that he loved me and that he didn't mean anything that happened when he thought Gabe was dead. Still, making him sweat just a little wouldn't hurt anything. I had continued to avoid him since our run-in, mostly because I wanted to know if that was a fluke declaration or if he really felt that way. I didn't think I could take anymore wobbling from him.

I had been wandering the house the whole morning and I hadn't really seen any of the guys. I actually thought they left the house until I wandered down a set of stairs and heard grunting. At first I thought someone was having sex, but then I heard multiple voices and figured that if someone was having sex, there was a massive orgy going on, and who didn't want to see that?

But when I rounded the corner, I saw a long hallway that led to an open gym area. There was a basketball court where a few of the guys were shooting hoops. Then there was an area with weights, but nobody was over there at the moment. Around the entire gym was a track. That was where Jackson was and damn, did he look hot. He was wearing just a pair of black gym shorts and sweat was glistening down his chest.

I pushed back against the wall so no one would see me and stared unabashedly at the man that took over all my fantasies. I licked my lips as I watched almost in slow motion. The muscles in his legs were strong and flexed teasingly with each stride. The sweat that ran down his face dripped to his chest and slowly slid down his rigid abs until slipping into the waistband of his pants. And then he slowed to a walk and ran one hand through his hair. Good God, even his armpit hair was sexy. I remembered laying in bed with him and it tickling me.

I checked out the tattoos that wrapped around his biceps and seemed to flow right down his back and around his rib cage. I hadn't really checked those out yet, but I really wanted to. I just had to get him alone and pounce. He shook out his leg, then bent over giving me a nice shot of that ass. He ran his hands up and down his injured leg, pressing his thumbs into the muscles. If he needed a massage, I would gladly give it.

He stood and spun toward me. I pushed back against the wall and moved into the shadows, hoping he hadn't seen me. I held my breath as I waited, counting to twenty, figuring he had probably moved on by now. I slowly walked back to my earlier position and was sad to see that he had in fact moved on. I decided to just go back upstairs, but then he quickly came around the corner, caging me against the wall.

"Were you watching me, baby?"

"I...uh..." I couldn't think with him so close to me. After watching the way he moved and his body dripping with sweat, all I could think about was getting him upstairs and into my bed.

"I really need a shower and you happen to be very good at cleaning me. Care to join me?"

I bit my lip to keep from jumping up and down with my hand in the air, begging him to take me back with him, even though he had just asked me. I didn't want to seem desperate. In fact, I wanted to seem like a sex kitten. I let my hand slide down the front of his chest and then gripped his waistband, pulling him as I moved out of his arms and down the hall to a door I had seen.

Pushing it open, I was relieved to see it was a locker room with showers. Perfect. After he fucked me, I could take him to the shower for a second round. I hopped up on a massage table and pulled him in between my knees. "What do you say we skip the shower and get right to the fucking?"

He didn't need another invitation as he slammed his mouth against mine and climbed up on the table, pushing me down with his body. I spread my legs wide, wanting to feel his body as close to mine as possible. My hands slid across his sweaty back down to his shorts. I slipped my hands inside and squeezed his ass, thinking I would feel some fat, but instead it was all hard muscle.

"Holy shit," I breathed against his mouth as he ground his cock against my pussy. He did it again and again, my juices flooding my panties until it seemed almost pointless to be wearing anything at all. My heart was thumping harder and harder and my breathing was so ragged that my throat had gone dry. I moaned and started pushing down his boxers and shorts, needing to get his cock inside me now. He took the hint and yanked the pants from my body, then ripped my shirt over my head.

I laid naked on the table, spread bare for him, but not feeling at all self-conscious. The way he looked at me made me feel like the most gorgeous and tempting woman he had ever seen. But right now, he was staring at my breasts, which were still enclosed in my bra.

"Have you ever been tit fucked?"

I shook my head no, my eyes widening with wonder and need. He quickly removed my bra and then he was pushing inside me, fucking me hard, fucking me to the end of the table. I was so close, but then he pulled out and climbed up my body until he was straddling my stomach. He pushed my breasts together and gave me a wicked grin.

"Open your mouth, baby."

I did as he asked and watched in fascination as he slid his dick in between my breasts. The tip of his cock slid into my mouth, but I wanted more. I lifted my head off the table, straining forward to take as much of him into my mouth as possible.

"God, that's so fucking sexy. Hold your tits, baby."

I did as he asked, holding my tits in place as he continued to fuck me. Then I felt his fingers on my pussy, shoving inside me and playing with my clit. I moaned as he shoved inside my mouth again and something flashed in his eyes. Suddenly, as if a wild beast had been unleashed, he was fucking my tits fast and hard. His fingers strummed my clit until I was screaming with my release. I thought he would come in my mouth or on my chest, but instead he pulled back and slapped the side of my hip.

"Roll over, baby. Stick that ass in the air for me."

In a flash, I was on my stomach, pushing to my knees. His hand ran up my spine until he was pushing down on the back of my neck as he slid inside me. That was the last time he took things slowly with me. His hips started pistoning against my ass as he slammed into me over and over. I held onto the table for dear life as his cock hit me so deep that I thought I would go flying off the table. Then his hand was in my hair, fisting it into a tight ball as he held me once again.

It was brutal and rough and I had never been so turned on in my life. The table started screeching across the floor with the force of his thrusts, making me worry that he was going to send the whole table crashing to the ground. His fingers found my clit again and worked me until the sensations were so blindingly magnificent that my whole body clenched and spots were flying in front of me in a dizzying haze. I felt him slam into me two more times, but it barely registered in the midst of my bliss.

I felt the weight of him pressing down on me and then he was pulling me up, his cock still lodged firmly inside me. His hands massaged my legs and up to my breasts. Kisses flowed across my shoulder and up my neck as his hand lovingly caressed my breasts slowly.

"I love you so fucking much," he whispered in my ear.

"It's about time you said it right," I panted.

"Because I didn't say maybe?"

"Nah, throwing *fucking* in there just makes it seem like you really mean it."

"I fucking love everything about you. I fucking love fucking you. And you can bet you're never fucking leaving me."

"See? So much more believable."

A throat cleared and I jerked in Jackson's arms, but he was already covering me up with his large hands. I peeked around Jackson to see

Gabe, Burg, Sinner, Derek, and Cazzo were all standing just inside the door.

"Not that we're not all enjoying the show," Sinner smiled, "especially Gabe, but we were kind of hoping to use the showers today."

"Go use your own fucking showers," Jackson growled.

"I think we should just hang out here," Gabe said, leaning against the wall with a grin. "They'll have to get up from that table eventually. Could be quite a show."

"If anyone looks at my woman's pussy, you'll wish you were dead."

"Ah, sorry," Cazzo said teasingly. "We already got a pretty good showing. I'm not usually into porno flicks. I saw one before with my sister and I wasn't really into it. But this was interesting."

"You watched your sister in a porno?" I screeched. Cazzo flushed red, shaking his head no.

"It wasn't like that. Gabe was fucking my sister while they watched a porno. I walked in on them. It practically blinded me."

"Believe me," Gabe grumbled, "it wasn't exactly my favorite sexual experience either."

"I'm sure it wasn't nearly as embarrassing as when Derek got caught fucking Claire in his Superman costume," Burg joked.

"At least I don't fuck sheep," Derek shot back.

"Hey, you know that's not fucking true."

"Oh, right. You just take men home to fuck."

Burg lunged for Derek, but Cazzo held him back with the help of Sinner. Meanwhile, I was still sitting, wrapped in Jackson's arms and if I moved even a little, everyone was going to get a show.

"Hey!" Jackson yelled. "Get the fuck out so Raegan can get some fucking clothes on."

"Not a chance in hell," Gabe grinned.

"Baby," Jackson whispered in my ear. "Turn slowly around in the other direction until you can straddle me. I'll make sure no one sees you."

I nodded and did as he said, blushing furiously when I felt his cum sliding out of my body. He managed to get down from the table with me wrapped around him like a monkey, and then shoved right past the guys and walked down the hallway with me. Stark naked.

"What the hell are you doing?"

"Getting you to your room."

"Everyone's going to see my ass!"

"Baby, they'll see a whole lot more if we go back."

"I am so going to kill you for this."

"Nah, you fucking love me too much."

And it was true. I did fucking love him.

It became my routine over the next few days to sneak down and watch the guys work out. However, today was different. When I got down to the gym, several of the other ladies were already there. Only, they weren't hiding like I chose to. No, they were sitting against the far wall and blatantly staring at the men. Well, if they were going to do it, so was I.

Claire patted a spot next to her and I willingly took it, also taking the popsicle that she offered. She had a cooler sitting next to her and from the looks of it, she was planning on a horde of women coming in here or she would be here for a while.

"Why is everyone down here today? I thought I was the only one that came here to watch."

"We were getting bored and Sinner told Cara what he walked in on in the locker room. We figured maybe we would have some fun too."

"Not all at once, right?"

Claire chuckled as she shook her head. "I may like role playing, but I'm not into orgies."

"What a shame, and here I was thinking my very first orgy would take place with my new found friends at a secret hideout where dirty things happen that no one talks about."

"Ooh, that actually sounds kind of fun," Claire said excitedly. She turned to me, pulling her legs into a crisscross shape in front of her. "We could have a theme night where everyone dresses up like it's a masked ball and we pretend we're all strangers. And then the men could take us back to our rooms and do dirty, nasty stuff to us."

"Yeah, that definitely sounds like a good idea. We'll all wear masks and then someone will go to a room, not realizing that they're with the wrong spouse until they start making out or fondling each other. Then the guys would start a huge fight and the girls would-"

"Watch with popcorn!" She clapped excitedly, bouncing up and down.

"I was being sarcastic."

"I wasn't. I love watching a good fight. Why do you think I'm down here today? It's not for the exercise. I love to watch them working out, sweat dripping down their bodies while their muscles flex with every movement."

"They? You mean Derek, right?"

"Sure," she giggled. "If it makes you feel better."

I stared at her wide-eyed, but she just shrugged. "Look at them. Can you honestly tell me that you don't think they're all hot? It's not that I want to sleep with all of them, but damn, talk about lighting my panties on fire."

"And do you all feel this way?"

"I don't know. Hey, Maggie." Maggie turned and smiled at me. "Are you checking out everyone or just Sebastian?"

"Everyone. I'm doing research for a new article I'm writing."

"Kate?" Claire asked.

"I'm taking notes on their workouts for their medical records."

"Lucy," I said, "Hunter isn't even down here."

She shrugged. "So? I'm keeping tabs on Knight for Hunter. He asked me to make sure he didn't overdo it."

"Isn't that why Kate's here?" I laughed.

"Hey, we all look out for each other. Besides, Knight has this crazy, psychotic demeanor about him that makes every woman either terrified of him or flaming hot."

"Well, it's good that you're willing to share, Kate."

"I'm not worried. Knight is laser-focused on Raven and me. He won't let us out of his sight for even a minute. He has this watch on that tracks our every move with a camera. He thinks I don't know about it."

"That man is absolutely crazy when it comes to you," Lucy said. "I'm not even sure how you ended up with him. The man stalked you and snuck into your house all the time just to watch you sleep. It's creepy."

"Seriously?"

She shrugged. "What can I say? I always felt safe when he was around. I know it sounds weird, but I knew he would always protect me because he was always watching."

I nodded, biting my lip, wondering how the hell someone responded to that. It was so strange and I wondered if Jackson did that to me if I would still be with him.

"Well, considering that my first experience with Knight was him holding a knife to my throat, I'm not quite as enamored with him, but I will say, the man's body moves like silk across my skin."

"Does Sebastian know that you watch the others work out?"

"Hell no! And don't you dare say a thing. It was hard enough to convince him that I wasn't having an affair with Sinner."

I glanced around the room and when I saw him, I had to fan myself. "Sinner is definitely..."

"Sinful?" Claire said helpfully.

I sighed, resting my chin on my balled up fist. "All this man candy in front of us and we can only have one. It seems wrong somehow, doesn't it?"

The other ladies sighed in agreement as we watched the men flexing their muscles for us. It was such a sexy sight. "What do you think they would do if we all played a little switch up?" Lucy asked.

"How exactly?" Maggie asked.

"Well, each of us could go flirt with someone else just for fun."

"Aren't you worried that one of them would flirt back?" I asked.

All the girls laughed like it was the most ridiculous suggestion in the world.

"Trust me," Maggie said, "when these men find *the one*, that's it for them. No other woman exists to any of them. The only thing that would happen is a giant fight that we would have to break up. Then we would spend the next month with them tailing our asses to make sure that we weren't doing anything we weren't supposed to."

"I take it you have experience with this?"

"The tailing? Unfortunately, Sebastian seems to think that I always need protection. It doesn't matter how many guns I keep on me or how many times he sees me shoot someone, he still thinks he has to protect me."

"Shoot someone?"

She shrugged. "It happens."

"More times than it should," Kate pointed out.

"Hey," Maggie said indignantly, "I can't help it if trouble finds me. I'm a magnet for danger."

"Jackson doesn't trust me with guns. I sort of shot him the last time he gave me one."

"Did he call you fat?" Lucy asked.

"Or look at another woman?" Maggie added.

"Were you on a super spy adventure?" Claire asked excitedly.

"I bet he deserved it," Kate said. "Men always deserve it."

"Actually," I stared at their eager faces. Never had I seen women so enthusiastic about knowing how a man was shot. "We were running from these guys that were chasing me at the hospital and Jackson gave me the gun to protect myself. Not that it would do much good. I know how to shoot a gun, but it's not like I've been training for it."

"So, what happened?" Claire asked, practically bouncing out of her pants.

"Well, we were running through the parking lot at the hospital and these men were catching up to us. Jackson shoved me to the ground between cars and gave me the gun. I assumed that he gave me the gun so I could be his backup."

"That's what any normal woman would think," Maggie nodded.

"Right, so I followed him after he ran out like a crazy man, but people started shooting at me. I ducked behind a car and then stood and fired, screaming my head off as I fired."

"Badass," Kate said with a smile.

"Right, well, I also had my eyes closed. I may or may not have shot Jackson."

"Hey, if he was in the way, that's his fault," Claire said supportively.

"How many did you take out?" Maggie asked.

"I don't know for sure. I think at least two."

She nodded, "Yeah, you should have had a grenade. You could have wiped them all out at once."

"I was in a parking lot," I said slowly.

"Right, and cars provide a great cover. You just toss that bad boy and boom," she made an explosion with her hands as a smile spread across her face. "No more bad guys."

"Has anyone ever told you that you're a little trigger happy?"

"It's the thrill of the chase."

"You mean the story?" I asked.

"Sure, we'll say that. Honestly, ever since I met Sebastian, I've had this really weird fascination with guns...and grenades. Grenades are my favorite. I've wanted to use a rocket launcher, but only Sinner has let me try that. Apparently, Sebastian thinks that's too dangerous for me."

"Yeah, I know I've always wanted to try a rocket launcher," I said in mock agreement. "You know, they had bb guns for kids and lawn darts, why not a rocket launcher?"

"Okay, so Sebastian built this rocket launcher for the kids. It's not at all what you think. So boring. Anyway, it's got this air tank and then three PVC pipes that come out the top. He puts paper rockets in them. So, you use the pump to build up the pressure and then you press this button and they go flying into the sky. It's really fun for the kids. I've modified it slightly. I don't use two of the pipes and then I put nails in the third pipe. Man, you should see those kids run when I do that." She was laughing hysterically, mimicking kids running around and screaming.

"Aren't you worried that you're going to kill your kids?" Kate asked.

"Nah, I put helmets on them and they've been trained enough at Reed Security. It's actually good practice for them."

"Knight would never let me over to your house if he knew you did that. It's okay for him to teach Raven dangerous stuff, but nobody else better do anything that could potentially harm her in any way."

"Just wait until you have more than one," Maggie said. "I swear, Sebastian keeps knocking me up, but then he wants to wrap them in bubble wrap. They're kids. They have to be able to run around and get hurt."

"Yeah, well, Knight won't have to wait much longer. I'm just about twelve weeks pregnant and I'm not gonna be able to hide it too much longer."

"Why haven't you told him?" Claire asked.

"You've seen Knight. I won't be able to go anywhere without him. Last time, he followed me into work and picked me up every day. I just need as much time without the crazy as possible. Luckily, this pregnancy has been very easy."

"Don't look now, but we've got a pack of angry looking men coming our way." Lucy pointed to the corner of the gym that was filled with men coming toward us.

"Do you think it was the popsicles?" Claire asked. "I wasn't purposely trying to seduce Derek. Well, maybe I was, but I really like eating when he's standing or sitting. Sometimes when he's just talking on the phone. Everything he does is so sexy."

Knight was the first to reach us and he was staring heavily at Kate. His eyes were dark and angry and his stance screamed that he was ready to kill. I just couldn't understand why he was looking at Kate that way. Derek, Sebastian, and Jackson all followed suit. The only one not there was Hunter.

"Pregnant? When were you going to tell me?" Knight snarled.

"How did you..."

He held up his wrist, showing off his watch. "Did you think I wouldn't put in audio? Imagine my surprise when I overheard my wife saying that she was keeping her pregnancy from me. For twelve fucking weeks."

Kate scrambled to her feet, pulling Knight to the side. "Technically, it wasn't twelve weeks. I found out eight weeks ago."

Knight took a menacing step toward Kate, pushing her back against the wall. "Do you think I give a shit how many weeks it's been? I should have fucking known. This body is fucking mine. This baby in your belly is fucking mine. We're in the middle of a fucking war and I didn't even know that I had a reason to worry about you miscarrying. You could have been taken at any time. Do you remember the last time this shit happened? Vanessa was pregnant and she lost the baby. How the fuck would I deal with it if that happened to you?"

His face was just inches from hers, and even though we had our own men staring at us, none of us could tear our gazes away from them. It was fascinating and terrifying as hell, but also a turn on. I could see now why Kate was so in love with Knight.

He pressed her hard against the wall and pushed his pelvis against her. His mouth moved sensuously down her neck, nipping and licking her as if he was a dog marking his territory. His hand slipped down her body until he was cupping her pussy as he whispered in her ear. I didn't have to guess what he was saying. He pulled back and yanked her behind him, dragging her out of the room. I was fanning myself by the time they had left. Until I saw Jackson glaring at me. I glared right back.

"Nails, Freckles?" Sebastian snarled.

"Staring at all the men? Those eyes are only supposed to be on me." Derek told Claire, then he turned to Lucy. "And playing with all of us, wanting us to get in a fight over your sex games?"

Before Jackson could say anything, I stood and held my ground. "Don't even say anything. I didn't do anything wrong."

"You listened to their stories," he growled. "They put ideas in your head that you don't need."

"Like they wouldn't have gotten there on their own," I snorted.

"You don't need to be listening about things they've done in the past. Look at Maggie's hand. Do you want to walk away with three fingers? Do you know what that did to Sebastian?"

I looked at Maggie, "Grenade?"

"No, knife," she said with a grin, waggling her eyebrows. I looked at her strangely, but she just shrugged. "Battle scars."

Sebastian pulled her away, grumbling about her being insane and how the men were supposed to protect the women. Jackson grabbed me by the chin, forcing me to look at him.

"They all find these stories funny, but trust me, they aren't funny in the moment. Some people don't come back, and for a while, you saw what that was like. This isn't a game."

"I never said it was, but they all have a point. You guys are so over-protective that it's suffocating. Now I get why Isa, Lucy, and Lindsey acted the way they did when they thought their husbands died."

"And how did they act?" he asked me in a dangerous tone.

"They acted like their husbands were assholes for leaving the way they had. And I quite agree. You all will do anything to protect us, but you don't seem to do the same for yourselves. Any risk is worth it to you guys."

"You don't know shit."

"Yeah? How many times have you been shot over the years, Jackson?" He didn't say anything and I took that for my answer. "That's what I thought," I said as I walked away.

Chapter Twenty-Four

JACKSON

"I've gone over all the pictures that you've given me and have profiles on all of them," Becky said as she brought up the first picture on the screen. "Okay, the first three guys are just low men on the totem pole. They don't really have any contacts that can help us."

She flicked to the next slide and Storm spoke up. "That guy used to come into the club with some other guys. I think he was there for the poker night that Morgan worked."

"His name is Dexter Corgan. He was a distributor of anything sold on the black market. He had connections all over the world and has been on pretty much every government's radar for years, but for some reason, nobody could touch him."

"How can you be untouchable by every government?" I asked.

"Maybe nobody actually wanted him caught," Cap offered. "They kept him on their radar for security purposes, but in the end, if he was doing business that helped them, they kept him happy."

"Did he travel under aliases?" I asked.

Becky shook her head. "Never. The man had some huge balls. He went wherever he wanted whenever he wanted. I've watched video feed at airports and security gates. He was never stopped or checked out. As soon as he was seen, he was just waved on through."

"Where did he travel the most?" Cap asked.

"Central America was a pretty big supplier for him, along with Southwest Asia and Afghanistan for heroin. Russia, China, Belarus, Venezuela, and Iran are the largest countries for human trafficking. The largest population of sex trafficking still comes from eastern Europe, Asia, and Africa, although Venezuela is also getting up there. Pakistan is the largest supplier of illegal arms and the Middle East is flooded with their weapons. Columbia is currently the top producer of cocaine."

"So, basically, this guy was everywhere," Cap said.

"Yes. He had a few competitors, but he was the largest fish before he was killed." Becky flicked to the next screen and a new face came up. This picture was a profile picture instead of one of the images of dead guys. "Now, this guy was his number two-"

"I know him," a feminine voice said from the doorway.

I turned in my chair to see Raegan standing just inside the room, staring at the screen.

"You've seen him or you've met him?" Cap asked.

"Met him. In the last year, Xavier was trying to make bigger deals, gain a bigger part of the market. This guy met with him a few times."

"Xavier was a mid-level supplier," Cap said. "Why would Corgan get involved with him?"

"He was planning on going up against the largest supplier, or that's what I heard."

"How would he do that?" I asked. "He didn't have that many men working for him, and most suppliers are a helluva lot more cautious. We walked right into Xavier's house."

"Xavier was cocky," Raegan snorted. "He always thought that he was going to take over the world."

"This man is Ben Curtis," Becky informed us. "He's a DEA agent, working on a joint task force with ATF. On the streets, he goes by Joseph Ramos."

"Is he dirty?" I asked.

Becky shrugged, "It's hard to say. He's been undercover for so long, I doubt he even knows."

"How did you get this information?" Storm asked. "Usually that stuff is-"

"Yeah, I know, but I'm good and I may have had Knight helping me. Seriously, Cap, you're wasting that man's talent."

Cap just huffed in response. "Is there anyone else we can work with? This guy seems untouchable."

"Unfortunately, he's our best option."

"Did he take over for Corgan?" I asked.

"It appears that he has, but it's hard to say if Corgan's contacts are as friendly to him. Corgan had the power of his name and his reputation. Agent Curtis is walking a fine line taking over Corgan's role."

"How do we even get in with Agent Curtis? That seems like an impossible task."

"We don't," Cap said, staring at Raegan.

"No." I stood and walked over to Raegan, standing in front of her as if that would protect her from what Cap was thinking. "There's no way you're using Raegan."

"Use me how?" Raegan asked curiously.

"If you've met Agent Curtis, Ramos, we could have you run into him."

"Did you just hear what I fucking said?" I snapped. Raegan pushed around me, completely ignoring me.

"He knew that Xavier was abusive. We could use that against him." Raegan sat down at the table by Cap, the two of them strategizing like no one else was in the room.

"Have you run into him, really play up the abused woman on the run," Cap nodded.

"Just one problem," I snarled, "she doesn't have any fucking bruises."

"That can be fixed," Cap waved me off.

"You're not fucking beating my woman up."

But no one was fucking listening to me. Raegan and Cap looked like two excited grunts planning their first mission together.

"And then I could convince him to let me stay with him for a few days."

"Becky," Cap barked. "Does Ramos have someplace local he stays?"

"He has a place in Texas."

"She's not going," I said forcefully.

"I could pretend that some of Xavier's men took me when Xavier was killed. I knew too much, which I do. I know all their meetup locations and the warehouses they use."

"Except they would have killed you."

"I could say that I escaped and have been on the run ever since. I could tell him I just need someplace to stay for a few days until I get my next plan in place."

"He wouldn't leave you alone in his house. Not unless he really thought you weren't a threat. It would have to look realistic, like you were seriously injured."

"So, if he leaves me alone in his house, what would I be looking for?"

"Nothing." I walked around to Raegan, pulling her out of her chair. "You're not going. Do you get that? You could get killed."

"Yeah, like I wasn't in that position before," she said sarcastically. "I can do this and then maybe we'll make some progress on finding Chance. Don't you want that?"

"Not if it means you get killed," I said angrily, shaking her slightly. It was like she didn't get it at all, that I couldn't lose her too.

"I won't get killed. You can give me a gun-"

"There's no fucking way you're getting a gun."

"And one of those knife thingys that gets strapped to your thigh. I could pull that off, no problem."

"This is fucking stupid," I yelled at Cap. "Just take Ramos and interrogate him. We've done it before."

"We can't take a federal agent. And if he's undercover and really isn't dirty, then we'll blow his cover and put him in danger."

"And we wouldn't be doing that by sending her in? Don't you think that Curtis is going to be watching her closely? If he and Corgin were meeting up with Xavier, his men will know who she is. If anyone doesn't completely trust Curtis taking over and they see Raegan, they'll be suspicious and want both of them dead just to be on the safe side."

"Then I'll just have to get the information fast and get out of there. You can give me a spy cam and some crafty microphone that's

disguised as a button on my pants. Then you'll always know what's going on."

"Including when you take a piss," Storm laughed.

"Okay, so maybe don't put it on my pants, but you get the idea. You were in the military. I'm sure you know how to stay hidden and keep an eye on me."

I grabbed Raegan's hand and dragged her out the door and down to a private room where I could talk to her away from everyone else. After slamming the door, I firmly moved her into the corner and then paced in front of her while I tried to get my emotions under control. I was so fucking pissed and she was acting like she was heading to a fucking spa day.

"You would think after all that time you spent with Xavier that you would have learned your fucking lesson," I snapped. Her eyebrows shot up in surprise and she tilted her head in that pissed off way that warned me I was on dangerous ground. I didn't give a fuck. If she wasn't going to look out for herself then I would.

"What lesson was I supposed to learn exactly?"

"Why would you offer to put your life on the line like that? Do you really not understand how dangerous this is? This isn't like when we were running through the parking lot or the woods. And that was fucking dangerous enough. I won't be there to protect you. If this guy realizes who you are, he'll put a fucking bullet in your head before I can get to you."

"If he's not dirty, he's not going to shoot me."

I scoffed, shaking my head in disbelief. "Do you really think that? He's undercover. He's not going to blow a seven year operation to save a woman that's trying to steal information from him. He's going to get rid of you and think about it later. And if he is dirty, he'll either shoot you right away or he'll torture you until he gets everything he needs from you."

"This isn't the same as Xavier."

"How the hell can you say that?"

"Because it would be for you!" she shouted. I took a step back, stunned by what she was saying. I shook my head, but she continued. "I stayed with Xavier because I was too stupid to leave when I should have. Or maybe I was just a coward. Maybe I didn't want to admit that I had been wrong. I have no fucking clue why I stayed with him as long as I did. But I knew after he started to change that I was going to die if I stayed with him. And guess what? I still stayed."

"So, what? Is this about redeeming yourself?"

"No..."

She shook her head and for the first time since she had been with me, she looked vulnerable. That shell that she had built around herself was starting to crack and that sarcastic demeanor was slipping away. I wasn't foolish enough to think that I would see this side of her very often. It was like admitting defeat for her.

"Raegan," I said softly, brushing my hand across her cheek. Her eyes lifted to meet mine.

"I saw what it did to you when we thought Gabe was gone. These men are your family and I know what it's like to lose family. I walked away from my family and over the years, I always wondered how my parents were. I wondered if they were hurting because I wasn't there. I wondered if they even thought of me anymore. I can't stand the thought of you not finding Chance, of always wondering if he's alive or dead."

"We can find another way."

"No," she shook her head. "This is our chance. We may not get another opportunity like this ever again. Are you telling me you're really okay with not doing this? With possibly abandoning Chance because you're afraid I'll get hurt?"

"I can tell you that I'm really not okay with the woman I love putting herself in danger. What the hell am I supposed to do if something happens to you? Do you know how much that would kill me? To know that I would never see you walk through my door again or drink coffee with you in the morning? I would never kiss you again or hear your sarcastic comments. I would never get the life with you that I want, that I've known since the moment I met you that I wanted. All of that would be gone and it would be my fault because I allowed you to do this."

"You're not allowing me to do this," she said with a sad smile. "I have to do this for me just as much as for you. I would never be able to live with myself if I let this opportunity go. I would feel like a coward for staying behind when I could have done something. I was already a coward for too many years. I won't be one again."

I swore, taking a step back from her. I didn't know what to say. I didn't know how to convince her that this wasn't the way. But one more look at her and I knew that I could argue all I wanted and she wouldn't listen to me. She was determined to do this.

She stepped into my space, pushing her body hesitantly against mine. Her arms wrapped around me, enveloping me in her comfort and warmth. I squeezed her body to mine, trying to come to terms with the fact that she was doing this just as much for me as she was for herself.

I cupped her face in my hands, bringing my lips softly to hers. "You are the bravest woman I know, and as much as I really don't like you doing this, I also know that I can't stop you."

"Don't get the wrong idea," she snorted. "I'm terrified. I'm not the badass that Maggie is, but I can do this. I know I can."

"Just promise me that if you change your mind you'll tell me immediately. No one expects you to do this."

"I promise, but I won't."

Chapter Twenty-Five

CHANCE

My head drooped again and I jerked it up, trying to stay awake. I had been waiting close to a week for an opportunity to get out of here. I watched how often guards walked by and kept track of which ones were vigilant. There were a few guards that didn't even glance my way. They must have thought that there was no way I could get out. As of yet, I hadn't found a way, but it was good to know that when I did find a way, I would just have to wait for the right moment to leave.

I had been doing everything I could to keep moving in my small space. I did push ups with my knees on the ground and sit-ups as long as I could. As for my legs, that was harder to do with the cramped space, but if I sat against the wall, I could do leg lifts. It wasn't the workout I was used to, but it would keep me in shape until I could escape. The major problem I had was the lack of food and water. It was sapping my energy and if this kept up, I wondered how long I would be able to keep up with my workout routine.

It started raining hard around midday and the ground quickly turned to mud all around me. I had never been so filthy in all my life. Even during my military days, I had never been in conditions like this. I remembered getting Morgan out of that well and how she had been after just two days. I was lucky in comparison. I had food and water at least.

I had dug a latrine in the corner, but it would only last so long before I would run out of space and need to dig another. The smell was terrible, not just from the latrine, but from me. I would never take a shower for granted again after this.

My eyes snapped open when I heard the rustling of leaves. There was a guard walking toward me, but no one ever came this early in the morning for me. He was carrying a bottle of water and my slop dish. He was one of the guards that never paid attention to me, and by the look of things, he didn't pay attention to much in general. I moved as close to the bars as I could. If I had a chance to take this guy out, I was going to take it. He had to have something on him I could use to get out of this cell.

As predicted, he didn't pay any attention to me as he leaned in to set my bowl down. My hand shot out between the bars and latched onto his shirt. I yanked as hard as I could, slamming his head into the bars. When he didn't collapse right away, I shoved him back and yanked again. This time he fell to the ground and his eyes stayed closed.

I pulled on his shirt until I could drag him close enough to look through his pockets. He had a knife in his pocket, small, but still useful in a dire situation. He also had a handgun on him. Checking it over, it wasn't the best handgun and it didn't have many bullets, but I could work with it. There were no keys for the cell, which I kind of expected. There was nothing else of use and he was too fat for me to fit into his clothes. His feet were also too small, so I'd be running naked through the trees. It would most likely be painful, but at least I would have a chance at getting out of here.

I looked around outside one last time. As far as I could tell, it was all clear. Moving as far back in the cell as possible, I took aim and fired at the lock. It didn't break on the first shot, so I fired again. The damn thing was rusted so badly that it hadn't moved, even though the lock was broken. I kicked with all my strength at the bars. It took several tries, but the door finally opened slightly and I was free. The dead weight of the man made it hard to push the door open all the way and

I had to squeeze through, barely getting out without scraping my dick on the metal.

With no one in sight, I took off as fast as I could, darting into the trees and hoping I was running in the right direction. After a few minutes, I heard men screaming. I wasn't going to have much time. I could climb a tree and wait it out, but if they found me, I would have nowhere to run. I pushed myself harder, ignoring the bite of sticks burrowing into my feet. I had slashes across my entire body from leaves and branches thrashing across my skin.

I was fatigued much sooner than I should have been, but the lack of food and water had drained my body. I didn't know how long I had run when I finally had to stop. I was leaning against a tree trying to catch my breath when I heard the shouts again. I didn't have time to stop and rest. I had to keep pushing. I shoved myself away from the tree and ran harder until I could see a break in the trees up ahead.

Bursting through the tree line, I could see water ahead. I stopped just before I would have gone over the edge of a very high cliff. I ran along the cliff's edge, searching for someway down, but there was nothing. I spun around as the men burst through the tree line, guns drawn and ready to fire. I still had my gun, but I only had two bullets left and that wouldn't help when I was up against twenty-some men.

"Put your weapons down!" one man shouted. "There's nowhere to go. You're on an island."

I glanced over the edge of the cliff again. I had to make a choice. Did I stay here and pray that someone would come rescue me or did I jump and hope for the best? The fall would most likely kill me. There were large rocks along the shoreline that I would probably land on. Still, a quick death would be better than staying here and rotting in that shitty cell. With no intentions of being taken back and held until I died, I turned completely toward the water and said a quick prayer for Morgan and the rest of my friends and family.

"I wouldn't do that if I were you," a familiar voice said.

Looking back, my eyes narrowed in on The Broker. He had a huge grin on his face that I would love to have the pleasure of removing.

"There's nobody around to help you this time," he chuckled.

"You're pretty confident in yourself. I would love to fight you one-on-one, without all your lap dogs fighting your battles for you."

He waved me off, obviously not caring that I would kill him in two seconds if he came near me. He slowly started coming toward me, but stopped far enough away that I wouldn't be able to reach him before I was shot.

"You fight for honor, family, and friends. And what has that gotten you? You're on an island that you can never escape and no one knows where you are, and they never will. I would guess that after a few hours of you going missing, that little tech genius of yours realized that you would never be found. I'm guessing they're already bandaging their wounds and moving on."

"That's not how we operate," I growled.

He nodded as he chuckled. "You're right. They'll no doubt waste every resource they have in the hopes of finding you and your little stripper friend. See, you should have learned by now that you fight for yourself and no one else. You're fighting lazy by relying on others and you need to be smarter than that. I pay others to do my fighting for me and look at where I am. Not a scratch on me. No one can touch me because I don't get my hands dirty and I make sure I pay people so well that they never turn on me."

Doubt started to creep into my mind about whether or not my team was coming for me. I knew deep down that they wouldn't give up easily and that's why I needed to stick to my original plan and jump off the cliff before they could take me back to hell.

"I see what you're thinking, but I still wouldn't do that. I have something that you want, something that you are desperate to get your hands on. In fact, it's right here on this very island. Jump and you'll never know what it is."

I shouldn't care. For all I knew, he was bluffing. I glanced back at him, trying to see past his calculating gaze, but the man hid every emotion when he needed to. His grin turned sadistic when I didn't make a move to jump.

"Just as I thought. You like playing the hero too much to walk away. Like I said, you should be fighting for yourself."

"Why do you care if I jump and kill myself?"

"I don't, but someone else does. He's not ready to kill you, but he doesn't know what to do with you either. And it's no fun to just tell you what's been going on from the start. This is much better. Allowing you to escape, giving you hope that you'll make it back to your little family. Then I snatch the rug out from under you when you realize that you're on an island and you'll never get off here alive."

"How do you know that I still won't jump?"

"Because I have something you want, something you've been searching for."

My whole body tensed when I understood his implication. Was it possible Payton was on this island with me? If she was, I couldn't just kill myself. What if Reed Security found my location? They wouldn't know she was here. Morgan would never get her little girl back.

"You can't do it, can you? Knowing she's here, you won't do anything to put her in danger or leave her here when you still have hope that you can escape one day. You just have to ask yourself, are you willing to stay, knowing you'll be tortured painfully and you'll die here, but Payton will still be alive. Or do you want to take the easy way out and end it all now?"

I looked around at all the men. There was no way I would escape from them now, but there was a chance I could in the future. I didn't know how or when it would even happen, but he was right, I did have hope that Reed Security would find me one day, and since it wasn't just me, I had to stay and pray that one day I would get Payton off this island.

I dropped my gun and knife to the ground and took a few steps forward. Surrendering felt wrong, but taking the easy way out was worse. The men rushed me, shoving me to the ground harshly and yanking my arms behind my back. The Broker knelt in front of me, smirking at my naked, helpless body. He had me cornered, exactly as he wanted.

"I would get a good night's sleep if I were you. The fun begins tomorrow."

Then everything went black.

Chapter Twenty-Six

RAEGAN

We had to wait two more weeks until Ramos, or DEA agent Ben Curtis, was at his home in Texas. Becky had been able to track him down within a day, but he was out of the country. When he booked a ticket home, she alerted us immediately and we were on our way to Texas. We couldn't take the chance that we would miss him if we drove, so we booked flights and hoped that no one was keeping tabs on me. If someone was, there was a chance that our plan would be blown.

Jackson, Gabe, and Knight accompanied me down to Texas. Knight was mainly there to fill in for Chance's absence, but if I could get Ramos out of his house, Knight could get in and hack into his computer. I stopped by a thrift store while I was down there and picked up some clothes that would make me look like I had been living on the streets for a while. I made sure to not eat anything the night before so that I was hungry to make it more believable. I also had to take a little dive in a dumpster to get a nice garbage smell to me, all for authenticity of course. After Jackson threatened to kill anyone that laid a hand on me, we decided that I would have to go in unbruised. I would have to find another way to get him to trust me enough to leave me alone.

We waited down the street from his home until he left for the day, and followed him into the city where he stopped at a restaurant. I got out and sat down against a wall, waiting for my chance to run into him. Knight had given me this super tiny earpiece that I almost lost the moment he handed it over. I also had a microphone attached to the jacket, but I couldn't see where it was placed. I guessed it was better if I didn't know so that I couldn't be self-conscious of it.

"Raegan, remember, Ramos is a DEA agent undercover. He's paranoid about everything. He's probably got cameras all over the place, along with a dozen other security measures. You wait until you know you have a good hour to search and you haul ass to find what we need. If you need help, you call us. Don't hang around too long."

I rolled my eyes at Knight explaining everything to me for the tenth time this morning. "I'm so glad you keep going over the plan with me. With all this other useless crap in my head, I don't know how I'll ever store those simple instructions in my brain."

"Don't be a smartass," Knight snapped. "I'm going over this for your safety. Do you understand?"

"Sir, yes, sir!" I said it harshly, but quietly, so I didn't draw attention to myself.

"Where do you guys find these women?" Knight grumbled.

"The normal way," Gabe shot back. "At least I do. I didn't stalk my wife and I didn't bring her home from a mission."

"I didn't meet Kate randomly on the street," Knight growled. "She was taking care of me, if you remember."

"Right, and you just happened to see her around town every single day, all day long," Jackson laughed.

"She was in danger," Knight snapped.

"Yeah, not until you started following her around like a puppy dog," Gabe joined in.

"Is that really how you met Kate? You just started following her everywhere?"

"Not only that, but he shot a man that was trying to get into her clinic for drugs. He just happened to be watching from a distance and just happened to have a sniper rifle on him."

"Laugh all you want, Jackson. You moved your girlfriend and her parents into your house without ever having spoken to Raegan."

"Because I knew," Jackson snapped.

"Knew what?" I asked.

"So did I," Knight growled.

"Knew what?" I asked again.

"It was like that for me too. After Cazzo beat the shit out of me, of course," Gabe added.

"Knew what?" I was really losing my patience. It was like they were ignoring me on purpose.

"I'm just saying you should own it." Jackson was poking Knight, trying to get a reaction out of him. I just wished I understood the context.

"Yeah, Knight. Stop being a hardass all the time and join the rest of us shmucks," Gabe jeered. "You have your job. You have your woman. Now, you need to learn to chill and laugh a little."

"I laugh at you every day you step into the ring," Knight replied.

"Hey!" I shouted, glancing up and seeing people staring at me. Great, people were going to think I was an insane person talking to myself. "What did you know?" I asked.

There was silence on the other end until Knight finally said, "Heads up. Ramos is headed your way."

I stood up and ducked my head, walking toward Ramos. "Just so you know, this conversation is not over. I will find out what you knew."

"Just keep your head down and do your fucking job," Knight growled.

"You know, I always liked you from day one," I muttered to Knight. "You have that dark, twisty thing going on and you literally growl. Not many men can pull that off."

"We'll be talking about this later," Jackson snapped.

I smirked, laughing to myself that I had gotten to Jackson. Served him right for not telling me what the hell he was talking about. I wiped the smile from my face and kept my head down. I was just a few more feet from him and...I stumbled, falling into Ramos. As expected, he caught me and grimaced when he smelled me.

"I'm so sorry," I said, peeking out from under my hood and looking at him. I saw a flicker of recognition on his face and pretended not to notice.

"Hey, you're Xavier's girl," he said, grabbing onto my arm. I looked closer at him and made my eyes widen like I figured out who he was. I took a step back and looked around like I was scared there were people coming for me. "What are you doing here?"

"Please," I begged, "let me go. You're hurting me."

His grip loosened and I took a step back, rubbing my arm.

"What are you doing here?"

"Xavier's dead," I sniffled, "but his guys thought I was a liability. I just barely got away."

His eyes narrowed slightly and I let the tears build in my eyes. It wasn't difficult to cry on demand. I just had to think about what an idiot I had been over the last few years and it brought on the water-works. Ramos grabbed me by the arm again and pulled me along with him.

"What are you doing?" I said, acting like I was panicked and didn't want to go with him.

"Taking you someplace."

"Wait, please, I can't go with you!"

"You can't stay on the street. Are you trying to get killed?"

"You're not..."

He stopped and looked at me, his face murderous. Now I really did take a step back because the guy in front of me was the one that met with Xavier over the last few years.

"I'm not what? Going to kill you? Going to turn you over to Xavier's men?"

"I..." I ducked my head and shook it slightly as I let the tears slip down my cheeks.

"Come on. I just want to ask you some questions. Maybe give you a shower so you don't stink so fucking much."

He dragged me along and then shoved me into the passenger seat of a car. It was easy enough to pretend that I was scared being in the car with him. For all I knew, I wouldn't be seeing Jackson ever again after this. I fidgeted with my jacket and shifted in my seat. My stomach growled loudly and Ramos looked over at me.

"When was the last time you ate?"

I shrugged, playing it off like I had been on the streets with no food for a long time. He pulled into a local burger joint and ordered for me, not bothering to ask what I wanted. It didn't matter. I was so hungry at this point that I would eat just about anything. It turned out, he ordered something that sounded really good. We drove back to his house in silence and when we pulled in, I got out and hesitantly followed him into his house, hoping that Jackson could still hear me.

"Why don't you take off your jacket," Ramos said.

I shook my head quickly, knowing that if I took it off and walked away, the guys wouldn't be able to hear anything that was going.

"I'm not going to steal it from you," he said irritatedly.

"I just...I'll keep it on for now."

He nodded, obviously not happy with my decision, and jerked his head for me to follow him. I went with him into his kitchen and took a seat, pulling the bacon cheeseburger out of the bag with the cheese fries. He even got me a strawberry milkshake, which went perfectly with my meal. I devoured my food, ignoring his penetrating gaze and didn't stop until I had finished every last bite.

"What do Xavier's men think you know that's so dangerous?"

"Um...drop off locations, warehouses, people involved. Stuff like that," I said with a shrug. "But I don't care about any of it. I just want my freedom. I never wanted to be involved in that part of Xavier's life, but he dragged me into it and forced me to stay."

He watched me for a moment and then came to sit down beside me. "What if I told you I could help you get that freedom?"

"How?"

"I want names, drop locations, warehouses, everything you know."

"What does that get you?"

"It will wipe out anyone that works against my goals."

"And in exchange?"

"When everyone's gone, you'll be free to do as you wish."

Everything that I knew I told to Sebastian already. None of it had been useful to us, but maybe it was useful to this guy. If I told him and got him to trust me, I could get into his office and look on his computer, maybe find something that could help us.

"Okay, I'll do it."

His eyes gleamed in satisfaction as he leaned back in his chair.

"Good. You can stay here while we're working on this. I've got a spare room you can use. I'll have to get you some clothes and you need a shower."

"Thank you," I said quietly, letting some tears slip through again. I had him hook, line, and sinker.

Chapter Twenty-Seven

JACKSON

"I don't like this," I said as I paced around the hotel room we were watching from. Knight had a laptop set up for us to watch everything that Raegan was doing. He had placed a tracker on Raegan's shoes and put a camera on her necklace. Logically, I knew we were covered. There was no sign that Raegan was in danger from the DEA agent, but something in my gut was screaming that this was wrong.

"Relax, it's been two days and nothing's happened yet," Gabe said. "We've got a handle on this."

"Nothing's happened yet. Yet. I'm not really happy with that statement. Would you be okay if nothing had happened to Isa *yet* if she was doing something that could get her killed?"

"Both of you shut up," Knight growled. "I got in last night and placed mics all over the place and tapped his phone."

"Yeah, you're fucking lucky you didn't get caught," I spat back at him.

"I don't get lucky," he said as he stood and glared at me. "This is what I do and I'm damn good at it. We have eyes and ears. We're within a mile of where she's staying. The only way we could be watching her any closer is if we were in the fucking yard all night."

"I wouldn't be-"

"We're not staying in the fucking yard," Knight said. "Sit the fuck down before I blow out your kneecaps."

He sat back down and started working on his computer again when we started picking up some chatter again.

"Raegan, I have to run out for a while."

That was Agent Curtis coming over the line. He sounded like he was putting on a jacket and it was interfering slightly with the sound.

"Okay, just let me grab my socks," Raegan replied.

"No, you won't be coming with. Just stay here and take it easy. Eat something and watch tv."

"What's that like?" she laughed.

"Now you can find out. I won't be gone long. Just lock the door behind me."

"Sure," she said. We heard him walking and then the door closing. After another minute, there was some more rustling. "Did you guys get that? I'm going to his office right now."

"We got it," Knight responded.

She walked into the office and I waited patiently while she shuffled through paperwork and opened cabinets. Gabe started snapping, getting our attention and pointing to another computer that was monitoring Agent Curtis's phone. Knight and I sat down and Gabe put it on speaker so we could all hear.

"Carlos, I've got Xavier's woman."

"How the fuck does that help us?" Carlos replied.

"She knows a lot of shit that will help us track down every last person that betrayed us. We wipe them out and we get in his good graces."

His? I mouthed to Gabe. He shrugged.

"What do we do when we're done with her?" Carlos asked.

"We kill her."

"When do you want to meet?"

"Two o'clock tomorrow at The Greasy Spoon. We'll make her feel comfortable and I'll introduce you as my associate. Just act like you don't want to kill her and we'll be fine."

"Xavier killed my sister. When I get my hands on her, I'm going to make sure the last thing she sees is my face, but not before I make her wish she was already dead."

"Listen, I don't care what you do to her, but you keep that shit locked down until we have everything we need."

"Fine. Two o'clock tomorrow."

Agent Curtis hung up and I immediately walked over to the other computer and picked up the handset. "Raegan, get whatever you can and get the fuck out of there. I'm on my way to get you now."

"I'm working on it," she said hastily. "I can't get on his computer."

"Is it password protected?"

Knight walked over and hit the speaker button. "Tell me what you see."

"I don't see anything. The screen is black."

"Did you try turning the computer on," Knight said, trying his best to hold back his irritation.

"I would if I knew how to turn it on. I swear, this computer is hiding the power thingy from me."

"What kind of computer is it?" Knight asked.

"It's black with a black screen and a black keyboard."

I thought Knight was going to explode. He rolled his eyes as he dropped his head back and blew out a harsh breath. "Are you fucking serious? You don't know how to turn on a computer?" he practically yelled. "Where did you find her?" he said as he turned to me.

"Look, I've sort of been restricted from using any technology for the past like six years or so. Sorry if I don't know how to use the computer."

"Look for a button," Knight said, holding back his anger.

"Okay, I think I've found it." Raegan squealed when the computer turned on and then we waited while it booted up. "Alright, what do I need to do now?"

"Are there any folders on the desktop? Anything that would stand out?" Knight asked.

"No, it looks like it's all personal folders."

"You're going to have to go in through the backdoor and plant a code for me."

"Why would I go through the backdoor? I'm already inside," Raegan asked in confusion.

"Jesus," Knight swore. He was about to explode, so I intervened.

"We're coming to you," I said before Knight could lay into her again. "Just hold tight."

"She thought I was talking about the fucking house," Knight growled.

"She hasn't been around technology. Give her a break."

We packed up quickly and headed for the truck. Knight looked like he was going to kill someone and Gabe was trying his hardest not to laugh. "You got something you want to say, fucker?"

Knight spun around and pushed me up against the truck. "Next time your woman volunteers for something, don't listen to her suggestions. Just lock her in the fucking basement and be done with it."

He jumped in the truck and slammed the door. I glanced to Gabe and then we both burst into laughter. Knight was taking it just a little too personally that Raegan didn't know about computers. It took us just a few minutes to get to Raegan. We parked down the street and quickly made our way to Agent Curtis's house. Once Raegan let us in, it was just a matter of Knight hacking into his system.

"Gabe, you watch the back and I'll take the front," I said as Knight headed for the study with Raegan. It had only been five minutes when I saw Agent Curtis coming back down the road. I ran for the study.

"Curtis is back. Move your ass," I shouted at Knight. I ran back to the front door, taking up my post by the front door. I whistled for Gabe and he quickly joined me on the other side.

"How do you want to play this?" Gabe asked.

"I was hoping we could just slip out the back, but that's not going to happen."

Knight walked out with a gun pointed at Raegan's head and his arm wrapped around her throat. She had tears streaking down her face and her eyes pleaded with me to save her. I almost didn't get it.

"Trash the place," I said to Gabe and then ran over to a table, throwing it over and then making a mess in the living room. Gabe had quickly knocked stuff over in the kitchen. We were just headed back to the front door when it opened and Curtis stepped in. He stopped right in the doorway and stared at the four of us. Gabe and I had our guns pointed at him and Knight was still holding Raegan.

"Okay, everyone just calm down," Curtis said.

"Stay the fuck back or I'll shoot her," Knight sneered.

"You're not going to shoot her. She's too valuable and you know it."

"She's only valuable if she's on our side, which I now know she isn't," Knight continued. "A bitch that snitches is only good for one thing and I happen to know the perfect market for her. I can make quite a bit of money off her."

"You're not taking her anywhere," Curtis said calmly. "We can work something out. I have-"

He didn't get to finish his thought because Knight shot him in the shoulder.

"What the fuck?" I shouted.

"He was delaying us."

I shook my head, reminding myself that Knight was anything but conventional.

"Let's move," Gabe said, rushing past Curtis to the door. I stepped aside to allow Knight through and took up the rear, keeping my sights trained on Curtis the whole time. Once we were outside, Knight gripped onto Raegan's hand and ran for the truck. Just when I thought I was clear to turn and run, Curtis stepped out the door and started firing right the fuck at me. I returned fire immediately, but I had no cover and unless I figured out how to outrun a bullet, I was going to end up in the morgue.

I moved backwards as much as I could as I returned fire, but when my clip ran out, I was fucked. I reached for a second clip and quickly reloaded, ducking behind the mailbox, which only provided minimal cover. Bullets pinged off the metal of the mailbox, one ricocheting and skimming my cheek a little too closely to my eye. I returned fire, turning to run when Curtis ducked back inside.

I could see Knight up ahead in the truck, barreling toward me. He wasn't close enough yet and now Curtis was out of the house and running after me. I spun and fired again, hitting him once in the side, but the fucker didn't even stop. Something pierced my ass and then I was falling to the ground, watching as Curtis fell just seconds later.

I stood and hastily hobbled over to the truck. Knight was holding a fucking sniper rifle. "Did you just fucking shoot me in the ass?" I yelled as I yanked the door open and lifted myself inside.

"You were in my sights. I had a clear shot of Curtis until you stepped right in front of me," Knight said calmly. "Relax, it was your ass. It's just muscle. It's not like I did any major damage."

"You fucking shot me! I'm gonna be sitting on a fucking donut for weeks."

"Stop being such a fucking baby. It's the job," Knight sneered.

"It's not the job to shoot your fucking teammate." I turned to Gabe who was fucking laughing. "See, this is why we shouldn't have brought Knight with us."

"It could have been worse," Raegan added. "If he hadn't shot you, Curtis might have gotten you."

"You're on his side?" I said incredulously.

"I'm not condoning shooting teammates, but he did what he had to in order to get you out of the situation you were in."

"Just like he held a gun to your head?"

"That was actually my idea," Raegan grinned. "Good plan, huh?"

"Yeah, until Knight shoots you," I grumbled.

"I really think you're being just a bit dramatic," Raegan said. "He did you a favor. You should thank him."

"That's it," I said to all three of them. "None of the women go anywhere near Knight. He's brainwashed them all."

We had been driving for about fifteen minutes when Knight spoke. "Just so you know, you're going to have to pay for the truck to be detailed."

"Why the fuck would I have to pay for it? You're the one that fucking shot me."

"It's your blood. You clean it."

I just stared at him, wanting to fucking shoot him. And that's just what I did. Before he could do anything, I pulled my gun and shot him right in the ass. The bullet most likely ended up in his seat. Knight quickly pulled his own weapon and we were suddenly in a standoff.

Knight was barely watching the road as he pulled over to the side. I kept my weapon on Knight and we just stared at each other, wondering who was going to give in first.

"What's going on?" Raegan asked Gabe. "Is this a normal thing that you guys do? Like waxing?"

"This is new," Gabe said calmly. "Damn, I wish I had some popcorn. This is better than any tv show."

"Should we, I don't know, lay down tarp or something? I think we passed a hardware store not too far back."

"Nah, we'll just buy the truck. It's easier that way."

Knight's eyes were wild and dark, just like when I first met him. I knew I was playing with fire, but sometimes you had to stand up against someone that thought he was untouchable. Finally, Knight started to lower his weapon and then set it on the dash. I lowered mine and put it back in the holster. Knight sighed and shifted into drive. "Split the cost?" he asked.

"Deal."

Chapter Twenty-Eight

JACKSON

I limped into the house with Raegan and Gabe trailing. Knight followed a minute later, walking with the same limp I had.

"What happened?" Cap asked.

"Knight shot me in the ass."

"What happened to you?" he asked Knight.

"Jackson shot me in the ass."

"What the fuck? It's not bad enough that other people are attacking us, now we're shooting each other?"

"Cap, it's all good." Knight turned to go, but stopped, tossing him the keys to the truck. "Oh, by the way, the truck needs to be detailed." He smirked at me before walking away.

"Gabe, please tell me that between them shooting each other, there was actually something gained from the trip."

"Turned out pretty good. I mean, Raegan now has someone else that wants to kill her, but overall, it was a successful mission."

"Who wants to kill her now?"

"Carlos Guerrero. He's an associate of Agent Curtis. Apparently, Xavier killed his sister and now he wants to kill her. Quite painfully, actually," Gabe added. "But Knight was able to hack into Curtis's computer and do his computer shit. He should be able to tell us more after he goes over the information."

"This is why I don't send Knight into the field," Cap muttered. "Alright, get some sleep and get your ass checked out by Kate. We'll go over the mission tonight."

"Sounds good, Cap."

"Uh, maybe go to Rocco. I'm thinking that showing your ass to Kate right now would only get you shot by Knight again."

I tapped the side of my head. "Good thinking, Cap."

I took Raegan's hand and dragged her back to our room. After this trip, I was ready for things to be normal for just a little bit with us. I stripped my clothes as soon as we got in the bedroom and laid down on my chest. I was too tired to go find Rocco right now and taking a shower was out of the question until I got some sleep.

"Hold on there." I opened my eyes to see Rocco in my room. "Take these before you drift off to la la land." He held out a bottle of water and some pills. I took them and quickly drank them down while he set out his medical supplies.

"I hope you gave me the good stuff," I grumbled.

"Why, feeling a little butt-hurt at the moment?" he chuckled.

"Ha ha, you're so fucking funny."

"Come on, you gotta admit, it's not every day that someone comes back with a bullet in the ass."

"Yeah, I'll be sure to laugh the next time someone shoots you in the ass."

"Geez, you spend a few days with Knight and you've lost all sense of humor," Rocco mumbled.

I watched as he took a needle to numb the area, but I drifted off soon after that. I must have slept for a long time because I felt completely refreshed when I woke up. There was something soft and warm on my ass and it felt really good. It must have been Raegan's hand.

"Baby, that feels so good," I mumbled as she continued to rub my ass. I laid with my eyes closed, just enjoying the massage. She put something on my ass and started smoothing her hand over it. I tried to figure out what it was, but then screamed as something was ripped from my body. It felt like my skin had just been peeled off me.

My eyes flew open and I lifted off the bed, spinning to face her. Jules was standing next to me with a white strip that had my hair stuck to it and Hunter and Ice were sitting in chairs laughing. Raegan was on the bed next to me, biting her lip to keep from laughing.

"What the fuck is going on? Are you waxing my ass?"

"Hey, I just wanted payback," Jules grinned.

"For what?"

"Well, Chris and Ice did it to me. I figured it was only right that I get a turn."

I stared at him in disbelief. "But I wasn't there!"

He shrugged like he didn't give a shit, and based on his grin, he really didn't. I turned over and he held out his hand, blocking him from seeing my junk. "Whoa, man. You might want to cover up. We don't need to see the whole package."

I pulled at the covers, but stopped and stared at my own dick in shock. There was no hair around my dick. My gaze shot to Jules. "You waxed around my dick? You're fucking sick!"

"Nope, that was me," Raegan said cheerily.

"Why?"

"Well, I wanted to see why you all seemed so fascinated with who was waxed and why this was so entertaining. I get it. This is really a great....bonding experience."

"You waxed my dick," I said slowly. "That's not....I can't even..."

"That's not all she waxed," Hunter chuckled.

I looked over my body as horror swept through me. She had waxed my arms, my legs, my chest. I quickly felt my hair, relieved when at least something was still there. Then I felt my face and started shaking my head.

"No. No, no, no, no! You waxed my beard?" I shouted. "How could you do that?"

"Oh, it's not that bad. You have a cute sort of baby face with all that hair gone." Raegan patted my cheek as she mumbled baby talk to me.

"Raegan, what did you do to my eyebrows?" I said hesitantly.

"Now, that wasn't my best work. It took a few tries, but I think they're mostly even now."

"Raegan," I growled. "Hand me a mirror."

"I don't have one."

I pulled the sheet from the bed and flung it around my waist, marching off to the bathroom. When I flicked on the light, my mouth dropped open and I was pretty sure tears were in my eyes. There were two thin lines where my eyebrows once were. I shook my head in disbelief and just stared at myself. I didn't look anything like myself anymore. I walked slowly out of the bathroom and clenched my jaw, trying my best not to yell when I saw not only Ice, Jules, and Hunter in the room, but now every other fucking member of Reed Security.

Lola snorted, not trying at all to hold in her laugh. "Holy shit. That is not a good look on you."

"Dude, you're all smooth and shit." Sinner walked over to me, his eyes studying my face and then my arms. "Can I feel it?"

"Do you want me to break your wrist?"

"There's no need to be hostile. You just look so smooth and..."

"Like a baby's bottom," Cazzo laughed.

"Yeah, exactly," Sinner nodded. "Lola, go get Ryder so we can compare whose skin is softer."

"Don't you fucking dare," I growled, but Lola was already out the door. She ran back in the room with Ryder and quickly undressed him, diaper and all. "Keep that fucking kid away from me."

"Oh, stop," Lola waved me off. "I just want to feel."

She put her hand on her kid's bottom and then she was feeling my face. "Wow, that's amazing. What did you use to get his skin so soft?"

"Argan oil," Raegan grinned.

"Sinner, seriously, you have to feel this." Lola waved him over, but Cazzo and Burg joined in.

"Stay back," I commanded. "No one is feeling anything on me. This shit ends right now. I mean it!"

Ten minutes later, I was sitting on the edge of the bed as everyone was taking turns petting me and feeling my silky soft skin. I was glaring at Raegan, who just leaned against the wall gleefully. Sometimes I really hated this woman.

After going through our mission with Cap, we all split up for the night. Despite my nap this afternoon, I was still pretty tired and just wanted to get some shut eye. After taking a shower, I laid down gingerly in bed, sighing when I found a position that was comfortable. Raegan slipped into bed beside me and snuggled up to me.

"What are you doing?"

"I'm getting comfortable."

"Not on me. Not after that stunt you pulled this afternoon."

"Chill, that was funny and you know it."

"I look like a fucking woman!"

"No, you don't," she laughed. "So I messed up your eyebrows. Who cares? The rest of you looks fantastic."

"The rest of me looks like a newborn baby, only adult-sized."

"I still find you sexy." She ran her hand down my abs and under the covers to my dick. I quickly shoved her hand away.

"No sex. You made me look like a woman."

"I did not. Look at yourself." She pulled the covers back and slipped her hand around my shaft, slowly stroking me. I watched as my cock hardened in her hand, swelling until it was thick and long. "See? You look so much bigger like this." She climbed on top of my body and bent over, taking my whole length in her mouth.

"Holy shit," I bit out. She swirled her tongue around, licking and sucking as her fingers slowly played with my balls. I groaned as she shoved her mouth all the way down and I felt her throat hitting the tip of my cock.

I pulled her off me and rolled over so I was laying over her body. She spread her legs, then quickly wrapped them around me, pulling me closer to her.

"This is new for us," she smiled. "We're actually going to have normal sex."

"What are you talking about? We have normal sex."

"I mean, no one's chasing us and we're not about to go do something really dangerous. We have nowhere to be and we can sleep in tomorrow. It's like we're a normal couple."

"Is that what we are, baby? Are we a couple?"

"Well, after I shot you, made you kill me, you fucked me in the mud, and I pretended to be homeless for information, I think we've worked up to couple status."

I kissed her, letting my tongue slip inside her mouth just as I pushed my cock inside her pussy. She sucked in a breath as I hit deep inside her, thrusting into her over and over again. Her fingers combed through my hair and she held my mouth to hers. Her taste and her warmth wrapped around me until all I could think of was her and having her by my side for the rest of my life.

"We're not a couple, Raegan. We're so much more. You're mine and you always have been. And when we get back home, we're going to find someplace else for your parents to stay and I'm gonna fuck you every minute that I'm home on every surface of the house."

She paused, drawing back from me. "And?"

I looked at her quizzically. "And what?"

"Is that it? I'm yours and you're going to fuck me?"

"Oh. Did you want more?" I asked with a grin.

"Well, I think I deserve it. After all, I did make it fifteen miles on foot back to Reed Security. That has to earn me something."

"Hmm." I nodded like I was thinking. "You might have a point. Alright, let's negotiate. What is it that you want?"

"Well, first, I need someone to teach me how to use a computer."

"Done."

"Let's see. If you're going to be running off all the time playing hero, I want lessons in badassery."

"Badassery?" I grinned.

"Yeah, I want to learn how to properly use a gun. You know, so I don't shoot you again."

"I think that's a good idea. But let's keep grenades out of it."

"Maggie knows how to use a grenade."

"Maggie's not exactly the best example to follow."

Her eyes narrowed in on me and no matter how hard I tried to resist, I just couldn't say no to those gorgeous blue eyes. "Fine, we'll put grenades on the table for now, but I have a few requests of my own."

"I'm willing to listen."

"First, you will never refer to Knight in any way other than that man that is married to Kate. You can't call him the Black Prince or say how hot he is."

"Is this negotiable?" Her eyebrow raised in question and I smoothed it out with my finger.

"Not at all, baby."

"Well, it'll be a hardship, but I could do it for you."

"Good. Second, no more offering to go off and do something that could get you killed. I don't care how good you are with a gun after I train you."

She sighed dramatically, "The things I give up for you."

"And third, we need to set a timeline for when we'll have our own little rugrats."

"Are you in a hurry?" she grinned.

"Well, everyone else is having them, so we have a lot of catching up to do."

"Well, if that's the way it must be, I think we can agree that the sooner we start, the better."

"Now all we need to do is sign the contract."

I got up and walked over to the desk, pulling out the box that I had hidden in there. I opened it and smirked when I saw the diamond inside. It was exactly what I thought Raegan would like. Pulling it from the box, I walked back over to the bed and laid down between her legs again. Taking her left hand, I slipped the ring on her finger.

"When did you get this?"

"Would you believe that I've had this since the second week you were at my house?"

"No."

"You'd be right, but I was thinking about it even back then. You have no idea how much shit I had to go through to get Cap to agree to let me off the property. So, I hope you like it."

She shrugged. "Eh, it's okay."

I slammed my mouth down on hers, rubbing my cock against her entrance again. When I had her good and dizzy, I yanked my lips from her mouth and started kissing down her neck. "Just okay?"

"Uh...it's..."

My tongue slid across her skin, licking her salty flavor and nipping at her breasts when she shoved them toward my mouth. I wrapped my hand around her thigh, pulling her leg up to wrap around me again. The wetness from her pussy leaked down her legs, rubbing against my cock. I couldn't hold back from her any more. I slammed inside her, ignoring her screams as she gripped my hair and yanked on me, trying to bring me closer to her mouth.

"Tell me, Raegan."

"It's..."

I gripped the headboard and held on tight as I thrust into her harder and harder as I pushed her higher toward bliss. "Tell me," I huffed between thrusts.

"It's...God..."

"Not God, Raegan." I slipped my hand down to her clit and teased her, taking her just to the edge and then I moved off her, pulling my dick from her warmth. She sat up, her mouth in a pretty little O.

"What was that?"

I jerked my cock as I stared at that gorgeous body. "You haven't told me what I want to hear."

"Fine, it's a nice fucking ring. I love it, but I don't give a shit about it," she yelled. "I wanted you. You could give me anything else in the world and it doesn't mean shit to me if I don't have you. Hell, I would live in this little room with you for the rest of my life and not care as long as I had you."

I grinned. That was the perfect fucking answer. What happened next could only be described as a flurry of sex on every surface of anything we could fuck on or against. My dick had never been in a pussy for so long and I had never had to think of so many different things to distract myself from coming. Every time I pushed into her, I was in danger of blowing my load. By the time I was done fucking her, we were both worn out and didn't even have the energy to move from our spot on the floor.

"Jackson?"

"Hmm?"

"Please don't make me have a big wedding. I just want it to be you, me, my parents, and your friends."

"Sounds good."

She sighed against my neck, her warm breath puffing against my skin. "It's a shame we don't know anyone that could take care of this now. Everyone's already here."

I looked down at her, her eyes closed and contentment all over her face.

"I think that could be arranged."

Chapter Twenty-Nine

RAEGAN

"It's not even legal. I don't see why I have to wear a dress." I grumbled as Claire fussed over me.

"Because it's your wedding and you don't know that it's not legal. I think Hunter may have been ordained online after he married Gabe and Isa."

"Seriously? He married them?"

"Well, sort of. It was more Hunter and Lucy yelling at each other while saying the vows for Gabe and Isa. It was pretty funny, but we all just kind of assumed it was the real deal after that."

Claire finished adjusting my dress that had been picked up at the nearest town. It was not something I would normally wear, but I did like the way I looked in it. The dress was royal blue and tight fitting, hitting just below the knee. It had a boat neck and no back. At first I was worried what my parents would say, but then I remembered that they were already in love with Jackson and wouldn't care what I wore as long as I walked down that aisle and married him.

"I knew this dress would look perfect on you," Claire said excitedly.

"Yeah, it's beautiful, but what are the chances that Jackson will show up in jeans and a t-shirt?"

"I doubt the guys would let him show up like that. At least, I hope not," she mumbled under her breath.

"This is ridiculous, really. I mean, we don't even know if this is real. I think we should just-"

"Don't even finish that thought," Jackson growled from behind me. "You are fucking marrying me today and we're going to be fucking happy. You got that?"

I nodded, not really knowing what else to say. Jackson looked amazing. He was wearing black dress pants and a white shirt that was left open at the top. A black suit coat was left open on top of that.

"I don't know why you're so nervous. I'm the one that has to marry you with eyebrows that have barely grown in yet."

I chuckled slightly. He was still a little upset over that. Most of his hair had started coming in again, but we'd had to wait almost two months. His eyebrows weren't as bad as he thought. They just weren't as full as they normally would be. And he looked really sexy with the scruff that was dirtying his jaw.

"Just promise me that this is low key. I can't take anything flashy."

His eyes glimmered slightly until he saw that I was dead serious. His brow started to sweat and he paled slightly.

"Oh, shit. You did something big, didn't you?" I started hyperventilating. I wasn't ready for this. I didn't want a big wedding. I wanted it to be like any other day with us. I just wasn't one of those people that did well under pressure or when the spotlight was on me. I needed to not be the center of attention.

"Baby," he chuckled nervously. "You've got nothing to worry about. I wouldn't let you down."

He took a step back and looked at his watch. "Ten more minutes," he grinned, and then he turned and fled the room as fast as possible.

"Oh God. This is going to be bad. I can't go down there. I can't walk in front of everyone when they're all staring at me and expecting me to be this sentimental, blushing bride."

"Calm down," Claire said. "Seriously, it'll be fine. These guys are experts at giving a woman what they need."

"You're sure?"

She waved me off like I was insane. "Trust me, Jackson's got this covered."

Chapter Thirty

JACKSON

I raced down the stairs, almost slipping and breaking my neck on the last step. I had eight minutes to get everything out of here and make it look like I hadn't just tried to give her a dream wedding. When I flung the backdoors open, everyone looked over at me.

"We have to get rid of it all. She was fucking serious about not wanting all this shit."

Everyone just stared at me, not sure what to do. I clapped my hands as I yelled, "Move people. We only have eight minutes. I want this whole place cleared out!"

The women started grabbing the white chairs that had pink fabric draped across it and moving them to the shed. Cap helped me grab all the flowers and we tossed them into the pond. I grunted in frustration when they floated, but it kind of made the pond look cool, so I forgot about it and ran back to get more flowers.

"Shit," I said as I saw the swans in the cage. They were supposed to wander around the property, but I couldn't have that happen now. "What the hell am I supposed to do with all these swans?"

"Open the cage," Hunter said from his chair.

"They'll just wander around."

"Trust me."

I didn't have any other ideas, so I ran to the cage and opened it up. The swans waddled out, not going anywhere. Then chunks of dirt and grass flew from the ground as Hunter fired at the swans. They quickly ran, making their way to the pond. At least over there I could just say they wandered over here.

"Get rid of those doves," I yelled to Derek. He opened the cage and let them all fly free. I looked around frantically, seeing what else I had to get rid of. Shit, there was gauzy pink fabric draped all over the place.

I ran to the house and started ripping it from the roof. Sinner ran over and started helping. "What else do you want?"

"We need to look casual. Grab beer and hand it out to everyone."

"On it!"

Sinner took off and I started gathering up all the fabric, tripping over it multiple times before I was able to get it all over to the shed and shove it in with other decorations. I checked my watch, relieved when I saw I still had two minutes. I walked over calmly to the group, trying to slow my heart rate, and wiped the sweat from my face. I was fucking hot now and had to get rid of my jacket. I rolled up the sleeves of my shirt so I looked more casual.

When Raegan stepped outside, I almost had a fucking heart attack. She looked hot. I had seen her inside, but my brain had short circuited when she started asking about the wedding. But now, the way her hair was pinned back on one side and draped over her shoulder, and the way that dress fit all her curves just perfectly had me rethinking my choice to go commando for easy access after the wedding.

I stared anywhere but at her so that I didn't grow any harder than I already was, but eventually I would have to look at her. Hunter was sitting in his position, ready to marry us, and everyone else was standing around casually, holding their beer. I hoped like hell that this was more what she was hoping for.

She smiled at me when she stood next to me and leaned in close. "How much did you have to get rid of?"

"Nothing. I kept it casual, just like I promised."

"Is that why the pond is full of flowers and there are swans all over the place?"

I looked over and sure enough, the swans were out of the pond and wandering around. "I...uh..."

"Ladies and gentlemen of the...Reed Security party," Hunter began. "We are gathered here today, as we are every day, to witness the marriage of Jackson and Raegan. It only took them a little over a year to get their shit together, but now that they have, we can finally drink some beer and pretend that we all want to be wearing monkey suits today."

I glared at him and he shook his head before continuing.

"When you meet that special person, it isn't usually when she's all beat up and shit, but she's pretty cool, so we'll just pretend that these two met under normal circumstances."

Hunter was completely fucking this up. He told me that he knew what he wanted to say and he said it was *romantic as fuck*. I should have known that his version of romantic was different than everyone else's.

"Hunter," I motioned for him to keep moving.

"Right. So, Raegan, do you promise to stick by this fucker through bloody times and boring times? Do you promise that you'll bandage his wounds and make sure your kids are fully trained by Reed Security? Do you promise that when the shit hits the fan, you'll still be there for him, even if he loses a hand?"

"I do," Raegan laughed.

"Cool. Jackson, do you promise to always care for your woman? Make sure she's properly fucked so that we can expand the Reed Security crew? Do you promise that when she's pregnant, you'll remember to keep all the fat comments to yourself so that we don't all get bitched out by our wives? Do you promise that you'll invite us all over for your mother-in-law's cooking, as we all know how fucking fantastic it is?"

"I do."

"Oh, yeah," Hunter cleared his throat before he continued. "Do you promise to love one another and all that bullshit until one of you inevitably gets blown up by one of Maggie's grenades?"

"I do," we both said.

"Good, then fucking kiss her."

That was the only traditional part of the ceremony. It wasn't short and it most definitely wasn't the kind of kiss you wanted your in-laws witnessing, but it was everything I felt about her. Maggie tapped me on the arm, breaking our kiss.

"Here," she said, shoving two grenades at us with a grin. "Kind of like fireworks, right?"

"I'm not sure-"

"Awesome!" Raegan said, snatching the grenade from Maggie. "Alright, let's go blow shit up!"

3 months later...

"I've gone over everything on Agent Curtis's computer and I'm not finding a whole lot," Knight said as he sat around the table with the rest of us. "There are names, but I looked into them and they're all dead. None of them seem to be connected and I've searched their backgrounds for hours. There's nothing there, no connection or relation to anything that has to do with Raegan, Chance, or Morgan from what I can tell."

I was starting to lose my mind. Chance had been missing for almost six months and we were no closer to finding him than we were when he went missing. "How does someone just fall off the grid like that? How is it that there's no trail left behind? None of this makes sense."

"I looked into Carlos Guerrero," Rob said. "I've been tracking him for a long time and trying to figure out what his end goal is. I couldn't really find out a whole lot about him, but he lives in Mexico. If he was entangled with Xavier, it would suggest that the guy operates out of Central America."

"So, we don't know what his role is in any of this?" Cap asked.

"He doesn't show up in any databases and I couldn't find any ties between him and Curtis. I don't know if he's friendly or part of the trafficking ring. There's just nothing there."

"He can't be a friendly. He wants to kill Raegan."

"But if he's on the government's payroll, that suggests that he's either an operative or he's a scout of some kind."

"You haven't found anything on him, though," Cap said.

"That doesn't mean he's not working with our government."

"So, basically we're back to guessing," Knight scowled. "I hate fucking guessing."

"Bossman!" Becky ran into the conference room, panting and smiling like she had just finished her first marathon. "I think I have something. Okay, remember that Craig was saying that when he was taken they said something about praying at the altar?"

"Yeah." Cap looked to Craig, but he just shrugged.

"I figured they thought I was Catholic."

"That's what I was thinking too, but then I got to thinking about the fact that you said the guy made a slicing motion across his throat, which had me thinking about human sacrifice. See, altars in a Catholic church are for praying, but in other cultures, altars were used for human sacrifice. So, I did some research to find out which cultures practiced human sacrifice. There were the Etruscans, Chinese, Celts, Hawaiians, Mesopotamians, Israelites, Carthaginians, Egyptians-"

"Becky," Cap interrupted. "Get to the point."

"Okay, so those I ruled out because of location or who they sacrificed, which were mostly children. But, then there were the Aztecs, Incas, and Mayans. The Aztecs were located in Mexico and the Mayans were in Central America. The Incas were in South America and I ruled them out because they also sacrificed children."

"What does this have to do with Chance?" I asked.

"I'm getting to that. This is the good part." She squealed and clapped her hands excitedly. "Now, the Aztecs mostly sacrificed by laying someone on the altar and cutting through their abdomen and pulling out their heart. But the Mayans used the altar and beheaded their human sacrifices." She drew a line across her neck with a big smile. "See?"

"No," Cap said blandly. "That sounds like a lot of coincidences."

"Okay, I understand that it's not enough, but what if I told you that the human sacrifices were usually prisoners of war?" Everyone just stared at her. "Oh, come on! Craig was a prisoner of war and the guy said something about praying at the altar and then made a beheading motion." Still, everyone just stared. "Okay, you're still not convinced. There are six prominent sites for the Mayan cities that still stand. Chichen Itza, Coba, Copan, Calakmul, Tikal, and Uxmal. Now, four of those sites are in Mexico. One is in Guatemala and the other is in Honduras. Obviously, we could look into any one of those areas, but Honduras happens to be the murder capital of the world. That's where I say we start looking."

No one really looked like they were too convinced of anything she had said, but we literally had nothing else to go on.

"So, what do we do with this?" Knight asked. "We go search for an altar and that's where we'll find Chance?"

"Well, I don't know exactly. I was thinking that maybe the altar was just a stopping point for the ring. Maybe the people that get executed by the trafficking ring for snitching or whatever their crimes, are used to send a message. They're taken to the altar and executed."

"It sounds far fetched." I wasn't sure that any of that was right. "I mean, these guys are traffickers. What the hell would they have to do with Mayan traditions?"

"Maybe nothing," Becky said. "Maybe he's just from Honduras and was using it as a scare tactic, but either way, I think we should check into it."

"Well, fuck," Cap sighed. "We have nothing else to go on. Becky, do some more research on the altar and the area. Before we go on any missions, we need to get back up to strength. We'll plan over the next month and Knight will make sure everyone is where they need to be for the mission. Derek and Cazzo, work with Becky and start planning as soon as you have something to go on. Ice and Hunter, you're going to have to sit this one out. Lola, we need a weapons check. I want an inventory of everything that we have at our disposal. We need to figure out how many trips we can take before we run out of supplies."

"Cap," Cazzo shifted in his seat, obviously uncomfortable with his next question. "How long are we staying here? I know that we need to rebuild and everything, but I think we all need to know if this is becoming our new home. The ladies have left everything behind for us and at this point, none of them really have a job left to go back to. Vanessa lost her job, Kate's clinic is in her partner's hands, Claire was supposed to be running the library and they've probably replaced her by now. Lucy was notified that she lost her teaching job. Ali lost her nursing position. Lindsey had to shut down her bed and breakfast and Emma had to close her bookshop. Isa lost her position as a real estate agent."

"Not to mention that Ryan hasn't been able to contact Logan about their construction company," Lola added.

"What does everyone want to do?" Cap asked.

We all looked at each other. None of us really knew what the best option was at this point. "If we go home, we still need to protect everyone. We can't take any chances right now. Raegan is still a target and most likely, so are we."

"Let's put it to a vote," Cap said. "Who wants to stay?"

Pretty much everyone raised their hands, but Cazzo was hesitant. Eventually, he raised his hand also.

"We stay," Cap nodded. "Now, what do we tell our women?"

"However you decide to do it," Sinner said, "make sure Maggie doesn't have any weapons on her."

"Are you seeing anything?" I asked Gabe over the mic.

"Nothing. What are we looking for exactly?"

"Anything that looks off," Cazzo replied.

We were at Copan in Honduras searching for anything around Altar Q that might give us some hint as to where Chance was or who took him. So far we weren't having much luck.

"You know, we should have brought Claire with us," Derek sighed. "She's great at solving shit like this. She's got an overactive imagination."

"Okay, so let's think like Claire," I suggested. "What would she say was going on?"

"Shit, I don't know," Derek grumbled. "Her mind doesn't quite work like other people's. She gets lost in these imaginary worlds of spies and thievery."

"Alright, so think like a spy," Cazzo suggested. "Spies would send information in secretive ways. So, let's look around the altar for any hidden papers or...whatever shit spies use."

"That was very articulate," Gabe laughed.

"Shut the fuck up."

We all converged on the altar and looked around the outside. "It looks clear from here. Who's going to get down on the ground and wiggle underneath?"

We all looked at each other and laughed. None of us were small enough to get all the way under this thing. I got down on my back and pulled out my phone, using the flashlight feature to look underneath. I wiggled all around the damn thing, but there was nothing.

"Nothing," I sighed, standing up and brushing off the dirt. "Where do we go from here? We've already looked around the entire site and we've been through town."

"Well, the locals aren't talking and with nothing here, we have nothing else to go on," Cazzo said.

"Maybe we should hang around for a few days," Gabe suggested.

"We've already been here a week. I think what Becky found was just a coincidence," Derek said. "I'm sorry, guys. We all want to find Chance, but I think we're wasting time here."

I knew he was right and it sucked. I had really been hoping that we would find something. It had been too long since Chance had been taken. We'd planned this trip out and looked into every aspect of Altar Q. We'd all been training and getting back in shape for this mission, but it was all a waste of time. There was nothing here.

Watching from nearby...

This was a fucking disaster. Whoever had led them down here was a fucking fool. I had been using this location as a drop for the past two years and it had proven to be safe. But someone fucked up. If I hadn't seen the men from Reed Security earlier in the week and called off the drop, they would have found what they were looking for today. Now I had to set up a new location. This one was no longer safe. Even though they didn't find anything, that didn't mean that they wouldn't be paying attention from now on. And since they were looking in this area, chances were they would continue to look in Honduras. I would have to lead them in a different direction. The Middle East was a perfect location for a few former military personnel to disappear.

The last six months had been absolute shit for us. We'd gone out on mission after mission and we still hadn't found a damn thing about Chance. We had searched most of Central America it seemed, and we had intel that was pointing us to the Middle East, but it was more difficult to get in there undetected. I wasn't sure how much longer we could keep this up. We were running low on money and supplies. The women were getting pissy with being stuck at the house all the time and it didn't help that we had so many changes around here.

Maggie had our baby a few months ago, a son we named Gunner. Lindsey was pregnant, as was Lucy, Kate, Cara, Vanessa, and Isa. It was a hormonal nightmare around the house and none of us could do right in their eyes. I guess that's what you get when there's nothing else to do but train and fuck.

I went over our numbers again and tried to figure out how I was going to keep stretching our money when we weren't bringing in any jobs. The fact was, we couldn't stay hidden if we wanted to survive, but we couldn't make ourselves vulnerable either. Pretty soon, we were going to have to make a decision because none of us were getting paid as it was and we still only had a month or two left.

My phone rang and I didn't recognize the number. I let it go to voicemail and pulled up my personal assets to see if there was anything I could liquidate. My phone rang again with the same number. I slid the green button and answered.

"Hello?"

"Is this Sebastian Reed?" It was a male voice, shaky and quiet.

"Yes."

The line was silent for a moment and I considered hanging up. I wasn't sure who could have my number, but if they did have it, it was most likely someone that was friends with someone I knew.

"I know where Chance is."

ALSO BY GIULIA LAGOMARSINO

Thank you for reading Jackson and Raegan's story. There's still more to come further down the line, so keep reading. The Reed Security gang will be back in Chance's story!

Join my newsletter to get the most up-to-date information, along with new content in the Reed Security series.

https://giulialagomarsinoauthor.com/connect/

Join my Facebook reader group to find out more about my obsession with Dwayne Johnson!

https://www.facebook.com/groups/GiuliaLagomarsinobooks

Reading Order:

https://giulialagomarsinoauthor.com/reading-order/

To find the individual series, follow the links below:

For The Love Of A Good Woman series

Reed Security series

The Cortell Brothers

A Good Run Of Bad Luck

Made in United States
Orlando, FL
10 April 2024

45670651R00157